WITHDRAWN

MY MOTHER'S HOUSE

My Mother's House

FRANCESCA MOMPLAISIR

ALFRED A. KNOPF   NEW YORK   2020

Library of Congress Cataloging-in-Publication Data
Names: Momplaisir, Francesca, [date] author.
Title: My mother's house / by Francesca Momplaisir.
Description: First edition. | New York : Alfred A. Knopf, 2020. |
Identifiers: LCCN 2019017546 (print) | LCCN 2019018686 (ebook) |
ISBN 9780525657163 (ebook) | ISBN 9780525657156 (hardcover)
Subjects: | GSAFD: Suspense fiction.
Classification: LCC PS3613.O5226 (ebook) |
LCC PS3613.O5226 M9 2020 (print) | DDC 813/.6—dc23
LC record available at https://lccn.loc.gov/2019017546

Jacket images: (details) jayk7; alvarez; bunhill; Koron, all Getty Images;
Ranta Images / Alamy; (background) Rolau Elena / Shutterstock
Jacket design by Jenny Carrow

Manufactured in the United States of America
First Edition

FOR THE ONES WHO TAUGHT ME TO LOVE

AND THE ONES WHO TAUGHT ME TO SPEAK

America. God bless you if it's good to you.
America, please take my hand.
Can you help me underst——?

                    —KENDRICK LAMAR (FEATURING U2), "XXX."

Zero

THE HOUSE screamed, *"Fire!"* from every orifice. *Difé!* Melting windowpanes rolled down the aluminum siding, dripping polyurethane tears. Orange, blue, and yellow flames hollered their frustration into the icicles along the struggling gutters. The two-story (three, if you counted the basement), one-family (two, again, if the basement was included) House had had enough. Fed up with the burden of Its owner's absurd hoarding, inexcusable slovenliness, and abuse of power, It spontaneously combusted everywhere a power source sprouted unkempt. The matted nest that passed for a fuse box in the basement; the half-assed hose that connected the gas stove to the wall in the upstairs kitchen; the shaved pipes that pulled natural gas from its source to the boiler and radiators throughout the House; the power strip in the upstairs bedroom that powered a tenant's hot plate, microwave, refrigerator, stereo, television, DVD player, cable box, computer, and electric shaver and toothbrush; the tangle of Christmas lights left plugged in and blinking as a deterrent to robbers over the holidays. The House blew it all up and burst into tears It had been holding back for decades.

It cried and laughed at the same time, watching the owner scurry out of the basement. When the tenant jumped out the upstairs window, the House doubled over and shook in amusement. It nearly keeled over from being tickled by the rodents and roaches racing one another into and out of their hiding places, confused which would be best—crackle in the fire or crack in the icy January air outside while trying to make it to the safety of a neighbor's house.

The House listened for the loud cries.

"*Anmwey! Difè!*" the owner hollered as he ran Its circumference.

It tracked the movements of the owner, who ran around like a man trying to keep his pants up after having missed a belt loop while getting dressed. It watched as Its pajama-clad owner rushed from the backyard up the skinny driveway to the front stoop, then through the frozen garden in the empty parcel where another house could have been built, then around to the backyard again. The House didn't see where the tenant vanished to, but he was gone before the ambulance arrived. It had a hard time emoting and keeping eyes on the owner simultaneously, but the House continued to cry and laugh convulsively.

"*Anmwey!*" the owner shrieked as he waited for help to arrive, help the House did not want.

It tried to figure out how to drown out his cries. It screamed in different ways for different reasons until sirens overwhelmed them both. The fire trucks pulled up out front and, mercifully, the drivers silenced the blaring. But the night was far from still. The House blinked rapidly as the engines' discordant lights made a visible noise of their own. It closed Its eyes to shut out the annoying but necessary red and yellow spinning that cracked the dark freezing night. Desperate for attention, It pumped out flames with renewed vigor like a toddler in a tantrum forcing herself to cry harder.

It wished It had been built with the ability to speak, since people-talk always trumped Its performances. It huffed as the owner continued screaming in his native language: "*Pitit mwen yo!*" It wanted to shut him up. But a firefighter came across the half-frozen man while inspecting the perimeter of the House for points of entry. The House rolled Its eyes as the owner spoke English to ensure the firefighter understood.

"Hep! *Difé!* My sheeldren!" His accent protruded like a boil through taut skin.

It looked down at the two men and easily deduced that the heavily masked rescuer was white by his blue eyes reflecting the frosty glint of aluminum siding in the January night. The firefighter chased the owner back through the rock-hard soil of the hibernating snow-covered garden and out to the front of the House. The man finally stood still, watching powerlessly as his house blazed before him. *Difé!*

The House ignored the outside entertainment and, refusing to be defeated, It tried to turn Its efforts inward. It spread flames through every corner of Itself to produce Its cry of fire for onlookers to see. It kept an eye on the owner standing outside in the subzero air bawling and mumbling to himself. It drooped to see the hydrants give more easily than expected. It recoiled as the hoses gushed against Its battalion of flames fighting for their right to be and be seen. It had earned this catharsis. It had endured and witnessed, had stood silent and been complicit. It deserved to explode publicly, to commit suicide grandly. It harnessed and funneled the flames to fight off the water like hell itself.

It followed the firefighters as they focused on the left side of the House where most of the windows were. Their hoses lined the narrow driveway that separated the opportunistic flames from the closest neighbor's house, a tacky yellow eyesore with brown trim. Ambushed on Its left, the House strained to push fire out of the singular window on Its right. Its flames stretched their fingers across the empty parcel, trying to reach the tips of the dormant leafless apple tree. That was Its only hope of spreading Its fury: extend Its fire to high-five the tree, set it ablaze, then jump to the next house just inches away. If Its flames could reach the branch tips, they could skip to the almost-elegant pale blue cookie-cutter structure and take out half the block toward the main boulevard at least. At least.

The House longed to level all Its neighbors that should have known about Its suffering. It knew that they'd also been in pain, but they'd done nothing to help themselves or It. It would be the brave one, the one to put an end to it all. It would euthanize them, take them out of their misery, in the only way It knew how. The people were a different matter. It wanted to tear them down for putting their houses through the same suffering It had endured; the same misery that had been replicated in the various shades of brown, languages, and accents of the neighborhood's inhabitants. How could *people* want to live through all of that? What was there to live for after all It had seen and been through? Why prolong the pain? What were they trying to prove? Perseverance? Resilience? To what end? Why stand outside in paper pajamas in the middle of a blocked-off street, in the mean January air, in the middle of the goddamned night, shouting, "There are people in there!"

The House changed tactics. It retracted the flames. It inhaled and held the smoke in Its chest, tricking the firefighters into believing that they were winning. For now, It would have to settle for self-consumption. Like an unseen hell, It would devour Itself without the fanfare of sparks. *Lanfè.* It would revel in the blue and yellow hues of Its dark interior. *Hellfire.* It would swallow molten glass and metal as salves to soothe Its regret at not having destroyed other houses whose inhabitants surely should have known the hurt being heaped upon It. It held Its breath and allowed the flames to do their worst inside to make Itself forever uninhabitable. It allowed them to eviscerate all of Its wood paneling, floors, and furniture. It took one hard gulp of fuel from the kerosene heater to burn through the floorboards in the cold upstairs bedrooms. No one would ever sleep there again. *Difé!* One long lick with ten tongues through the shotgun first floor, blackening the foyer, living room, dining room, and kitchen. No one would ever be welcomed, invited to sit, presented with a plate, and allowed to dip a tasting spoon there again. One jagged cough through the basement, a hiccup of final fumes, skipping over and in between defunct TVs, stereo turntables, eight-track tape decks, and heaping crates of unsorted junk. No one would ever stoop through the tight tunnel to thrift shop among the owner's dusty collection again.

The House floated in and out of consciousness, waiting to die. It would no longer have to stomach wickedness, deviance, and injustice. It looked forward to the demolition that would level and free It at long last. It sighed and quietly stuttered, *"Di-di-di-di-difé."* It closed Its eyes, ignoring the embers' red glow. It didn't feel the water pounding around Its gutted insides. Even if It had given credence to the owner's incessant pleas, It wouldn't have felt the tickle of a small child or the heft of a few adults crouching in one of Its corners.

One

LUCIEN

Well into his sixties, Lucien was arrogant enough to wish there'd been songs written about his birth, so he would know that he had been a miracle. He remembered only being abandoned in the care of his aunt La Belle by his U.S.-bound parents before his first birthday. Newly settled into his true complexion and curly hair texture, he'd become the perfect light-skinned, silky-haired toddler that Haitian families welcomed and worshipped. As he aged, he'd retained his color that was the creamy beige of traditional flour-thickened vanilla porridge—*labouyi*—boiled slowly and sweetly, eaten from its cooled-down edges to its enticingly hot center. His light brown eyes looked hazel in sunlight, proof of the centuries spent preserving the mark of miscegenation that had produced his lineage during centuries of slavery. His last name, Louverture, was the other legacy of that epoch.

Tante La Belle had been the same color. She should have been pretty given her light skin, smooth hair, green eyes. She believed that she was, but even Lucien's merciful and grateful gaze could not make it so. Her features had come together awkwardly on her flat, round, wide face. Her eyes protruded like two egg yolks in a pan. Her bottom lip hung open, exposing the pink inside with its blue-green and purple veins. As much as she'd tried to hide her freckles, the three-dimensional skin tags around her nose resisted the heavy face powder. Her hair should have made up for some of her ugliness, but it had been so thin that it exposed her scalp.

As downright ugly as she was, she liked to think that Lucien resembled her. But his features had come together to make him a gorgeous toddler and, later, a pretty preadolescent boy. But he didn't remember his face. Who and what he'd been between his childhood and his preteen years were murky. He couldn't recall if La Belle had been kind to him or if he had made that up. But she'd bathed him like a baby until he was nine years old, slathering lotion over his skin in a way that had made him feel awkward and aroused at the same time. She loved to touch him because of the way her hands felt again his creamy skin. He would wait with anticipation as she slid off the rings she wore on each finger. She would end by running her fingers through his curls to remove the remaining oil. He would stand in her full-length mirror to bask in the sight of his shiny naked body, taking his time to get dressed, never looking at his own face.

He had not been able to resist the way she had doted on him, reminding him how beautiful a boy he was, how he looked like a prettier male version of herself. He'd once asked her why she'd had no children of her own and she'd responded that she hated all children except him. He'd been flattered at the odd compliment that had raised him to a status just above special. Her attention had approximated love, and the responsibility she'd placed on him had resembled trust.

He vaguely remembered the deeds that she'd made him commit. But he recalled with precision his early love of counting and his giftedness at math. He still relished the calculation of money and the appraisal of the value of things. He was an intelligent boy, but by age eleven, Lucien was only sporadically attending the clean, pricey Seventh-Day Adventist seminary for which his parents dutifully paid tuition twice a year. He'd never enjoyed time behind the doors of the pastor-led school. He'd even found the freedom of recess in the yard confining. Instead he'd wandered throughout the roughest parts of Port au Prince, daring shirtless slender boys—muscular despite days without meals, with skin as dark as the bottoms of their bare feet—to attack a well-dressed, well-fed, well-heeled cream-colored man-boy like himself. From the same dirty streets gorgeous indigo girls rose and ripened like curvaceous eggplants. With a frightening hunger in hand, he harvested the loosest ones and fucked them before bringing them to his newly adopted home, the brothel at Bar Caimite. He'd claimed the entryway to the place, which smelled of rum and frequent and corrupt sex. Leaning against the doorframe, he'd become a permanent fixture like the knob and hinges. A mature teenaged toughie, he'd installed himself as a handsome recruiter and de facto bouncer and earned his way to part ownership in only two years. He packed an old pistol and liked to watch the American and European soldiers, peacekeepers and self-proclaimed rescuers of his people. They unabashedly entered his bar to enjoy their favorite overpriced liquor and even more expensive ladies of the dawn, *bon matain,* afternoon, and evening. He'd owned these women and even some soldiers by means of blackmail and the pistol he bragged about but never brandished.

Lucien had always preferred reclining against walls to sitting in chairs or on high-backed barstools. A burgeoning narcoleptic, he needed to stand to stay awake. He remained vigilant to watch the prettiest little brown-skinned girl he'd ever seen, a precociously dressed two-year-old whose father was a rising military man in François "Papa Doc" Duvalier's personal guard. From his post in the doorway, Lucien watched the coddled Marie-Ange Calvert grow up for more than a decade beside the general who drove, carried, and held the hand of his baby-doll daughter to the elite Catholic school up the only green hill in Port au Prince. Lucien was puzzled by his amorous feelings for such a young girl but determined to wait until she was of age to court her. For this reason, he hadn't taken any girls seriously until he was twenty-four. By then, Marie-Ange was fifteen, old enough for him not to be embarrassed by his slow chase—stalking, really—of this maturing untouchable beauty.

Why she'd married him was one of the many stories he'd rewritten upon arrival in America. He preferred to focus on how well he'd dressed back then. The sharp creases in his linen slacks. Panama shirt starched as crisp as *kassav*. The collar tips as hard and pointed as sharks' teeth that would later devour daring or stupid Haitian boat people. From his open collar, a hypnotic gold chain beckoned to passersby. He flashed new greenbacks that hid his wad of ratty Haitian *goud*. The bills tempted beggars, hungry hookers, and ambitious marriage-age schoolgirls with no acceptable suitors. Not that he was suitable. But he looked like he could get somewhere.

Yet he'd always known that calamity, not his good looks and exquisite dress, had forced Marie-Ange into his embrace for protection. Fear tightened around her waist, forced her to bend over his left forearm, allowed him to give her the most painless, pleasure-filled, doggy-style fuck any virgin had ever experienced. He had not expected the day to end that way, but, a natural opportunist, he was always ready for the unexpected. He was one of the first to see the eight armored trucks along the Palais Nacional road, carrying expendable blue-black Haitian soldiers strapped with U.S.-supplied machine guns. Behind them, an American exported tanker and a band of Union Jack–bolstered combatants stomped the dirt road smooth, ready for a fight. Many assumed that this was just another episode of grandstanding by the newly appointed president for life Jean-Claude Duvalier. But it turned out to be one of many attempts to overthrow the demon president bent on slaughtering his real and imagined enemies and terrorizing ordinary citizens. It was merely a single song set to play over and over again on the aging record player in Bar Caimite.

Because baton blows were hard to count amid chaos, Lucien had paid less attention to the potential eruption of random beatings of innocent street peddlers and truants. Instead, he looked at the ground in front of the bar near his left foot, where he had scattered just enough sugar to draw out a line of soldier ants. These he counted obsessively while waiting for dropped treasure. He would forever advise those under his care or influence to look down when walking so they would never miss dropped coins or bills. Standing outside his own bar, having counted women, money, and ants, he would catalog the shoes of polished private schoolgirls.

Their footwear boasted water droplets from the lush wet grass of the school grounds. Sturdy English garden greenery taunted the browning tufts of weeds drying out on the lawn of the national palace. Both greens mocked the gray dust of the rest of Port au Prince's streets, where the only verdure to be seen were the plantains lounging on market tables. If Lucien had been paying attention to the landscape, he would have been counting the disappearing trees, an occupation that would have grown easier with each passing season until Haiti's trees quickly became endangered and then extinct. But he'd been more concerned with the shoes that would bring his beloved to him.

A third of the girls wore the same standard-issue Mary Janes purchased from a flabby market woman with New York ties—Buster Browns with chunky rubber soles and cutesy patent leather low block heels. Some sported the odd white Keds for the one day of mandatory physical education in which they were forced to participate. Lucien knew how many shoes each girl owned. Most of them were awarded three different pairs at the beginning of every school year. Everyday BBs, ineffective cloth-topped sneakers that sucked up street dust like a Hoover, and patent leather for church. The church pairs were so shiny the girls could use them as mirrors for applying Vaseline to their lips. Beyond his obsessive need to count, he wasn't interested in these. He waited to spy the pair of matte leather French kitten heels better suited to a teacher than a student. But even the teachers at the most expensive Catholic school in Port au Prince couldn't afford to buy them. The shoes Marie-Ange sported were one of many pairs purchased by her father during his presidential trips through Paris en route to Switzerland.

After counting the shoes and the girls, Lucien counted the days of the week on his fingers. On this day, the day of the coup attempt, he confirmed that it was indeed Friday. Bored but patient, he even started to count the boys, scrutinizing the face of one, Marie-Ange's baby brother, to deduce if something had happened to make her late. Had their father unexpectedly sent his chauffer on this particular Friday? Did he forewarn her of what the line of soldiers had been planning? The boy's face surrendered no clues. Instead, his attire reminded Lucien of himself as a schoolboy, in a white shirt, plaid tie, and shorts too short for an adolescent boy; they exposed his legs and thighs that were more curvaceous and elegant than a girl's. As he thought back to those times, he heard someone whisper, *I am nothing.* The soft sound came from within and resonated outward. He needed to count.

He looked over his shoulder into the bar behind him, taking inventory of the patrons. Startled, he turned around fully to recount the women leaning over and chatting up men, deliberately doling out copious amounts of cleavage. He counted the ones sitting in the laps of patrons, throwing back shots of diluted rum. One of them was missing, but so was one of his regulars, a sloppy-fat gray-haired white soldier who paid a monthly retainer. Lucien heaved his relief without letting on that he had been worried. He turned back around so he would not miss Marie-Ange passing by.

Growing impatient, Lucien started walking toward Marie-

Ange as soon as he spotted her distinctive shoes amid the early-dismissed upperclassmen. She was still at least five hundred yards behind, making her way down the last green slope. His headstart allowed him to make it to the bakery, where he would watch her enter to secure the pastries for which he had prepaid. Given her status and wealth as the daughter of one of President Duvalier's most trusted generals, he didn't want her to see him handling dirty bills. He knew that she would refuse to accept a gift from him, a hang-about nearly a decade her senior with no known profession.

He would never meet her standards. He was a vagabond—a dead one, if her father ever caught a whiff of him on her uniform. The general would know. Her father had first figured out that she went to the bakery on Fridays by sniffing her imported cream cardigan. He could smell the butter, flour, and even the salt water and oven heat that was used to make her preferred patties. Papi General had spies in the area, failed ones who told him only what Lucien had paid them to say about his distant liaisons with Marie-Ange. Which is to say they told the general nothing except what she had eaten, if she had also opted for a beverage, and whether she had shared with her younger siblings. Dirty money aside, Lucien never wanted Marie-Ange to see him deep in one of his counting spells. If he'd had to pay the girl behind the counter in Marie-Ange's presence, she would have misjudged him as a penny-pincher instead of the well-dressed, mysteriously moneyed suitor she couldn't look in the eyes.

Lucien entered the bakery and leaned against a tall, skinny refrigerator that grunted as it forcibly slurped electricity from the generator like a thick milkshake through a stirrer straw. He stared at the wind chimes that would announce her arrival. When they finally tinkled, he watched as she walked in with three of her little sisters and her youngest brother. He winked at the boy to disarm his disgusted, dismissive stare.

He turned his attention to the baker, who handed Marie-Ange the same pastries she always ordered. She nodded gratefully and gracefully as she handed a bag to each of her siblings and kept one for herself. He was glad to see the children run out when they heard the sound of military trucks passing. They were hoping to glimpse their father driving by on his way home, so they wouldn't have to walk. If they saw him, they knew to make excuses for Marie-Ange, who stayed behind shamelessly pretending to avoid Lucien's stare. The trucks were headed toward the capitol instead of away from it, which was unusual. Lucien and Marie-Ange knew something was amiss when they saw her siblings freeze in the doorway. He let her walk outside alone, so he wouldn't be accosted by her father. He followed when she started to run in the direction her siblings were sprinting. Spotting confusion up ahead, he ran behind her. He was on her heels immediately and took the opportunity to hold her waist to guide her away from the dustup. They lost the children they were trying to catch up to amid the running shop owners and the army trucks that tried to speed through thick traffic. Even with the cars giving them priority passage, the envoy could go only twenty to thirty miles per hour in short sprints.

With one swift movement Lucien swooped Marie-Ange up and over his shoulder and accelerated in the opposite direction to get her to safety. Although she would never learn how, she would eventually admit to herself that, in the years she'd grown from girl to near woman, Lucien had followed her even to the safe place her father had chosen for such an occasion as this. She fell asleep in the crook of his arm, in the most secure place she'd ever known, a place so far outside Port au Prince it could have been another country.

In the morning, Lucien woke Marie-Ange and handed her the traditional remedy for extreme shock: equally traumatizing bitter black coffee in a covered *emaillé* cup. He watched her eyes flicker as she tried to recognize the squat hut where she'd slept. The countryside that buffered Port au Prince was equally unfamiliar. He could see that she recognized two people—him and her godmother, Nen-nen, who was safety itself. The newly bound couple would spend nearly a year hiding there, too afraid to let anyone know where the general's daughter was after he had been "disappeared" or assassinated. There were rumors of both and one equaled the other. Lucien and Marie-Ange assumed that her siblings had met the same fate, gorged on by the indiscriminately lustful vampiric militia who fed on the blood of children and adults alike.

When Lucien recounted the story of his immigration to New York, he liked to say that his parents had rescued him from an economically declining dictatorship. He'd left Haiti right after Papa Doc had died, making his vicious nineteen-year-old son president. In less than a decade Lucien would opine on the sensationalism of America's six o'clock news that dubbed the juvenile president "Baby Doc," trivializing the experience of those brutalized, erased, or massacred throughout Haiti. Lucien's parents had really rescued their grandchildren from the trouble they'd known Lucien had gotten himself into back home. In fact, he'd immigrated when Haiti was still a country much like other Caribbean islands—pretty beaches cradling neat hotels that rose like champagne glasses on glittering trays. Behind the paradise, mean dirt roads, hungry hovels, squat donkeys, and skinny cows held themselves together as sturdily and desperately as the proud, undernourished dark waiters serving maraschino-cherry-laden Shirley Temples to the bratty children of French and American tourists.

He'd never bothered to analyze why his parents had left him behind. It was common for immigrating parents to leave their kids while establishing themselves unencumbered in a new and unfamiliar place. Mothers and fathers would promise to send for their children when they reached school age and expensive all-day American childcare was no longer necessary. They would excuse themselves for leaving the children a little bit longer while they amassed enough to rent a proper apartment or even buy a house. By that time, it was too late to try to integrate an adolescent into such a new environment. Sometimes they decided to spare themselves the embarrassment of a rebellious teenager's behavior. They still sent hefty remittances to the relatives caring for and putting up with lost, resentful, and recalcitrant children. They absolved themselves of the sin of abandonment that left their children with oozing wounds that would never close.

I am nothing.

Lucien had opted to become what he'd believed his parents had seen in him even as an infant—a wild, soiled boy whose insides would never be as clean as his perfect light skin. He'd grown up thinking of them as the source of the countless luxuries he'd enjoyed all his life, and becoming the child his parents had written off as a worthless and shameless embarrassment. It was too late to make him into the son they would have liked to bring to the United States much earlier for schooling. Instead, by the time he'd gotten his passport and plane ticket, he'd been living as deep in rural Haiti's soil as the mahogany tree roots surrounding the cement-block hut. His pregnant wife was still nursing their first child. He didn't see anything wrong with his circumstances and was comfortable with the fact that he had squandered his elite seminary education to pimp hopeless women at a brothel watering hole. Earning nothing but dust in Bois Droit, he manipulated his parents into listening to well-crafted recorded messages. The cassette tape missives did not require the flawless French and impeccable penmanship of handwritten letters. He was capable of both, but the tapes and photographs messaged the intimacy and urgency he wanted to convey.

He'd choreographed poses for the photos of him and Marie-

Ange under an emaciated almond tree with their dusty bare legs evidencing their desperation. They were holding hands, her head on his chest, his free hand on her belly. He knew that these would scare his parents into rushing him to the States. They were nearly as incensed at the sight of their high-yellow son with a beautiful brown country dweller as they were at the story of her escape from Port au Prince amid a failed coup d'état. That her father was one of Duvalier's closest generals was nearly as frightening as the fact that he had been disappeared. Lucien knew the things that would tug at his parents' hearts as they weighed their decision to bring him to America. Entire families had been known to vanish in the wake of a patriarch's assassination. To add to their fear and worry, he'd considered counting coins in the background while Marie-Ange recorded the section of the message he'd scripted for her. But her succinct explanation of what had happened to her father sufficed. He preferred to count in private and in his head anyway. He had learned to dismiss the breath at the back of his neck eschewing the foreign yet familiar words, *I am nothing. Nothing—until I count.*

Zero, un, deux, trois . . . He always started at zero. He'd counted the many coins and then the soiled wrinkled bills that resisted his attempts to smooth them out. "This is enough to get me into town to pick up the money transfer."

"Are you sure they sent the papers as well?"

"Guaranteed. With this belly"—he ran his hand along the width of her stomach—"they would be cruel not to. I'm going and soon so will you."

"And my children. I am not leaving them behind." Marie-Ange cast a glance at Veille, their first daughter who had not yet turned one.

"We'll all be together. I won't let them leave my girls behind. Or my boy." He patted her stomach again.

"Girls. I can feel it. This one is a girl too. Nen-nen also said—"

"You listen to that old woman."

"Yes, I do. Do you have any idea how much magic is keeping us safe here?"

"Ezili. I know, I know." He was tired of hearing about deities masked as saints. He especially despised Ezili, the goddess who exerted her dominance over men.

"You know, but you don't believe. Someday you will. Mark my words."

"I believe. I just don't worship. I won't submit."

"You sound like my father," she said for him to hear. Under her breath she whispered, "But you'll never be the man he was." She didn't articulate the rest of what she was thinking, that she was pregnant with a baby in her arms only because he was her ticket out of hell's hunger and the devil's danger.

"I couldn't bow down to anyone, even at the seminary."

"Anyone except me."

"Precisely."

"To do that, you must love her too."

"As long as she gets me to New York, I'll do whatever she requires."

"Go then."

"I'm not leaving yet. I have to take a bag with me in case I can't get a bus to come back tonight." He silently enumerated everything that would be needed.

LUCIEN COULD tell that his parents did not recognize him as he came down the Jetway at JFK Airport, despite having seen the carefully orchestrated photos he'd sent. He barely recognized them in their heavy coats, wool hats pulled down over their eyebrows, and scarves wrapped up to their bottom lips. Rather than hug him, they helped him put on his coat, each one holding a sleeve as an excuse to touch him. But he felt nothing even when skin met skin. Especially then. What he felt were the tears that arose from nowhere inside him. He swallowed them with the words he didn't acknowledge, *I am nothing.*

Within a week of his arrival, he was rolling coins into long bank-issued paper tubes. He licked his lips as he counted over and over the tips he'd earned as a newspaper delivery boy. He contemplated how he would miss them when he started working his manly job as a steelworker at a plant in New Jersey that was too far to get to by bus and train. Only two months later, a week before he started work, he made a trip back to Haiti to hold his first child again and to have reassuring sex with Marie-Ange. He stayed long enough to rub the sides of her stomach and the small of her back when she went into labor with what neither of them knew at the time would be twins. A year later, he imported her and their three baby daughters to New York.

He loved that there were four of them, four women specifically, enough to count and to manage. A lot to feed, but Marie-Ange would start working as soon as they could find childcare for their girls. They agreed that they would not depend on his parents. They didn't even want to continue cramming their family of five into the small apartment. They could not have predicted that the upper Manhattan tenement would someday be turned into luxury housing for Columbia University professors. Anxious to be out from under the strangers who were his parents, Lucien made the right connections with the lower Mob loan sharks who ran the union at the steel plant where he worked. From them he secured a loan for the down payment on a house in South Ozone Park, Queens. Once established, he and Marie-Ange inadvertently helped transform the once Italian neighborhood into a mixed immigrant community of primarily Caribbeans.

Through word of mouth about the compassionate and savvy young couple, newly arrived Haitians—mostly distant family members at first—flocked to SOP as they tried to find their way in their new country. Lucien had been the first to call the house Kay Manman Mwen, "my mother's house," KAM for short. The name stuck, and over the years he capitalized on what it had become: a welcome center, restaurant, motel, halfway house, off-the-books job brokerage, legal office, and casino. Veille, Clair, and Dor, born in that order, were Lucien's motivation to hustle and secure his foothold in New York. He never liked the city. He always longed to return home to Port au Prince, where he could stretch his legs while leaning against the doorframe of Bar Caimite, counting ill- and easily gotten gains from gambling and pimping. But his girls, which included Marie-Ange, were different. They were enough. They would always be enough to keep him in America, to make him happy in a hostile place. For them and his precious house he'd sweat in 150-degree steam at the plant. He would lose all of them, his three daughters, Marie-Ange, and his house, one decade at a time. He knew because he'd counted the time to the day.

The house was the last to be taken from him.

LA KAY

The House hadn't always been like this. Suicidal ideation does not come naturally or easily to a house, let alone the guts to kill itself to stop the hurt. It used to be happy and tolerant of families' faults and conflicts. In Its early days, It tolerated the garden-variety types of tussles: sibling rivalries, visiting in-law beefs, same-house different-bed spousal separations, the anomalous slap on the hand of a misbehaving child. It had even stomached the odd fistfight between best friends and the locking out of husbands who'd stayed out too late. But It didn't know what to do when mobsters started torturing delinquent debtors in Its basement. It was gripped by helplessness witnessing rough touches of any kind, let alone wife beatings that required ambulances and the involvement of the police. It had seen things escalate over many decades since It was first built after the war, so the changes It later witnessed had nothing to do with the shifting ethnic demographics of the neighborhood. It always tried to understand what might have happened to Its inhabitants to turn the everyday goings-on behind Its doors toxic, sadistic, and even deadly enough to make It take Its own life rather than stomach the madness that had started to materialize.

Like most of the homes built in the neighborhood, It had

been constructed primarily of the wood that had been part of America's first source of natural wealth. It didn't start to care about why It was built the way It was until the everyday evil started unfolding. But when It started being used to conceal wickedness, when Its last inhabitant started turning It into the type of hell that even Satan wouldn't stand for, It decided that It could not go on.

It had rolled out its welcome mat to Italians, accidental transplants who, after supplying the labor to build the cookie-cutter two-story homes for soldiers returning from World War II, bought for themselves the houses that wouldn't sell. The veterans didn't want to live in SOP and opted for homes in New York City proper or in other parts of the state or country, so the immigrants dug their roots deep beneath the basements carved out through their toil.

The House had been one of these. It had watched as these early immigrants cozied themselves into their new enclave, dictating who could and could not live there. It didn't much care for the crazies who started abusing certain of its features for profit and sadistic pleasure. A bomb shelter had been hidden in the far corners of Its basement. According to the other houses, who were more connected associates than friends, they all had basements, and the shelters had been common features put in for their originally intended buyers during the era of mass production, under the assumption that U.S. soldiers returning from the war would appreciate the additional security. Not knowing if the war would come to U.S. soil, the builders had designed the homes to include safe rooms. Most of the occupants had used the spaces as extra storage, while the few wannabe rich ones had converted the rooms into wine cellars. The more troubling lot valued the metal soundproof back rooms for privacy and protection as they engaged in despicable deeds.

Although the sound of airplanes taking off from and landing at Idlewild Airport had been soundproofing enough, a few serious mobsters had added insulation to the safe rooms to seal all sound in and out. They hadn't trusted in the reliability of airplanes, which proved prophetic as several major crashes had grounded flights out of the airport every decade since the war. The conservative Catholics and the superstitious among them quipped that the crashes were God's revenge for renaming Idlewild after a dead liberal philandering president.

For a time, the House had given Its residents a pass. To protect Itself from the pain brought on by Its powerlessness to stop the hurt, It ignored their misdeeds. It couldn't afford the heartbreak of getting involved and instead allowed external forces to bring about the necessary reckonings. It was fearful of reprisal from self-proclaimed murderers who recounted the burning of bodies and buildings in other parts of the city. It felt vindicated when their offenses resulted in butt-kicking karma in the form of arrests, decades-long prison sentences, or hospitalization after near-death beatings. But when one of Its residents started getting away with all manner of murder—the dismemberment of minds, the fingering of souls like a nail in a deep wound—It started plotting rebellion.

It had started out in a very different South Ozone Park from the place It finally tried to die in. For a time, It had marveled at the flexibility of the neighborhood as it became a mixed community. Italians grudgingly lived side by side with newer, slightly browner immigrants like Lucien Louverture, a fair-skinned product of multigenerational inbreeding. The House had welcomed him as Its first nonwhite inhabitant with coloring that hinted at the slave-epoch rape and rage out of which it was produced. But that's not why It had opened Itself to the man. Besides having no choice in the first place, It appreciated Lucien because, in demeanor as in appearance, he was as sweet and harmless as tapioca pudding. With his curls and off-colored eyes, he had often been mistaken for Hispanic or directly biracial instead of the octoroon he really was. He had been easily, but distantly, accepted by the Italians who'd run SOP and the union at the steel plant where he'd worked. The House had been hopeful that he would bring warmth and harmony to smoke out like burned sage the evil and sadness that had been left behind by Its previous gangster head of household. This man had been one of the most brutal of a band of Mafia flunkies who'd beaten every penny out of his debtors the same way he'd beaten the spirit out of his black-and-blue wife without killing her.

Like the other SOP houses, It had been glad to hear that the evildoers had started providing prime loan-shark interest rate financing for houses they couldn't sell fast enough. The House thought that the neighborhood's transformation made the price-gouging loans palatable. The same lot also arranged for independent mortgages for honest, everyday Italian home-owners beating an early path to Long Island to get as far away as possible from the darkies, no matter how light-skinned. It all but threw a party when It heard about the group moving into SOP.

It had watched as the occupants of SOP's houses had evolved over the years, becoming every darker shade. The few Latinos who'd been able to move out of the neighborhood did. Only two Puerto Rican families had stayed. Haitians, Guyanese, Barbadians, and Jamaicans planted themselves firmly, occupying SOP like peacekeepers in Port au Prince after a natural disaster.

Lead among the other houses, the church, and the school, It danced like *kanaval* when the neighborhood changed hands and color. Having come from predominantly Catholic countries, Caribbeans gladly filled the church's pews while their children occupied the school's seats.

After the church and its school, the restaurants had been next to evolve under the still mostly Italian owners who'd been shaken down by their own brethren. The pizzeria started selling beef patties with melted mozzarella and later even cocoa bread. The always Chinese-owned Chinese restaurant paid its dues staffing its eatery with a slave-labor immigration racket ("human trafficking" was the fancy term developed later). It added fried plantains, green and sweet, to its menu to complement the fried rice that Caribbeans couldn't get enough of. The already diversified bodega's inventory expanded to include dried salted codfish and beans of every variety. To the few American blacks (the term "African American" hadn't yet been popularized), the corner stores still sold loose cigarettes, pork rinds, pickled pig feet, single sour pickles, and twenty- and forty-ounce bottles of malt liquor, all in the right-sized paper bags, never longer than a forearm, never wider than a palm.

A couple of African American families had crossed over from Southside to the lower-digit addresses of Rockaway Boulevard to escape the crack epidemic. Most had come as basement tenants dealing dime bags to chill Caribbeans who'd been too afraid to drive to Southside. The self-proclaimed decent immigrant homeowners had held their own, refusing to allow their little lawns and gardens, polyurethane white picket fences, and paved driveways, for which they made long bus-and-train commutes each day, to slide into hood ruins. They'd grown more selective about their tenants, renting to their own mostly unless they were in a pinch. They'd redesigned their basements into elegant apartments with lots of mirrors to make up for the lack of space and natural light from ground-level windows.

The House joined in the neighborhood's fete as more and more brown and black immigrants, who'd discovered how easy the commute from SOP to Manhattan could be, moved in. It hadn't taken long for Caribbean and African drivers to take over the Q10, Q7, and Q9 bus routes with faster, more frequent service in the Jamaica, Queens, area. It didn't mind being part of Jamaica. But the neighborhood had had a different opinion on the matter. SOP had once resisted being lumped into that geography. When it had been primarily Italian, the preferred identification had been with Ozone Park and Howard Beach.

But the name "Jamaica" made the Caribbeans feel at home. The real Jamaica, the country, was just a stone's throw away from the archipelagoes and peninsulas from which they hailed. But a generation ago, SOP would have brawled at the insult of being considered part of Jamaica. That was before the only white faces seen were those of the priests and nuns who still ran the only private school and maintained the church. The new SOP loved the affiliation and the double entendre, as did the House.

But by the time It had started calling Itself La Kay, the "*kay*" in KAM, the House had already decided that Its first Haitian and absolute last occupant needed to go or maybe even die. It started focusing Its attention on the holes Lucien had drilled through Its walls for his voyeurism. Watching him peek through openings as small and deep as an ear canal, It knew that he was more than a Peeping Tom. He liked to touch women, mostly voluntarily through gross persuasion, the imposition of guilt, and blackmail when necessary. Through leaking pipes, It soaked itself with tears of torment to know that that was just the beginning of his lasciviousness. Regretting Its very existence under his occupation, It decided that there had to be an end to that beginning.

There came a moment when La Kay wasn't just thinking about dying; It was devising ways to do it. It was so distraught over the happenings within It and Its own powerlessness to do anything. But It couldn't kill Itself without taking the innocents with It. It felt as if It were standing three feet away from the edge of a cliff with a fifty-ton anvil in front of It and a tangled rope net behind It in which Lucien's three daughters were coiled. It wouldn't have given a thought about killing Lucien. In fact, It was still more homicidal than suicidal at the time but figured that It didn't deserve to live. Its failure to stop what was going on had earned It a death sentence. Despite the neighborhood where It had been conceived, built, and evolved, It wasn't Catholic and did not believe in purgatory. It knew that it made no sense to worry about spiritual limbo when It was already in hell. And although It had skimmed the Bible Marie-Ange sometimes opened in her lap minutes before church, It had never been tempted to process, let alone believe, in its contents.

La Kay had spent decades reading New York newspapers over the shoulders of Its inhabitants. It learned French and Kreyòl from the Louverture family and visitors to KAM. To better understand them and where they'd come from, It even mastered L'histoire d'Haïti, books that Marie-Ange had insisted her children memorize. From this homework, It learned American and Haitian politics, culture, and social norms. It made a point of understanding the horrors in the history of both countries. Thus, It identified the aberrations in the behaviors of Its dwellers, what was the result of centuries of violent oppression, racism, and disenfranchisement and what was just the fucked-up-ness of individuals. With all this in Its heart and mind, It started to mount the resistance that had been building up inside for decades. However, It had been distracted by equally deviant, sometimes peculiar, and even triumphant happenings on the outside popping off gray news pages: unavenged full-blown beatings of black men, murders of the same at the hands of policemen, the countless abductions of white children, accidental and deliberate plane crashes, unpopular and fully supported wars, citywide blackouts, the demolition of twin towers by aviator bombers, the election and reelection of America's first black president, the defeat of the would-be first woman president, the mourning of a divided nation ready to build and tear down a wall. How could It have focused on rebelling against the goings-on inside when the outside offered so many reasons to fight?

LA KAY had finally succeeded at Its revolt and gleefully mocked the man whose egregious transgressions had driven It to suicide as Its only recourse. It celebrated Its own demise with sparks that lit up the dawn sky. Its fete angered Lucien so much that he produced his own fire that kept his bare feet warm on the frozen pavement. After laughing until It cried hydrant water, La Kay sat silent, watching Lucien as he tried to convince the firefighters to check his basement where he believed his girls must have found refuge. Knowing but mistrusting Lucien, It hesitated to check what, if anything, was happening in Its basement. It chose to wait to find out who or what might have survived in the shelter constructed to withstand military-grade explosives.

More fire!

LUCIEN

Lucien stood in front of his house, impervious to the cold. His memory flashed to the houses back home, all of which were built of cinder block, brick, cement, and, when available, stone. Even the smallest huts, the ones with cutouts for windows with no glass panes in Haiti's poorest provinces, were made of materials as indestructible as the will of a perpetually oppressed people. The roofs were corrugated iron whose thickness depended on the affluence of the owner and the honesty of the builder. He would have settled for the smallest of these even though he had grown up in a mansion with his aunt La Belle. Even her add-on quarters had been fortified. Its dense iron roof had taken away the pleasure of falling asleep to the melody of rain harmonizing with the all-too-familiar sound of her soprano screech that had the urgency of a woman on fire or in the death throes of orgasm.

Now, crumbling like stone to dust, as broken as the sheets of ice beneath his bare feet, Lucien longed for a dirge of rural rain to keep his house from dying.

Lucien channeled the sound of drops as heavy as hail on the roof of his childhood home as he ran around his still-smoking home, lamenting that it had fallen victim to America's abundance exploited to excess. Although he had not been back to

Haiti since 1975, forty-two years later he stood in snow falling like grains of sugar wishing for cinder block, stone, and brick. Yes, even brick like the one once thrown through his screen door as a welcome from the few remaining white neighbors who had been trying to hold their ground to keep South Ozone Park as homogenously, or at least mostly, Italian as neighboring Howard Beach. Lucien wished that the rest of his house had been built of the same bricks that formed the steps to his screen door. That screen had never been shattered again since black and brown immigrants like himself had bought up all of his block and most of South Ozone Park.

If only block and brick had supplanted the wood frame, he wouldn't be standing outside in pajamas as thin as the *Newsday*, listening to firefighters discuss the need for his house to be demolished. He overheard them explaining to one another that the only thing keeping the house upright was the aluminum siding that covered the ashen splintering structure beneath. His externally erect, internally crumbling house was a sadly laughable façade akin to the dream sold to immigrant aspirants back home.

He wanted to cuss, but he wasn't that type of man. He was perverse, just not verbally, and certainly not in English. He was angry enough to drop a Kreyòl f-bomb, "*Fout!*" But he pleaded with the firefighters who were packing up and the demolition team who was unloading. If his wife had been alive, she would have heard his suppressed anger. If it had been back home, his possessions would have been safe. He could have slept in his own bed later that night, on his couch, or opted to crash amid the comforting junk in his crowded basement. He wouldn't be absurdly holding back Kreyòl curses against American lumber or wanting to let loose against his neighbors, who had gathered to see the carnage and plot to buy the soon-to-be cleared double lot at a bargain.

Lucien pleaded his case to the fire marshal. "My things! My girls are in there!"

He braced himself against the shaky fence with his good arm. He could barely stand. It had been at least an hour since he'd crawled out of his dilapidated van on one good leg. His first stroke had done little damage five years ago. The second one paralyzed his left forearm to his wrist, leaving that hand and three fingers irreparably curled into a claw. He didn't bother with the walker Medicaid had paid for or the cane, preferring to limp while dragging his left foot along to get around. If his partially crippled state had not conveyed to the fire marshal that he was out of sorts, his hoarse ranting certainly did.

"My girls! Please, please!" He placed his claw on the man's shoulder. If he could have folded his hands in prayer and dropped to his knees, he would have. He struggled to speak over his Guyanese neighbors, who were explaining to the demolition team and departing firefighters that Lucien had been ill for years.

"Not just his body." The husband made the universal symbol for crazy—a pointer finger circling his ear and temple.

"Dementia," the wife said loud enough for Lucien and the fire marshal to hear. "I'm a nurse."

"A nurse's *aide!*" Lucien hollered hoarsely. "Not a real nurse!" Only the fire marshal heard his comment.

"Listen, sir, no one's going back in there. We checked as much as we could without endangering the lives of my men and there's no one inside. Anyone who may have been, I'm sorry to tell ya, is probably gone. As is protocol, we'll examine the debris for any remains. We'll let you know if we find anything."

Lucien chirped and then realized that the marshal, who was Italian, would not get the meaning of sucking teeth. "Let me go and see!"

"I'm afraid we can't let you do that. There's no way in. Even if there was, there would be no way out, and I can't risk lives trying to get to you."

On the verge of tears, Lucien dug his claw deeper into the marshal's shoulder.

The marshal did not recoil. "I understand. I'm sorry. I know this is tough. We have support. Some folks from the Red Cross should be here any minute. I'm really sorry for your loss, sir."

Lucien's neighbors came to where he stood.

"Man, I'm sorry. I can't imagine. I just can't imagine." The husband hung and shook his head.

"Is someone coming to get you? We can call . . ." The wife sounded as if she might cry.

"No, no. My girls are in there."

"How old are your girls now, Mr. Lucien? They're grown." The husband turned and spoke directly to the fire marshal. "His kids have been out of the house for more than twenty years. His wife's been dead for about as long," he added. "We've lived up the block since his girls were little."

"He's in shock. This is normal," the wife insisted.

"You ready?" The husband checked his watch, a too-shiny fake-gold timepiece that was out of place for his line of work.

The couple walked away but stopped to chat with other neighbors as the morning bloomed brighter, pushing everyone toward their respective bus stops.

Lucien did not lift his head to observe the morning exodus. It had been decades since his wife had had to make the Queens to Manhattan commute that required taking at least one bus and one train. Most commuters hadn't bothered with the bus in years. Instead, they boarded dollar vans, leaving the buses for those with time on their hands—patient students with school bus passes and elderly riders who paid discounted fares. He didn't remember the last time he'd ridden in anything besides his gray minivan or his yellow taxicab.

None of his neighbors had taken the two-time stroke survivor seriously, no matter how strong he'd tried to look without his walker or cane. With only a dry whisper to protest the refusals of the emergency crews, he crawled into the back of his cluttered van. His neighbors had added diagnoses of shock and dementia to his physical impediments, making him want to vomit and scream into their faces. He sat down in the ice-cold vehicle planning his next move. But before he could even recline, a car pulled up and screeched to a stop.

A woman hopped out in a huff. She was on a mission. Leona LaMerci, his girlfriend and caregiver, was as elegant as she was frustrated. She was dressed for work, where she'd been headed when a neighbor did what Lucien had not thought to do: call. With leather-gloved hands, she pulled her belt tighter around her thick coat, as if that would keep more heat in. She was fully covered, skirt over pants over tights, socks inside shearling-lined boots, coat over scarf over sweater over turtleneck, hat over kerchief over thick silken hair. What the necessary insulation could not hide was the prettiness of her youthful face, the watering of her chestnut eyes, her kissable ChapStick-laced lips. She turned the heads of onlookers from the smoldering house to the curvy girlish lover Lucien did not deserve. With worry and cold creasing her skin and quickening her step, Leona looked like a well-heeled and -groomed Christian mother who had come to beg her derelict prodigal son to come home one more time.

A concerned and lucid someone had called her to drag him from the front of his burned-down house, throw a coat over his shoulders, and drive him away. Lucien refused to get out of his van and into Leona's car. When he finally did, he didn't say a word. To shield himself from the onslaught of pelting pain, he retreated into his mind like a bullet reversing into its gun barrel. She wouldn't understand. She wouldn't believe that his girls were trapped in the basement. She was probably secretly glad that all of what she regarded as his distractions had perished in the fire. Maybe if he'd kept things clean or at least in order, she would think, he could have saved some.

Lucien found it disconcerting, even offensive, that Leona kept her vehicle and her house so pristine. He'd never been able to spend a lot of time at her place because of its cleanliness. He was repelled by her neatness. He let her believe that it was her good housekeeping that had led him to hire her as Marie-Ange's in-home hospice nurse. But it had been Leona's early tolerance of his junk that had earned her the job. That was one of the few times he'd been beguiled by a woman. And it had only been because he was already grieving Marie-Ange's impending death that came years later than the doctors had said it would.

The first time he'd met Leona, she'd been wearing a light spring coat, camel colored with a hint of peach, a shade darker than her skin. She was tall, two inches taller than him in her chunky nurses' orthopedic loafers. Her button-down A-line dress was cinched at the waist and held tighter by a wide, manly leather belt. Slivers of her camisole poked out of the gaps between the buttons of her dress that struggled to stay fastened all the way up to her collar. She wore a sky-blue silk scarf dotted with clouds on her head and tied loosely under her chin. Beneath it, her wavy hair showed like a poorly guarded secret. This would be the last time he would see her hair that way outside of her home. Thereafter she wore it parted down the middle and plaited in two childlike cornrows. He was fortunate to catch her blow-drying it after her weekly wash. On Saturdays, he saw nothing but her hair. It flowed over her clavicle, stopping at her breasts if she was wearing a bra or at her breastbone if she wasn't. The rest of it slapped her shoulder blades in the back. He remembered her face that first time. Her shiny black brows and lashes drawing her hairline into her face, leaving a two-finger sliver of a forehead. Her powdered face was all one shade including her lips. The cream of her teeth provided contrast. Her reddish-brown irises changed shapes and colors like a kaleidoscope.

She preferred to wear clothes that were one size too small than to accept her weight gain. Her clothes were of a good quality but modest. She wore mostly dresses and skirts even in the winter. Every so often, on days when the ice-sliced wind found its way into the space where her thighs met, she would wear pants under her skirt like the immigrant women from whom she tried to distance herself. Otherwise, when the wind was tolerable, when it fondled like the hands of a lover coming in from the cold, she wore thick tights that she changed out of immediately upon arrival at her destination. Although she usually wore pajamas to sleep, she'd started wearing nightgowns that were convenient for him.

If Leona's outfits were contrived, her speech was not. She started out speaking French, which excited him. As his charm overcame her formality, they slipped into the intimacy of Kreyòl. She had a mellifluous voice as if she should have been able to sing, but she couldn't. Her eloquence announced her education. She was as well-read and well-bred as Marie-Ange had been. But Leona, having had no doting father to inspire arrogance, was desperate for affection.

Leona had a fluid feminine walk and an aristocratic carriage. She stood like both the strict mistress of the house waiting to be served and the servant at attention waiting to be called. She'd sat comfortably among his clutter and entertained the cautious vulgarity he'd used to test her tolerance.

He'd come to regret allowing Leona to squeeze past his instincts during her interview. He'd been fooled by her willingness to sit amid his collection of junk, feigning tolerance of his mess. As his comfort with her had increased, she'd begun strategically hiding the spoils of his hoarding, secreting his stuff out of immediate view as best she could. At least she hadn't thrown it away. As he sat in her new-looking old car with lick-able leather seats, he sensed what she was thinking. *Leave them. Leave them. How many? Tell me, who, and how many?* She might indulge his delusion and let him enumerate who and what he'd left behind in the ruins of the fire. But, more than a decade into their relationship, he still refused to let her hear him count. And he never dared acknowledge, let alone whispered out loud to himself, the depth of the zero as the first number in his counting. *I am nothing.*

He listed for himself what and how many he could remember having in the basement. The decades-old thirteen-inch television sets with channel knobs were stacked, wobbling, nineteen sets high. The eight-track tape decks nearly toppling at thirty-two levels. The oblong first-generation Macintosh personal comput-ers in towers of twelve. Speakers of every dimension rose insepa-rable from the basement floor like stalks of sugarcane. The boxy relics bolstered one another to form a wall on either side of the narrow walkway he had created so he could use the bathroom in the back of his basement while sorting and taking inventory. The turntables, cassette decks, VCRs, DVD players, tape recorders, compact Walkmans, and CD players filled in the cracks like cement between bricks to keep his junk walls from toppling.

Still counting, Lucien moved his mind to itemize the cans of food he had last brought to the safe room. In his head he saw the candles, the gallons of spring water, the canned meat and fish, the preserved vegetables and fruit from his summer garden, and the backup blankets. He recounted these things two, three, four times, and then moved forward to the important things. He lost his place counting his women. He wanted to cry as he had done many times before when he hadn't been able to name the place from which he told himself, *I am nothing.*

Lucien sat in the back seat and reluctantly closed his eyes to nap in Leona's 1987 Toyota Corolla that looked as perfect on the inside thirty years later as it did the day she'd bought it.

"New, brand-new," she liked to tell people about her purchase. Lucien swallowed the tears that threatened to breach his façade in Leona's presence. He had never cried in front of her, not even when they visited Marie-Ange's grave, not even when they'd attended Marie-Ange's funeral as co-caregivers, not lovers. He was not about to start now.

"Lulou, why?" Leona insisted. "I'm sorry. I know. I can't believe it either. But it's okay. We have our lives. And at least Marie-Ange isn't here to see this. I'm so sorry."

Lucien didn't bother to answer. He barely heard her.

Leona was no substitute for Marie-Ange or even one of his girls. She was a good imitation of his wife—grateful to do his accounting with his Social Security, Medicaid, and Medicare benefits so he wouldn't end up penniless. But she refused to ride with him in what she insultingly referred to as his "smelly, piece-of-crap minivan." He went alone on his trips collecting empty cans and bottles and other malodorous trash in the city. Leona wouldn't hold her nose and suck it up for him like Marie-Ange had. She wouldn't allow gambling in her house either, nor was she a good enough cook or a patient enough hostess to turn her kitchen and dining room into a restaurant to feed comrades from back home and any needy associates they brought with them. As much as he referred to her as the second Madame Lucien, she would not allow him to turn her house into the second KAM. Lucien was disgusted at the thought of having to live with Leona, at least until he could repair or rebuild his scorched house.

He knew that his daughters would never visit him at Leona's, although it was clean. They would never visit him anywhere. The only thing that had brought them home had been Marie-Ange's funeral.

He'd wanted to hold them, three grown women who'd looked like little princesses memorializing their fallen queen at the church. His youngest daughter, Dor, had sung lead with her older sisters backing her up. Counter to her character, she'd even spoken up at the repast at the house, chiming in when Veille and Clair complained about the evidence of Lucien's hoarding that Leona had failed to hide well enough.

The girls had searched for and found Lucien's strays as well, sycophantic hang-abouts he'd taken in for days, weeks, or months in exchange for the sound of people talking, leisurely card games, and light petting when they were willing. The girls wailed at him over how he had tortured their mother with his collections of discarded junk and unworthy, usurious people up to her final living days. Why Marie-Ange had tolerated him at all was beyond words or tears. He could not argue.

He had dethroned Marie-Ange, the hardworking self-promoted queen who'd plunged them into debt to secure her throne in America. She'd dressed herself up and surrounded herself with three regally groomed princesses. She'd never imagined that she would die so young, at forty, in a hoarder's house. He had always known that he was beneath her, as she'd frequently reminded him by telling him stories about her father. He could still hear her favorite rant that, had her father been alive, he never would have permitted their courtship and eventual marriage. If not for the chaos of the failed coup that had separated her from her king, her doting general and de facto husband, she never would have fallen prey to Lucien's charming rescue. She'd known that it was only a matter of time before the baker and the spies gave up details of her clandestine flirtation with a barman. Only a matter of days before her father would pistol-whip it out of them and then beat Lucien down with his baton, cat-o'-nine-tails, fists, and kicks. This beating would have been personally executed in the presence of his lieutenants as a lesson about what happened to those who crossed him by even thinking about his prized daughter. That day, that discovery, and that beating never came, so Marie-Ange had been carried from the city that had disappeared her father straight to Nen-

nen's place, where she'd given birth to Veille, married Lucien, and then given him Clair and Dor to round out the threesome who would deliver their final performance at her funeral. How low—*how low!*—he had brought their mother. They would not allow him to do it to them again.

Lucien ignored Leona as she opened the car door, lifted her thin legs, and planted her feet on the icy pavement. She slammed the door as hard as she could to get his attention, but he pretended not to notice. He sat in the car in front of her house until dusk, refusing to go into what he knew would be his jail for months to come. He searched his pockets for her spare car keys, crawled into the driver's seat, and took off for home.

As he drove, he started his counting, hearing his daughters in the back of his mind. He counted the carcasses of decrepit electronics. Ten, twenty, thirty. What? Television sets? Turntables? Space heaters? Empty barrels to send stuff to Haiti for one of his customers? He could hear the demolition machinery from several blocks away. He sped up and arrived just as a backhoe was driving into the empty parcel next to his house. He jumped out of the car as if he'd never had one, let alone two strokes, limping like a three-legged cat that had mastered its handicap. Still hoarse, he shouted at the driver not to knock down the apple tree. He rushed to the tree and looked around. He was worried that he wouldn't be able to revive some of his bushes. The ground would be flattened by the trucks and harder to hoe by hand in the spring.

"Get out of here, man!" the driver shouted.

Two members of the demolition team held each of Lucien's arms, trying to drag him away from the base of his precious tree.

"Come on, man! Don't make us hurt you."

"Can I get some things out of the house?"

"Sure. As soon as we're done tearing it down." The men did not laugh, but their sarcasm was insulting.

"Okay. Okay. I'll move." Lucien snatched his arms out of the clutches of the men who may as well have been his jailers. He walked around the house, staying as low as he could, trying to peer into the basement windows, looking for a way in.

"You are not getting into this damned house, man! Not on our watch."

Lucien was incensed that the man had damned his house like any old structure. He tried not to cry out loud. *This isn't just a house! It is a life! My life! My dream! I am nothing. I am nothing without it, without them.*

But was he just dreaming now? Of his girls trapped in the basement? Of a family long gone? Was he having a nightmare of his house burning down? Had his life really caught fire? Was it really about to be leveled flat? Was this him or was it his house thinking, speaking? Did his house want to die? Did he? Was this a dream about his overburdened house? A house that had taken his girls and maybe even his wife prisoner? He counted: *Zero, One, Two, Three,* and stopped before *Four.*

The house creaked a little while Lucien squatted by the farthest basement window, the one closest to the safe room. He got stuck trying to get back up and had to call for help.

"We told you!"

Lucien did not thank the hard-hatted worker for helping him up. As he walked back to Leona's repulsively clean car, he heard it. The house buckled then chuckled: *Your family is gone, man.*

LA KAY

The House settled into a coma and waited to die. Something was holding It back. Something was holding It up. Its slumping aluminum siding, Its weakened steel frame, the crushed remnants of Lucien's hoarding: junk appliances stacked from the basement floor to Its ceiling, the same on the ground floor, more in the upstairs bedrooms all the way to the roof. Something wouldn't let La Kay die. Something inside wanted to survive Its suicide attempt. There were only two things It loved enough to live for—children and music—and It hadn't heard a whisper of either in a very long time. As far as It could feel, neither was present after the fire. It hurt so badly to think of life after. It knew that It was now uninhabitable. It also knew that Lucien's standards were low. He'd regularly slept in his trash dump of a van. But the smell of burned things, the wetness of fabrics turning musty and moldy, the crumbling floors and ceilings, would surely keep him away, unless he was being drawn in by someone or something inside.

La Kay wanted to get into his mind. It had done it before, outsmarted him and won. It wanted him to come back so It could find out what he knew, what had made him plead to be let back in, to risk being burned or buried alive. If It had to live while waiting to be demolished, It wanted to, at least, toy with Its nemesis and, perhaps, get him to kill himself.

It didn't care what Its neighbors thought. Their condescension, fear, and pity were of no consequence. It didn't give a damn if, like their owners, they wanted It torn down. It didn't give a single golden fuck what It looked like to them after the fire. Boarded up, KEEP OUT signs posted all over, spray-painted with graffiti by hood vandals or artists. It was way past the point of caring about anything, even music and children almost. It just wanted to collapse and let the demolition team end it all. But It wanted Lucien to come back inside and suffer the same.

He's the one who'd brought It to this point. He deserved to pay for inflicting so much pain on all Its occupants. He didn't deserve a second or third chance, a new life somewhere else. The misdeeds La Kay had witnessed warranted incarceration in the bowels of a crumbling building where his remains would mix in and be discarded with the decades of debris he'd collected. He deserved to be scooped up and dropped into a metal trash bin, indecipherable from the rest of his garbage. La Kay held firm to Its belief that he needed to be dismembered alive by Its broken windowpanes, crushed to death by Its sandwiched ceilings, and pressed into a junk pile while his mind remained alive to witness his own demise.

It had plans for Lucien, one final coup before resigning Itself to an undeserved death that would also be a well-earned rest.

Two

LUCIEN

——————

Lucien slept through first light. He missed the red rising of the sun shrugging off the night while basking in its own glow. He didn't even hear Leona step out of the taxi in front of his house. He'd known for decades that he couldn't hear anything over his motorcycle-engine-like snoring, including the snoring itself. He could remember Leona reminding him of what his now deceased wife, Marie-Ange, had said constantly: that he slept as deeply as death. He would always respond that this flaw was perfect for living in South Ozone Park, where low-flying planes sounded as if they were taking off from or about to land in their backyard. He'd never known the word for the condition, but he'd listened carefully when Leona had later explained narcolepsy to him. For decades, he'd lived with his condition and accepted that he could and did fall asleep whenever he was seated and still, wherever he happened to be—stopped at a red light; having a conversation that did not require intellectual agility, did not involve money, or did not require counting or calculations. Conversations with Leona especially had always bored him, and as soon as he'd known that he could trust her, which is to say that he could manipulate her into behaving the way he wanted, he hadn't bothered listening for her arriving or departing footsteps. He'd continued to sleep this way to keep from hearing anything she said, the same way he couldn't hear the voices of people speaking in his dreams.

His self-awareness had allowed him to judge his own features that helped produce the sleep sounds. He never believed that anything could compromise his good looks, including the flaps of his nostrils that were as wide as the wings of a Cessna. The shape of his nose spoke for itself—the visual manifestation of a plane engine roar when he slept. For the better part of his life, he'd been so absorbed in the privilege of his light skin that he hadn't seen that it was merely a superficial veil thrown over distinctly African features. When looking into mirrors, he had judged his lips as copious and pleasurably kissable, perfect for embracing targets by choice or by force. He would complete his assessment by looking deeply into his hazel eyes. He appreciated the heaviness of his eyelids that allowed him to pretend convincingly to be asleep.

Only the deliberate slamming of the car door woke him up. He saw no need to open his eyes to watch Leona walk from the taxicab to his van. He did not stir under the coarse gray blankets more suitable for wrapping and moving furniture than for comfortable deep sleep. He liked the feel of the three formerly scratchy covers that he'd worn smooth whenever he didn't want to sleep alone in his house. He burrowed his body deeper into the pile. Surrounded by the broken legs of a large table he had not had a chance to unload, he insulated himself against the January cold with an immaculate coffin-sized cardboard box that read HANDLE WITH CARE. On it was an outline drawing of a couch. He had picked it up from a gentrifying neighborhood on the border of Morningside Heights and Harlem—same neighborhood, different shades of people. He'd wished that the owners had also discarded the Italian nubuck sofa bed the box had once held. He thought he knew the type of people who wouldn't give a second thought to tossing good furniture when the style no longer suited their taste. These sorts were comfortable, well-housed owners with pampered pets more contented than the human being loading the empty box shell into his van. He'd considered his own privilege, knowing that he had no need for and was less entitled to that perfect carton that would have sheltered a homeless man more fittingly. He'd appreciated the irony of looking homeless while owning a home. But with his house ravaged by fire and about to be torn down, he had finally earned the box, that luxurious domain of the housed and well-fed, and the right to sleep outdoors as he had previously done out of insanity and vanity.

Lucien could feel Leona peering into the back of his van. Of course, she'd checked and hadn't found him in the front seat. He snored a little bit louder in the hopes that she would go away, although he knew she wouldn't. He tried to make himself small under the cardboard box. He knew that she wouldn't bother opening the back doors even though she could do so quite easily. His minivan's doors—driver's side, passenger side, and rear—had no locks. He loved how the unlocked doors kept people out, that it confused them as much as the look of the van. Whereas the even yellow of his taxicab made him itch, he found the chaos of his minivan's exterior soothing. A patchwork of dented salvaged steel in various shades of gray stitched together like the mismatched strays he'd pieced together into a family. But the odor that engulfed the van had been the real deterrent. He still enjoyed catching a whiff of stale swigs of beer in the bottles and cans he collected more to give him opportunities to count than for the nickel apiece that added up to hundreds a month. He could get three, sometimes four rounds of counting out of one haul. Once when picking them up behind closing bars and restaurants. A second when taking them out of the thick black plastic bag, large and opaque enough to conceal and carry a body. Then a third time when rinsing each one. And a fourth and final time when sadly packing them away for the trip to the recycling center. He used to get a fifth round placing them one at a time into the supermarket's crunching machine, but he'd been banned from bringing his loads there. He noted how many vessels he'd collected after every trip, adding up the numbers and then counting from zero until he reached the tens of thousands.

He heard Leona climb cautiously into the driver's seat and start the engine with the spare key he'd thought he'd lost long ago. He crawled out of his pretend slumber as the icy van warmed up. He didn't bother sitting up until he smelled Leona's perfume floating above the smell of stale, burning motor oil the van emitted. Her scent was rather ordinary, unlike the varied, expensive French perfumes that Marie-Ange had worn even in her coffin. Heartbreak and missing Marie-Ange's scent finally made him sit up properly amid his sleep pile. He didn't bother climbing into the passenger seat to sit beside Leona. It was easier to talk to the back of her head when he lied; not that he had ever had difficulty doing so to her face. He hadn't even told her his true birth date, that he had his mother's last name, Louverture, not his father's, or why his children had cut all ties with him after their mother's death.

He watched as Leona fidgeted, clearly unaware that he was awake until he finally spoke. "I'm waiting for them. They can't tear down my house!" he shouted, startling Leona. She was jolted and banged her neck against the metal of the stripped headrest. She gripped the door handle as if ready to run out. He didn't want her there anyway, but his words had given her all the invitation she needed to stay and get started on one of her monologues.

"The house isn't safe. Do you want to die in there? You have to care. You're too old for this . . ."

Lucien tuned out Leona's admonishing lecture. "My girls are there. My girls," he repeated in a whisper.

She ignored him but still felt the twinge of jealousy that he could be so worried about the daughters who had abandoned him. Despite her hurt, she tried to allay his fears.

"There are legal options to stop them from tearing down the house, Lulou. And there's a snowstorm coming that will delay everything. The temperature will drop below zero. No one will want to work in that weather. The house is in bad shape. But it won't fall down in a day or two. It might hold up for a few weeks or more. Even if it was about to fall, it wouldn't collapse straight down into itself. You don't see how it's leaning? To its right, toward the garden, not the neighbor's house. Let's go, Lulou. I have to get to work. Where are my keys? Lulou? Lulou?"

Lucien hated hearing Leona call him by one of Marie-Ange's pet names for him. At least she didn't call him by his favorite, Luci, which had been reserved for the bedroom. Marie-Ange had been his everything and, as far as what he understood of love, the real thing. Like knockoff perfume, Leona's was only an imitation of Marie-Ange's loving. But so was his.

Hearing the demolition crew arriving, he jumped out of the back of the van while Leona was midsentence. Before they could make it to his front gate, he started pleading. It was his turn to be tuned out. At some point, he stopped listening to their refusals and disappeared into his counting, taking mental inventory of the people and supplies in the back room.

There is at least one, no two gallons of water left. The confiture from last fall's fallen apples is good for another 365 days. There are at least two jars. The bread must be gone by now. Twenty slices in a loaf. Four for each of them. The canned sardines are likely still there. They never liked sardines. The cans didn't require a can opener. The Spam either. Even its jelly could be eaten in a pinch. Anyway, it had been only a day and a half since he'd seen them down there. *No, today is Monday. I saw them last Wednesday. The fire . . . Oh, the fire!* Toné! *Yesterday, Sunday. Let me see . . . Sunday, Monday, Tuesday, yes, Wednesday will make one week. They'll need water. One, two, three, four gallons. Four girls, grown women really. They mostly look like my Ange. Why did she leave me? Why did they? Don't they know? I am nothing. Nothing without them.*

"Lulou! Get in the car! Let's go. I have to go to work."

Lucien ignored Leona as she climbed out of his van and headed to her car. He could hear her keys jingle as she unlocked the driver's-side door of her immaculate Corolla.

"Let's go, Lulou!"

He didn't want to leave, but the workers hadn't even looked at him, let alone listened to his pleas. He ducked his head as he climbed into her back seat. He refused to sit next to her. He didn't want to see her, not even her profile. He liked her to be faceless, almost invisible, certainly inconsequential, even now that he had nowhere to stay. He didn't want to see her because that would mean she could see him. And he wanted to count. *Zero, One, Two, Three. Four is gone. One and a half gallons of water. Enough confiture. No bread. Spam jelly. Sardines, if they got hungry enough to eat what they hate.* He half listened as Leona picked up from where she'd left off.

"Lulou, you've done all you could. You did everything for those girls. And our Marie-Ange too."

Leona had claimed Marie-Ange as her own, not because of the time she'd spent caring for her, but because she believed, and told everyone she met, that it was Marie-Ange's spirit that had sent her to Lucien. She remembered conversations that had never happened between her and the dying woman. She'd received the wife's blessing before the husband even became a widower. Better yet, she'd been instructed to care for him in every way, even, and maybe especially, sexually.

"She's okay, Lulou. I know you think she's mad at you. The house. The way it is now."

Lucien hated to hear Leona speak about Marie-Ange, to hear anyone claim his saint besides him.

Marie-Ange wouldn't just be disappointed by the collapse of the house they had worked so hard for, borrowed against repeatedly, lost to the loan sharks while still living there, and then repurchased for three times the original cost. She would have died all over again to know that he couldn't rescue the girls.

Maybe she had been right. Maybe he had been distracted by his tenants, as she'd always insisted. Boss Dieuseul, the man upstairs who shared shifts driving his taxi and who rented their daughters' empty bedroom, was still there. Asante was "gone." After all the fuss over the downstairs tenant for whom he had displaced Marie-Ange's statues of the goddess Ezili and the glass-clad candles to the boiler room, leaving her nowhere to properly honor her deities. Maybe the fire was Marie-Ange's payback for that. Maybe she'd lit and knocked over some candles. But she would never harm his girls.

It could have been his obsession with his house that he'd run around drilling holes into, trying to make it perfect. Maybe his home, adversarial but beloved, had had enough and spontaneously combusted just to destroy all the junk weighing it down. But if his house could feel the burden of his hoarding and get pissed off enough to set itself on fire, then it had to know about his girls in the safe room. Maybe the room had been too perfectly insulated, so that even his overly sensitive house could not feel their heartbeats, their coughs, their dry-mouth whispers, the soft chewing of mushy canned meat, marmalade, and homemade Haitian *manba*. Maybe the room was so safe it had made itself smaller, quieter, invisible, undiscoverable, even by a hurting house on the verge of suicide. Maybe his house had never felt their pounding fists, their constant scraping at every crevice that looked weak and penetrable. Maybe that room was an amputated limb lying adjacent to, but no longer a part of, the body. Like him and Leona even when they were having sex.

He felt as apart from Leona during the act as he did sitting in the back seat refusing to join her in the front. Maybe she was not a reward but one of Marie-Ange's punishments. Maybe Leona LaMerci was no gift to be thankful for like her last name implied. Maybe she had set his house on fire to force him closer to her. They were like the house and its back room—adjacent but so separate that one could easily live without the other. She was the surviving appendage on a corpse, throbbing with blood, aching but determined to persevere. He did not experience her as a living limb but as the removable leg of a doll, the brainless, faceless plastic figure too dumb and needy to acknowledge that they were not together. He felt nothing for her, not even the shadow pains of dismemberment. He was the numb body that knew no emotion except for a hatred he could not acknowledge. He didn't even know that he had no true feelings at all, that he'd learned only to mirror those of others with none of his own. *Nothing.*

He could not shake the suspicion that Leona did feel their separateness and had been angry enough to murder his house to bring him closer. How much closer did she want them to be? They were practically neighbors. She lived in Ozone Park, close to the Brooklyn border. He lived in South Ozone, just a ten-minute drive away. The difference between their two neighborhoods was negligible. The row houses in hers were attached at the hip. The homes in his were detached. Most of them boasted spacious rentable basements with extraordinary back rooms, a peculiarity that he believed had saved his girls. He was neither insane nor suffering from dementia. There were women in that room, protected from fire and, for the moment, the collapse of an overwhelmed and suicidal house.

Leona revved the engine to try to cajole him into the front seat. He ignored the music she turned on to rouse him. He refused to meet her eyes in the rearview mirror. Instead, he lay down in a fetal position, which was easy for him with one hand and one foot already crippled. He felt like the deserted child he had always been. He'd taken in strays, as his children had called them, because he felt like one of them despite his still-living parents who'd mercifully brought him, his bride, and three babies to America. The people he accepted at KAM with or without vetting by Marie-Ange were like him. They had family. Some of them were even related to him or Marie-Ange distantly. He often took these relatives at their word, not wanting to have to probe his parents or theirs for the specifics. He could not remember if Boss Dieuseul was a second or third cousin, or if they were related at all.

"I haven't heard from Dieuseul." These were his first words to Leona as they drove to her house.

Leona perked up and turned down the radio. "I haven't heard from him either. I called his cell phone."

"I hate those things."

"That's because you never use yours."

"I never use mine because I hate those things."

"But when I need to reach you . . ."

"Nothing is ever that urgent."

"What about your life, your health? What about when the fire started? You could have called me."

"I wasn't thinking about calling anybody."

"Yes, you were. But that's okay. It's okay to think about your children no matter how grown they are or how far away. I would want to have mine right up under me." Leona cupped her breasts with her right arm as maternal confirmation, a gesture Lucien could not see.

"Me too" were Lucien's last words before his narcolepsy reeled him in like a minnow on a fishing pole.

He was never aware of the actual moment he fell asleep. Nodding off was natural whenever he sat for any length of time, so his daydreams, memories, and REM sleep ran into each other like an endless city block with no corners or crossings. His last thought before his closed eyes fluttered was of Dieuseul and whether they were related or just two men who had taken to each other more quickly than his other long- or short-term tenants.

Lucien had felt immediately comfortable enough to lease Dieuseul the morning shift driving his taxi without asking around about the newcomer to KAM and without requiring a deposit. The latter upset Marie-Ange, who'd already budgeted the funds, mentally applying one-third of the $1,000 to a new outfit. Years later, when Dieuseul's marriage to a black American woman deteriorated as rapidly as Marie-Ange's health, Lucien offered him his daughters' old bedroom upstairs. Marie-Ange was too exhausted to argue or even to question the decision. At least she knew and liked Dieuseul, who'd painted a portrait of their daughters from an old picture she cherished. He'd painted them as affectionately as he treated her, even though she was no longer beautiful or elegant.

Lucien had also appreciated conversations with his tenant and the man's attentiveness toward his wife, which would have made another man jealous or at least suspicious. But Dieuseul took the burden of caring for Marie-Ange off Lucien's shoulders. Dieuseul turned out to be the best company for Marie-Ange, who required extra help getting in and out of bed and climbing down the stairs to cook, something she insisted Lucien let her continue to do. Dieuseul had gladly held her under the elbow and obliged her all night long while Lucien sleepily drove the taxi during the night shift.

Lucien had not planned to still be driving a taxi at that stage. He'd planned to honor Marie-Ange's wishes not to take in tenants in the upstairs bedrooms or the basement. But the reality of their immigrant lives had fallen short of their dreams for their home, family, and community. In the beginning, they'd tried harder than anyone around them. New revenue streams materialized as quickly as Haitians stepped off planes and tipped out of boats onto America's hard ground. The food Marie-Ange prepared at KAM was only a welcome. Some thought it was a lure because of the perfume of her rice and beans, the crispiness of her fried green plantains, and the tenderness of her perfectly seasoned *griot* coaxed patrons who soon discovered the other offerings at KAM. Those who came for the promise of the best Haitian food in Queens, or a friendly moneymaking game of poker, dominos, or bezique, always needed and left with more than they'd come for. They were hungry for good food and company and downright desperate for immigrant services.

As Lucien slept, the memory of KAM rose like dough. His heart didn't swell; it stretched like a balloon being filled with air. He remembered how he had worked with Marie-Ange to increase their growing understanding of U.S. laws and institutions. He was the one who'd insisted they monetize their expertise and help KAM's patrons for a fee or for favors. While visitors ate and played cards, Lucien and Marie-Ange translated immigration documents, explained what FICA was on tax-eroded minimum-wage paychecks, arranged hookups for papers that an illegal immigrant could use for work, set up dates between green card holders and desperate *san-soulyé* undocumented seekers in need of spouses for plausible marriages that immigration officers would not question or deny.

Marie-Ange's English had grown so quickly and so eloquent that she had been paid to attend court hearings, citizenship interviews, and doctors' appointments. Lucien's domain had been all things vehicular—how to get a driver's license, where to get documents notarized, how to register a car, how to get insurance, where to get repairs made for cheap so the vehicle could pass inspection and be deemed suitable to insure and register. He connected buyers to sellers, held vehicles and money in his own form of escrow—the backyard for the cars and his locked briefcase for the cash. He ran raffles on Sundays for items he'd bought on credit or Marie-Ange's Avon products that weren't selling fast enough.

Lucien buried his head into the pillow of memories, dreaming of the good old days when he and his gorgeous wife worked to expand their bona fide cottage industry. They'd grown KAM into a marginally profitable business that didn't really earn them profits as much as it kept them flush with the cash of others as they brokered transactions. For a time, they'd thought they might be able to quit their jobs, but the medical benefits and the twenty-dollars-an-hour wage Lucien earned were indispensable. Marie-Ange had not wanted to leave her jobs on Wall Street, first as a cashier at a Duane Reade drugstore, then as a secretary in one of the law firms off Chambers Street. She'd landed the latter while translating and then filling out immigration documents at the Immigration and Naturalization Service office for a struggling Haitian grandmother. A lawyer in a priority lane had overheard her Frenchified English and the accuracy of her translation. Impressed with her legal advice, he'd offered her a job on the spot. That same afternoon, Marie-Ange had picked up two new suits from a Jewish-owned boutique on Delancey Street that she'd had on layaway for several months.

The following Monday morning she'd arrived at the law office better dressed than the long-tenured white paralegals with straight ponytails and impeccable bouffants. Although she never wore makeup, her flawless brown skin the color of coconut shells and her naturally plum-tinted lips made the few black cleaning ladies and bathroom attendants request the shade of powder and lipstick she used. To make her self-imposed Avon sales quota, she would pretend that her bottom eyelids were not naturally black, that her lips were not genetically tinted the same color as her gums. She would eventually double her target quota, selling products to women who wanted to look like her. But as the white secretaries struggled to keep up with her work quality and obscenely unaffordable wardrobe and the black cleaning staff tried to get their skin as smooth as hers, the envy of the two groups on both sides of the racial divide boiled over. Their unspoken competition against her would eventually explode after years of insufferable coveting of her exceptional typing skills, multilingual fluency, mastery of immigration law, and sexy diplomacy that allowed her to correct the partner who'd hired her straight from the INS line. They waited five long years to strip the pride that shone through her pricey wardrobe, natural beauty, and curvaceous figure.

Dubbing her the black Betty Boop, the women had been disgusted by the lust her thick thighs and legs elicited from the men in the office—white lawyers and black janitors alike. In their minds and closely guarded gossip, they hatched fantastic plots to put gum in her abundant hair that she tamed to look professional. They wished she'd leave some of it out of her loose bun, so they could put envelope glue in it, so she'd have to cut it, at least, in half. They imagined getting her Chaka Khan weave-like waves caught in a filing cabinet that they would lock, leaving only the option of a complete chop to set her free. The only comfort they had was that she had been going prematurely gray since age three. Most of the gray hairs were at the nape of her neck. She wore her hair back in a low ponytail most of the time to hide those. But an elegant shimmery line streaked down the left side of her head from where her temple vein throbbed, ending just above her left ear.

Lucien reached into his dream and grabbed at the hair he'd always loved. He could not let go of Marie-Ange's beauty, the very thing that had gotten her fired. And those people hadn't even seen the fullness of her looks. No one at work had ever seen her with her hair out. They would have murdered her outright to see her fresh from the salon. Only when she got a wash and set at the pricey Harlem beauty parlor did she indulge in a coif of soft loose curls. Only then could others see the length of her hair that hit below her shoulder blades, the hair that had made her marginally acceptable to Lucien's family. She was far too dark for the loosely inbred terceron clan. But her long hair, even before she had ever straightened or relaxed it, allowed her to pass for good enough. That and her spit shine polish—her private school education, impeccable dress, and high-class upbringing, enjoyed until her father was disappeared. Years later, while working in an alien country and office, she suffered another devastating disappearance. A pricey pair of shoes had gone missing and gotten her fired from her fancy office job.

Marie-Ange had pissed off too many people at the law firm. She'd physically rebuffed her bosses' passes one time too many. She'd ignored the Cameroonian janitor who called her *"ma soeur,"* hoping for the acknowledgment that would lead to coffee in the cafeteria, over which he would slip her his phone number and get hers, then maybe a date and so on. Not a single woman at the office had been able to tolerate the perfection she'd honed while serving fifteen years as the daughter of the first Duvalier's closest adviser. Her expensive wardrobe was a product of the same training, except less for being a good daughter and more for being a proxy trophy—a gentle, compliant, doting daughter-wife to her adoring father-husband.

Lucien had warned her to watch out when she'd started earning a few cents more than some of the white secretaries. He'd even told her to stop buying and wearing designer clothes that they could not afford. He wasn't surprised that she ignored him. She felt entitled to the pair of Chanel shoes, even if she used two weeks' pay plus funds borrowed from the escrow monies in his locked briefcase and the money for that month's phone and electricity bills. Madison Avenue shops did not offer layaway plans. They accepted cash, check, and American Express. She paid by check from the separate bank account she'd kept secret from Lucien. She had finally purchased the high-heeled, pebbled leather slip-on pumps she'd seen the most senior paralegal wearing months before.

That paralegal, a sneaker commuter, kept several pairs of shoes, still in their shoeboxes, under her desk. Unlike that paralegal, Marie-Ange would wear her new high-heeled shoes like a supermodel. She'd strut to and from work and all around the office all day in her highest heels. When she got bored with a particular pair of shoes, she'd switch to an equally expensive pair. The day she switched her shoes turned out to be her last at the office.

Marie-Ange never did learn exactly how the plot had been contrived or who'd hatched it. But the sneaker commuter's pumps had gone missing, possibly picked up and discarded in the janitor's bin by a partner who'd been working late and, seeing the shoes under a desk, assumed they belonged to the black girl who refused to bed a man of his stature and decided on petty payback. The Cameroonian janitor didn't want to throw the clearly new pair of shoes away, but he had grown tired of waiting for a wink from Marie-Ange. The next morning, she came in wearing her Chanels while the other paralegal was losing her mind looking for her own pair. She immediately pointed the finger at Marie-Ange, who knew that there would be no vindicating Cinderella moment of trying on a shoe to see whether it fit the true owner. Upon seeing the accusing eyes of the entire office, she left in a panic before she could be unjustly fired for theft.

That afternoon Marie-Ange boarded the A train with a slight bend in her neck. Sitting across from her were two women—one Haitian (she always recognized her people) and a black American who tried not to let her leather coat touch her neighbor. She stared at the Haitian woman, wondering if she would have to return to the life of a nanny-housekeeper after years of proud office work. She recognized the American woman's attempt to distance herself from her neighbor. It was the same way Marie-Ange had lived in Haiti, next to but apart from, different but akin to those believed to be less than. She could see that both women were staring at her feet, trying to figure out who and what she was and where she belonged. She had developed a close kinship with immigrants like herself, although they'd come from very different economic classes. However, until that day, she'd never felt an alliance with Amer-

ican blacks. She'd been stripped of her privilege, wrongly accused of theft, and ejected from the class she believed she'd
entered. She thought of the reciprocal prejudice between immigrant and America-born blacks, each group misunderstand-
ing the other, envy and resentment on both sides, separated by
how their Americanness had been obtained. Haitian immigrants
adopted the biases and stereotypes held by whites against black
Americans. Black Americans looked down on the lowly, ass-
backward, more "African" immigrants who struggled for better
lives in a foreign home, resenting them for attempting to rob
them of their birthright. America's native sons clutched their
tenuous citizenship with the power of a vise grip, as if immigrants could somehow purse-snatch their hard-won privilege.

Disdainfully and unsympathetically, they stood back and
looked down as their Caribbean and African just-come cousins
struggled for sponsorship by often reluctant or exploitative family members. A sibling or a parent might feel some allegiance,
obligation, absolute pity, genuine affection, or needy attach-
ment, or be simply worn down by on-their-knees pleas. The
desperate seekers might seduce, trick, or pay someone to marry
them. But the most they could become were naturalized citizens
of the United States. They could be converted but never native.
Never mind that black Americans had long been regarded as
second-class citizens. At least they were citizens by birth, not
by some mechanical conversion, some legally bastardized bap-
tism, some restoration of something broken or abnormal. The
foreigners were the abhorrent ones, rejected before they were
born by virtue of where they would be delivered. They would
go from aliens, legal or illegal, and, at best, become "unnatural"
American citizens. They might pass for black American if they
kept their mouths shut and adopted the proper garb. But their
contorted pronunciation of English words, accents as thick and
bumpy as oatmeal; their layers of sweaters, two or three hats, as
many strangling scarves, and ill-fitting winter coats would un-

mask them. Even their America-born children gave them away: little natives with kinky, basic-plaited hair, never braided then beaded; shiny shoes or leather sandals, never sneakers; knee-length skirts or high-water slacks, never jeans; thermos lunches of warm rice and beans, never sandwiches; proper English, never slang.

Marie-Ange looked at the two women and smiled in an attempt to make amends with and between both. She wanted to tell them that things would be okay and tried to believe the same herself as she rode home embarrassed and jobless. She waved as she stepped off the train. Neither woman waved back.

Lucien had understood why, even unemployed, Marie-Ange had resisted renting out their basement like their neighbors did. It wasn't only because she was a proud and deferential devotee who didn't want to displace Ezili's shrine. She had been saving that space for her most special women—their daughters. She'd planned for them to live there as college commuter students and then, one by one, they would move out to get married. She'd hoped that one of them would come back to raise her own family in the house when she and Lucien grew old and went back to Haiti or died. Marie-Ange had died. And, sure enough, Lucien had had his girls living in the basement. But none of it was as they had planned.

For the moment, he persisted in his waking dream in the back seat of Leona's car. Like hot breath blown close into his ear, he could feel Marie-Ange's wishes, her angst, and the humiliation she'd endured at the hands of others, including his own. Now he'd lost the house she'd debased herself for by cleaning white people's houses, wiping their children's noses, changing their elders' diapers, standing in their factories until her feet callused so badly she could peel thick layers off her heels with a knife, and serving these people as they made purchases from an overpriced drugstore, and finally been prejudicially indicted for stealing a pair of shoes that barely rivaled the hand-stitched Parisian pairs she'd worn since starting school at the age of three. She had been the general's daughter, dressed in French finery since birth. She had built KAM as the *manman* in Kay Manman. There was no other, no better, mother or wife to him.

Lucien startled himself awake, imagining Marie-Ange calling him, but it was Leona's voice letting him know they were approaching her house. He sat up to listen to whatever it was Leona needed him to know. Except for Marie-Ange, he had always been more enamored of his own thoughts than those of others, especially women. He was amused by the simplemindedness of the stronger sex, how easily he could manipulate them. Even Marie-Ange. While she lay dying, still showing her jealousy over their basement tenant Asante, he had already picked out a new wife—Leona, her caregiver—with the help of their daughters. He had had a mistress in the basement, a soon-to-be girlfriend running his home, and a dying wife in a bed upstairs. His grief and manhood had been the only things keeping the four-way arrangement from exploding.

He suddenly missed Asante but quieted the feeling, because the thought of his basement *bouzin* was a distraction from what he really needed to ponder. He sat up and stared straight ahead. The back of Leona's head kept him grounded in the present moment, so he could think clearly about how he would get into his house.

Leona would be of no use. She would, in fact, block his passage. She was a good nurse, had proven herself a proper jailer for Marie-Ange and him. He could blame no one but himself for his relationship with Leona. He'd picked her from the three finalists his daughters had offered as a nurse for Marie-Ange. After she passed, he'd kept Leona as his companion. She'd even attended Marie-Ange's funeral and visited her grave with him in the months and years after. Fortunately for Lucien, Leona, a long-widowed underachieving would-be physician who'd settled for becoming a trained RN, had been by his side during both of his strokes. But living with her until he sorted things out with his dying house would mean spending time away from his real life, his girls.

Lucien flicked his fingers to count in silence, *Zero, One, Two, Three.*

He climbed out of the car and all but crawled into Leona's house. He started coughing but hoped that she couldn't hear him. Homesick. Sick of home. This home. Her home. Sick for home. His home.

"Go straight to the bedroom!" Leona shouted.

He did not protest.

His boots were still on as he climbed into bed and pulled the covers up to his chin. Maybe he could make a home with his LeLe. Maybe they could unofficially adopt two or three young and struggling welfare mothers. Evenly light-skinned ones with syrupy curls who would resemble his family far more than Veille, Clair, and Dor. Leona's hair texture, complexion, and pure gullibility made her the ideal wife. But he couldn't let go of his house. It didn't deserve to be torn down, not after everything he and Marie-Ange had invested in it and planned for it. To have their girls, at least one of them, come with a family of her own and live there. To have that one take it over after their deaths or an indefinite return back home. His house deserved better, to be restored, nursed back to health. If it had to die, it deserved the same care Marie-Ange had received. It deserved Leona's prayers, stroking, and tears. Why couldn't she love it like she loved him? She could not truly love him if she couldn't love the only thing he had left.

He tried, but he could not get himself to admit that he had nowhere else to go. Leona's place would have to do for now. He would leave as soon as he could.

Deep in sleep under clean sheets, even his hacking cough did not awaken him. He didn't know when or if Leona came to bed. But she'd removed his boots, cleaned his face, hands, and feet with a washcloth, rubbed him down with Vicks and *luile maskreti*. He could have dreamed it all.

The next morning, he told himself that he didn't care if she'd done any of those things at all. Without acknowledging it, he knew that he was undeserving. Lucien lay awake with eyes closed, hearing the echoes of what he'd said in his sleep. *I am nothing*.

SOL

———————

"In case smoke starts to fill the room, stay as close to the ground as possible. The air is more breathable there." Sol remembered this from fire department presentations given in elementary school. It's not like she could get up if she wanted to. She could barely breathe. She wondered but could not see or hear how the others were managing with the smoke and cold that had made their way into the safe room. There had been no heat in two days. At least she thought it had been two days. She had started counting only from the time the smoke started to come in. That's when she'd begun to imagine the sky again. She hadn't seen it in the years she could deduce had passed only based on the size of the boy who had once been an infant.

She slowly raised herself on her elbows. She didn't know for sure, but she felt like she was dying. The crackle of calcified phlegm in her lungs stabbed her rib cage. It felt like the worst heartbreak made palpable, physical, by the cold air she breathed. Like a vertical glacial sheet, her hurt iced over, cracked a line down her torso, and rose back up toward her chest. She wanted to scream but had no voice. No point trying to over the sound of machinery and muffled voices coming from outside, the first she'd heard in years besides Lucien's and the others caged with her in the safe room. She didn't open her eyes. There was nothing to see that she didn't already know from memory. The shadowed faces of the others. The boy's decayed teeth that lit up the room when he smiled, just because he smiled. The steel walls that connected on the front and right sides of the room. The cavelike stone walls of the other two sides. And the sound-proof door like the entire insulated room. The intercom. The fucking one-way intercom. At least the sounds she was now hearing were not coming from his goddamned "sweet box," a steel perforated contraption built into the wall. She knew every one of the hundreds of dead glass botanica votives with the various iterations of Vierge Marie lining the walls, stacked, ready to topple and crack. They had once held wax and wicks lit over the years. They'd once held hope, prayers to the Black Madonna and the woman who had purchased all of them for her temple. Sol knew every crevice they had tried to penetrate to no avail. So, no, she didn't open her eyes, not even to see if the boy was smiling, because if she could hear the outside sounds, surely he, who had been out there more recently than they, recognized foreign voices and running motors. Was he imagining the sky?

She used to ask him if the sky looked the same as she re-membered. Then she stopped asking, stopped imagining. Be-fore the safe room, she used to look upward at the expanse, no matter its decor or dance except that once, that once when it had been pouring so hard that she had had to lower her head, run for cover under the gas station's steel awning, and wait for the sky to wring itself out. If she could have lived somewhere high enough that she could feel as if she could touch it, just low enough to stare at it from a distance, she would have given her soul. She had never flown in an airplane and couldn't imagine what it was like to cut through the sky's layers below or above the clouds. Despite having seen countless planes scar the ex-panse with their wings, it was impossible for her to know if she would have loved being truly *in* the sky. But she was so tall that she had been willing to settle for seeing it from the ground, except for that one day when she'd first forgotten to, then couldn't, then would never again look up and see it.

Whenever the boy returned from an outing, she'd question him about the sky as if asking about a long-lost sibling. It reminded her of her origins—not the country where she was born, but the place where she was not her body or her mind. Where she was only her soul. But after what felt like longer than a decade in the back room and a cough that held her chest captive, a fever boiling her very blood, sweat as copious as shallow water, she gave in and settled into being merely human.

The back room stole time. Its darkness allowed no knowledge of night or day, weeks, months, or years. Sol knew only that she was fifteen when she'd climbed into Lucien's van to keep from seeing her blood running in puddles of rain. When he'd dragged her into the back room, she'd found Asante, who was well into her thirties and had already given up trying to escape. A few years later, Sol hadn't known exactly how many, she'd stopped fighting after her sister, Chiqui, had been brought in. He'd tricked the twelve-year-old into his van, carried her out, and thrown her into Sol's lap—a gift tossed like trash. Cocoa had said that she was fourteen when she got there. Sol could only guess how old they were now. She'd seen snippets of newspaper brought in by My from his outings with Lucien. The greasy print had told her that he'd been eating French fries or plantains. It had also let her know that she must be thirty or more. She was six when Chiqui was born. Sol didn't bother with the subtraction. The last to be taken, Cocoa had kept close count of the years, at least she thought. If she had been free, she could legally vote, buy alcohol and cigarettes, and be chosen for *American Idol* without her parents' permission. Asante didn't want to know that she was now over fifty.

Sol chose to hear now. One of the others, Cocoa, was speaking again about finding a way out. She figured that, if they could hear outside sounds without the intercom, then maybe they could finally be heard. Sol could hear Cocoa starting to sob while mumbling to herself about their chances of rescue, if they would be buried alive once the demolition that she had heard snippets of commenced. Or maybe Lucien would make it to the house before that and slaughter them all. He had never been violent enough to break bones or draw blood, but anything was possible if he was scared enough. And the discovery of his girls in the back room would surely make him afraid. But he loved them in his own way, so maybe he would get them out and just let them go. Cocoa sucked up her tears because Sol, the sky lover, wasn't crying and she was worse off than any of them.

Sol spoke now, more of a rattling low growl. "Listen, I'm weak. I've already died. So find a way out; even if you have to leave me, just get out."

Chiqui overheard and trembled at the thought of her sister dying. "We're all getting out."

"It's okay." Sol consoled despite the pain that had taken over her body for weeks.

"No, it's not. It never has been." Chiqui didn't want to argue but she needed to speak. "But now we have a chance to make it so."

"Not even rescue can right this wrong, but we are getting out or we are going to die trying." Cocoa wiped her nose on her forearm.

"It's okay. I'm okay. I've made my peace."

"Then make peace with the fact that we're leaving. All of us. Alive." Chiqui seemed unable to stop crying. "I'm not going to let you die."

"Nobody's dying. If we can hear them, then they must be able to hear us. This is happening for a reason." Cocoa placed one hand on Chiqui's shivering shoulder and her other hand on Sol's foot. "I am going to sing us out of here as loudly as I can. And then I'm gonna dance my ass out of whatever hole opens wide enough. Doesn't have to be big because we're all skinny as hell now." She tried to laugh. "The back-room diet!"

Asante, Lucien's first, the mother with no maternal instincts, finally stirred. Sol had always known that Asante's internal deterioration was not unlike her own. Asante had been dying in her mind and overtly expressed her desperate wish for an end to her unbearable life. Sol had been trying to banish her own suicidality. But she had not reached that point because she could always compare herself with Asante, who had been in the back room the longest. Sol understood why Asante didn't speak much. She'd gotten used to the older woman's silence. At one time or another, Sol and the others had forgotten that Asante was even there. If they were getting out, her screams would never join their chorus to holler for help.

Sol's internal quiet and attentive spirit allowed her to hear Asante's whisper.

"Fuck all of y'all," she muttered under her breath. "Leave me here too. Ain't no point now."

Sol remained still hearing Asante echo her own sentiments.

He say Asante is Zero. Chiqui is Two. Cocoa is Three. Which one is me? Which one is My? I am not his first. Zero. She is gone, gone, gone. She is all thought, all body, all full of him. She is her Zero self. I am not her. I am One. I feel me. But not like before he took me. I am killed, dying, and dead. I am fever, sweat, and cough. I am ready. I am more than body or mind. I am knowing. Everything about everything. This is not thought. This is me. Knowing.

Sol sat upright for the first time since the fire. Unwilling to torture herself with thoughts of seeing the sky again, she focused on Zero, Asante, who had been living in Lucien's basement for two years before she'd found out that there was a safe room. Sol didn't need to open her eyes to see Asante, who was almost invisible in the candlelight. Sol had insisted that her cellmates conserve candles. For months she'd allowed them only one votive per day. If the house came down on them, if Lucien found a hole to plug, they might never see light again. So no more lighting up multiple candles at once, hoping that one of the saints or versions of the Virgin Mary or their guardian seraph Marie-Ange would save them. No more five, six, seven candles at a time. That was before, when they'd had real hope of getting out. Before she'd started counting like him—rations, lighter fluid, ounces of water in the gallon, shots from the gallon's cap, sardines, drops of Spam jelly on their fingertips, matches, sips of breath, minutes before he arrived, seconds before the intercom cracked on, footsteps and thumps before the music turned off, beats in their heads keeping time with silence made by the memories of sounds heard freely, outside and at will. None of them had taught four-year-old My to count, but still he had learned on his own as children will do in the absence of proper instruction. Asante hadn't taught anyone anything. She had even refused to tell any of them how she'd gotten in and how to get out of the back room.

Sol's memory of Asante the first time she'd seen her ran like wet paint dripping down a canvas. She wouldn't see the face or learn the name of her cellmate for months. Names and faces were meaningless inside the unsafe safe room. They were nameless objects in his curio, things he collected and owned, things he could admire or destroy. To scare her, Lucien had told Sol his version of Asante's story—how he'd first worshipped then wooed her, captured and then broken her down to Zero. That's who Sol remembered in the darkness, the outline of a disjointed sketch, a bowed skeleton in the far corner of the room, not a body but an unfilled husk, the Zero from which he'd always counted when listing the inventory of provisions stockpiled for the harem he would amass.

He was proud of his first, a woman to whom he'd rented his basement for a mere $300 a month. Marie-Ange had been as hot as her cooking pots when Lucien relegated her vodou peristyle to the boiler room so he could house his mistress in the finished basement apartment. Asante had lived there with her twenty-year-old daughter and one-year-old grandson. None of them had discovered the back room in the years they'd lived there. Asante used to laugh to know that she had displaced spirits masked as saints and yet another wife. But she had ended up in hell. Marie-Ange's payback. Ezili's last laugh.

Sol had seen Asante's torment that persisted even now. Asante continued to wish that Lucien's wife would really die and die forever, instead of living inside her head and telling her that she had been and still was zero by comparison. Just a quick fuck for Lucien when he was in a rush. Just a long suck when he'd had more time to make her earn the rent money that she had not been able to come up with. During the few times he'd spared a full hour, he'd fucked her like a porn star. Sol remembered every detail he'd painstakingly shared.

Asante had still had her salon back then. Marie-Ange had been able to walk in for her wash and set, chirping whenever Asante's boomerang boyfriend stepped in. He always wore Timberland boots, two pairs of pants, a gun in the small of his back tucked in the waistband of his underwear. If it had slipped down into his crack, he would have gotten fucked by his own gun. Asante never minded him stopping by. She couldn't have stopped him from coming if she'd wanted to. The shop had been more his than hers—a front for the real profit maker. He would come in with rolls of cash hidden in the lower pockets of the cargo pants worn underneath his designer jeans—the genuine article, not Jamaica Avenue back-of-the-van knockoffs. Asante would bring the money to the bank later, passing the money off as profits from her beauty shop. She would have had to complete ten weave heads daily at $500 apiece with five other stylists doing the same to earn that kind of money in one week. But she was fine with their arrangement. She was still getting laid by her first love, her baby daddy. She had had no more children after their daughter. He'd made sure of that. Paid the shady doctor to tie her tubes. Selfish prick. Making that baby girl an only child, at least on her mother's side. Marie-Ange had studied all this and knew what Asante was before Lucien came to explain why they needed to take her in and let her rent the basement. "She can sleep in her goddamned salon!" Marie-Ange gave in when she saw Asante's infant grandson. "*Tonère!* Go ahead. Don't break anything. And don't fuck that *bouzin sansavé* in my house." At first, he'd tried to conceal his involvement with Asante. But Marie-Ange had sniffed it out like rotting leftovers in the back of a refrigerator.

Sol recoiled at the thought of Lucien's treatment of a woman he had truly loved. If that was love, then it was no wonder he had done so much worse to others.

The memory of Lucien's descriptions oozed through Sol's mind like a rotten yolk from a cracked eggshell. Disgusted, she tried to scoop the slime back into its irreparable casing. The leakage persisted, and she thought of what he'd told her: the way he'd arranged the women in his love triangle, how well he'd manipulated them, so he could have them both simultaneously with minimal hassle. He'd explained this to her to ensure that she understood how skilled he was at handling women. With disdain for Lucien's version, Sol allowed the memory of Asante's account to come forth. It sprouted in her mind like a bean in a glass of water.

Asante had been a welfare mother before opening her beauty shop. She had been the kind that Marie-Ange and all hardworking Haitians hated—an able-bodied youngster who'd failed to take advantage of the country's limitless opportunities, a lazy girl who'd gotten herself knocked up, preferring government handouts to hard work. But she had also done hair in her small kitchen, which made Marie-Ange a bit more merciful with her criticism. The kitchen-salon had squatted above the store that would eventually become her shop. Asante had become

Marie-Ange's hairdresser the same week she'd stopped working at the law firm. No longer having to go into Manhattan to work and having been accused of theft because she was black, an immigrant, smart, alluring, and black again, Marie-Ange decided to give Asante's salon a chance. It was just up the road from the Q9 bus stop where she'd stood every morning to catch a dollar van to the Sutphin Boulevard E train subway station. When Asante told her that she was actually Haitian, born not raised, Marie-Ange had been pleasantly surprised and relaxed her judgment even more.

Asante had immediately felt Marie-Ange's prejudice. She had experienced it all her life among Caribbeans who cut her no slack because (a) she had spent less than a year in Haiti after birth; (b) she didn't speak Kreyòl fluently, although she understood it completely; (c) she was an academic failure (a high school dropout no less!); and (d) she'd had a baby in her teens. And that was just the stuff her mother couldn't hide from Haitian Brooklynites, which is what she had been when her stereotypical life unfolded.

Asante had been shown no mercy by black American kids in the 1970s either. They called her "African booty-scratcher" until they found out that she was Haitian. In the '80s, "Roll-AIDS" was the punch line to a joke about Haitians on skates. Asante's skin was navy into midnight, with eyes just as black. A man might fall into them as easily as a country well on a moonless, starless night down South. She started wearing colored contacts in the 1980s and kept them even when they went out of style. She changed her eye color to match her mood and clothes sometimes but, like her weave, they were neither natural-looking nor her own. She was pretty enough—petite, barely a hundred pounds, not even five feet tall. She had been lifted and thrown by angry lovers one time too many. Her taut, muscular body persisted without exercise. She had enough curves to convey that she was indeed female. But if she dressed in an androgynous fashion—boxy Lee jeans, Adidas sneakers, a white T-shirt—she could have easily passed for a teenaged boy from the neck down. She made up for that with her giftedness at the most feminine profession imaginable. She'd become skilled in changing her appearance, which had just become vogue, when Lucien started courting her.

She'd been enamored of Lucien even before moving into the basement. While doing Marie-Ange's hair in her salon, she'd indulged in fantasies of being married to a stable, respectable man with a house he'd bought legitimately with his hard-earned money.

Asante hadn't really hated Marie-Ange. She'd just thought that she was oddly stuck-up for someone who willingly displayed her vulgarity, discussing sex with beauty shop workers and patrons. She'd hated the way Marie-Ange would enter her shop on 135th and Rockaway Boulevard as if she both owned it and was embarrassed to be there. Asante's shop was in the black section of SOP, the poor section, the deep hood, close to the Van Wyck Expressway. A few blocks down, one street over from P.S. 96, was where the nicer part of SOP began. Once you hit the 120s, you were safe. You were in mixed Caribbean, hanging-on Italian, misplaced Latino, dislocated Indian, solid, confirmed hardworking immigrant territory. La Kay territory.

Her boyfriend had used her place and her body to satisfy his cocaine customers who needed a safe place to get high. She'd had so many men before and after her baby daddy, but Lucien had been her last. As far as Asante had known, Lucien had been Marie-Ange's only lover. She'd become jealous of Marie-Ange in earnest then. Feeling pretty and envious at the same time, she'd started strutting in front of Lucien's wife. Asante upped her game and styled her hair in drastic and dramatic coifs pulled back to accentuate her widow's peak, lengthened with horsetail weaves that slapped her ass. Her chiseled facial features and perfect skin looked severe and almost masklike. She couldn't accept that she looked like a Nigerian princess, not after years of booty-scratcher teasing, not after being dropkicked onto a broken bottle by a schoolyard bully, not after the five-inch keloid line she still boasted on her left triceps from that event. She got a snake tattoo to leverage and embellish the shape of her scar.

Sol saw clearly how Lucien had robbed Asante of what remained of her beauty. Just as her looks were becoming fashionably and acceptably pretty in the eyes of the dominant society and its subcultures, Asante had had to go underground to shake the cops who had been tipped off about the drug activity in and above her salon. She'd turned to Lucien for a place to rent, since it was no longer safe to live in the apartment above her shop. She'd left her boyfriend there but whisked away her grandson and her daughter to the safety of Lucien's basement. With money tight because the DEA was watching, she'd paid the rent with blow jobs, fast fucks from behind, and the occasional in-home wash-and-set and mani-pedi for stubborn and wise customers who would have no one else touch them but knew better than to go to her narc-surveilled shop.

Asante had been smart enough to know when the DEA would descend on her shop. She asked Lucien to hide her somewhere farther and deeper than the basement. Did he know anyone in Haiti who would be willing to put her up while things cooled down on the boulevard? Lucien said yes, but she would have to give him a couple of days, maybe a week. In the meantime, she might want to send her daughter and grandson down south where they had family. Asante had not seen her daughter and grandson or the light of day since. Only candlelight.

One, Two, Three, and My. I am not and can never be Zero. She is silent, empty. But she can scream. I used to hear her. Scream only when he says so. Be his Zero. Come! Scream now! Because I have no scream left in me. Only cough. I want to yell like I want to see the sky again. Even if I have to bring him flowers for the grave again. I

*want to go where I don't burn or sweat or ache. I want to see and be
seen like the sky.*

They had been invisible, Sol and her mother, but never as
invisible as My. He was truly undocumented—no fabricated
name to attend school under, no dilapidated passport with a fading visa stamp from a border crossing. No, they'd been nearly
as invisible. They'd crossed undetected. No one had known
they'd existed except the coyote who'd introduced them to
their employer and landlord. In New York, they'd been seen
in the one-room where they'd rented a bed, on the street where
they'd sold flowers and fruit, in the classroom where English
had seemed impossible. Sol had spent her time looking at the
sky for herself, never even looking at the flowers she sold along-
side her mother on the weekends. They would go out with the
pretty buds, bottles of water, and peeled oranges neatly halved
and bagged for drivers at red lights. Lucien and Marie-Ange
would patronize the roadside bodega.

Lucien had seen them. He had a knack for seeing the invisible. He was always looking down at the ground for treasure.

Sol had believed that she'd been invisible to him. Just a bar-
terer, a faceless girl, a hand stuck into his car window to give
him change, flowers, water, oranges. A hand pulling back with
bills, coins, the odd bag of new-like old clothes, some with tags.
Things his wife had bought for their daughters but they'd never
worn. Lucien would have Sol reach in instead of him reaching
out. Sol had thought that meant he was passive, harmless, welcoming. He had drawn her in one exchange at a time for nearly
a decade. He was just a middle-aged man, the color of butter-
scotch, with hair the same curly texture as hers. He could have
been her father. He could be. Who knew? Not her mother, who
could no longer recount the story because she had disappeared
into the custody of INS. No Department of Homeland Security,
the immigration abyss since 2002. She had vanished and been
made invisible to Sol. But, having been captured, she would

continue to be visible to and illegal in the eyes of DHS. It was better not to be seen, to be more invisible than My.

The stories of who they had been—Asante, her mother, herself—mixed together like swill in a bucket. Sol kept herself from tearing up at the knowledge that he'd contorted them into unrecognizable and then utterly unseen figures.

LA KAY

Sweet La Kay. There had been a tropical fruit cola named after It. At least, that's what It liked to believe. Sweet Home. It didn't feel like a home, just a house. Just any old house on 123rd Street between Rockaway Boulevard and Sutter Avenue in Queens. It was a cookie-cutter two-story structure with a basement, of course. It had white aluminum siding with red trim. Its favorite feature was Its six brick steps that rose to Its front door. It had always wanted a red door to match, but Its owners had placed and replaced the same ugly wooden door with an even tackier screen door that didn't match anything. Not that It could see Itself from the outside. It had only caught glimpses in the windowpanes of the house across the street.

As much as It liked to hear about the goings-on at the other houses, It never let on that there were maddening things happening on Its insides. But even though Its neighbors told only rose-colored versions of their inner disturbances, It guessed that they had their own troubles. How could they not? Every house was on the alert for sad news. La Kay listened as the entire neighborhood, borough, and city shook under so much trouble. New York's blackout had practically turned looting into a competitive sport. The Howard Beach Incident had confirmed that lynching was not dead and could and did happen north of the Mason-Dixon. Later, similar horrors befell immigrants like the ones who had taken over SOP.

The chief evil inside La Kay had unfolded on a sunny day, proof that darkness was not necessary for malevolence to over-run a place. It kept Its mouth shut and Its eyes peeled only be-cause of the music. It had always believed that the tunes had been the only reason It hadn't tried to kill Itself sooner. It would stay up late on Friday nights and rise early on Saturday and Sunday mornings to hear the sounds Lucien would play from around the world.

Three artists had kept It alive in the eighties—Michael Jackson, Kassav', and Rakim. Every song on Michael Jackson's *Thriller* moved It to convulsive catharsis. It listened as Lucien's eldest daughter, Veille, played "Human Nature" until the rec-ord skipped from scratches. It understood what she was trying to understand and cried with her every time. It knew why she'd never let the record get to "P.Y.T. (Pretty Young Thing)."

It had found relief when his second daughter, Clair, caught the vibe of zouk from Martinique and Guadeloupe, because It could dance instead of commiserating. It also got to see the Louvertures in action as a family. It watched and sighed as Lucien would snatch Marie-Ange or one of the girls from the kitchen. Zouk really was medicine, as the hit song said. It pre-ferred this to the kompas records that seemed to never end, leaving It feeling sorry for whatever daughter Lucien insisted on dancing with. Long gone were the days when he'd have his partner's feet on his, teaching her how to step and sway to Haiti's signature music genre. But, mercifully, fast-paced zouk allowed for separation between the dancers unless they chose to come together to *zouké*.

Most of all, La Kay had fallen in love with rap music that had yet to go mainstream as hip-hop. It preferred the rebellious-ness of a music still defining itself while resisting definition or even acceptance by the dominant culture. It learned about the hardships of the poor while listening to Rakim rhyme about his hunger for a plate of fish and resisting the past devious deeds he'd done to acquire it. It heard him make his DJ Eric B. president while Jesse Jackson forcibly etched his name on a ballot. It got a taste of what it must have been like to be inhabited by black poets in the 1960s. It applauded as Veille, Clair, and even Whitney Houston–crooning Dor made up dances to the new music. Their bounces, their hip-hoppin' poppin' and lockin' were better than anything they could have learned via formal dance lessons because it broke them out of the imprisoning expectations of their parents. La Kay tried to help by sealing the holes in their bedroom walls, so they could dress in their pinstriped Lee jeans and double-laced Adidas unobserved.

It would have shut down Lucien's weekend card games if not for the sound track. But even while appeased by the music, It had still tried to force him and his card sharks out. For three months straight, It conveniently sprung leaks in the bathroom pipes directly above the dining table–turned–card slab. From Friday night until Sunday midmorning, It had rained over the heads of delinquent dads, wife-beating husbands, and mortgage-gambling louses who played poker under beach umbrellas rather than go home. It finally succeeded at getting the gamblers out of Marie-Ange's house by forcing Lucien's casino into the garage in the middle of December. He had pleaded with Marie-Ange to let him host his low-rollers in the basement, but she refused to displace Ezili's temple. The basement was out of the question. His only option had been the garage, which was another matter altogether. Not all the houses had garages. But, regretfully, all of them had basements and some of those basements had safe rooms.

Over the years La Kay had been too busy trying to protect Its female visitors and inhabitants from Lucien's advances. It also saw no need to secure what had already been protected by the goddess Ezili. It wasn't going to mess with the perfection of a spirit who, when properly worshipped, had the power to boil and dissolve enemies into syrup where they stood. Even Lucien seemed to bow to Ezili's powers—that was, until Marie-Ange got sick. Their declining fortunes forced her to accept a basement tenant whom she knew was one of at least a dozen of his voluntary or coerced mistresses. With Ezili in the boiler room struggling to be seen under a single dangling lightbulb, Marie-Ange let Lucien have his way. She had already warned him of Ezili's revenge for his vilest violation, the line he had not only crossed but permanently stripped away. She had already told him that Ezili would whip him with his own strap. There had been no need to warn him again. La Kay agreed and went about Its business minding their teenaged daughters, who had been preparing to get the hell out of Lucien's house for their own safety and sanity. Fortunately, they were gone by the time Lucien's madness had reached its peak.

With two women and a baby boy inhabiting the basement, La Kay had to turn Its attentions downward. It had watched as Lucien breezed through at all times of the day or night to be serviced by a willing, even eager Asante.

La Kay had heard about her from KAM's gossiping patrons. But it wasn't until the first time she'd visited that It had seen for Itself that, even at her best, she couldn't compete with Marie-Ange. Even when Marie-Ange had gotten sick, even when she'd been a couple of years from dying, Asante had not been able to outdo Marie-Ange's elegance and had had nothing to rival her smile. Asante's own teeth were crooked and rotten from decades wearing gold fronts and caps as well as the occasional hit from her boyfriend's customers' crack pipes. The only thing Asante had ever had on Marie-Ange, post-sickness, was her walk. Men and women alike hurt to see Asante walk—sexy, coquettish, swishing and swaying in the highest heels possible. She had been determined to look five foot something. A hand on her hip with one holding a cigarette to her mouth had injured the egos of wannabe divas who just couldn't outdo her Marilyn Monroe–Olivia Newton-John bad-girl cigarette drag. A true beautician, Asante never sat down, not even on a high stool that would have kept her at the same height as her heels. Her walk did not suffer until the basement.

La Kay had devoted half of Its attention to watching the basement, while focusing on Marie-Ange, whose health had been declining. In the blink of an eye Asante's daughter and grandson were gone. Before It could properly search, Asante had also vanished into a corner of Itself It had always neglected. It had felt an itch like a mosquito bite in an unreachable, unknowable place.

Before It knew it, the music had started to play less often and more quietly. La Kay had settled into Its sadness, not wanting to kill Itself while Marie-Ange lay dying.

Three

LUCIEN

———————

Lucien awoke to the odor of Leona's cooking and mentholated ointment. The latter was an up-close, almost pleasant smell emanating from his body. The former was yet another of her attempts to make her cooking palatable. Her profound care and immense effort were as futile as her attempts to coax him into conversation. He could smell her eggs, nauseatingly fried in butter and oil despite her use of a nonstick pan. To give him a taste of home, she had bought ready-made coffee from a shop near his house earlier that morning. It was the closest thing to the Café Bustelo he preferred. (Later, he would be grateful that she even allowed him full-fat evaporated milk and genuine white sugar to make up for having dragged him away from his perishing home.) He knew that what he really needed was tea with lemon and honey to help his cough but appreciated that she'd resisted her natural inclination to forcibly nurse him. On the nightstand on her side of the bed, he saw the NyQuil she had not bothered to make him to take the night before. He never had trouble sleeping anyway.

Since all he smelled of himself was the vapor of Vicks, he figured that he must have acquiesced to the long hot bath she'd insisted on the night before. He knew that he must have first fallen asleep in the tub. The bathwater seasoned with VapoRub had been augmented by what she'd rubbed on his chest, his back, and the soles of his feet. It was clear to him that she was running out of genuine Haitian *luile maskreti* that was neither cheap nor easy to find in New York. Lucien rubbed his nose, feeling the greasy stripes of menthol on either side. Somehow, he recognized her efforts as love.

How Leona could love someone she didn't know was a mystery to him. Yes, she had practically lived with him during Marie-Ange's illness. But Leona didn't even know his actual age and had not met any members of his family except for his daughters, who'd barely spoken to her at Marie-Ange's funeral. He wondered: How could a woman not know, not ask, why his daughters wanted nothing to do with him? *She doesn't want to know. Why tell her what she doesn't want to know? Why scare her with the truth? Let her sleep. Let her dream that Marie-Ange had placed her hand in mine as a blessing.* He had no intention of disclosing or explaining anything. Some of his past would have further endeared him to her. The other parts might have sent her running but would have explained why he was still such a good lover in his sixties and so agile after two strokes. She knew and believed what he wanted her to know. That he came from a well-to-do family in Jacmel. That his parents had left him in the care of his aunt when he was a baby. That they had not sent for him until he was in his twenties, married, with one born child and twins on the way. Who he'd been back home was either a mystery or a falsified memory packaged as selective personal history.

Lucien had had many girls before Marie-Ange had given him three of his own. The doorway she'd always seen him leaning against after school on Fridays had been his bar. Not because he'd owned Bar Caimite outright, but because he'd owned all the women and girls who'd brought in customers for drinks that had helped fill the true proprietor's coffers. A small commission from the profits the girls turned over had helped Lucien maintain the façade of a legitimate proprietorship of an established watering hole. But that was just a snippet, a blip, an aberration, in an otherwise crimeless life, he would explain to Leona if she ever found out about that time. His Caimite girls had been his everything because he could count them. He could cry in front of them. He could let them hear the whispered words that they knew were true: *I am nothing. I am nothing without you.* He even let them hear him count as he took them in the darkest corners of the bar. *Nothing until I take, until I count, until I make you mine.* He found a more permanent way to push the tears and words down into the void inside himself. He turned himself into a family man in earnest, thanks to Marie-Ange, his parents, and a few exploitative lenders.

Lucien had chosen to become what he'd wanted to be, but had allowed his wife, his parents, and even his creditors to believe that they had made him. He'd done the same with Leona, who still held the conviction that she was a savior who'd been sent by Marie-Ange to care for him. He let her believe that her son, who looked more like him than his own, and granddaughter were the family he'd always wanted. That had always been his game—architecting false families, playing house, and appeasing women with believable lies and terrific sex.

Lucien was warmed by the thought that Leona's wasn't his second or even his third fabricated family. His second had been the Haitian immigrants who'd flocked to South Ozone Park based on word of mouth about KAM. They'd been craving community as much as Marie-Ange's incomparable home cooking. They'd wanted to do more than roll the dice at weekend-long gambling binges that had left their pockets as depleted as their homesick hearts. They'd wanted a home since they could not go *back home*. Not just a home because they were making one in America. Back home was a place in and of itself, a place they couldn't return to. Not yet. Not until they'd made it big in New York and could alight from the airplane stairs onto Port au Prince airport's scorching tarmac, uncomfortably attired in wool suits, hundred-dollar wing tips, silk shirts buttoned to the collar, and as many gold chains as they could afford or borrow from their friends who understood their need to flaunt their *ti-gran-negre* frontage. They couldn't go home until they had real INS-approved green cards and passports with expiration dates five or ten years into the future to ensure they could resume their janitor jobs and night school English classes. They couldn't make return visits until they could fill at least six suitcases—two covered by their airfare, two they would willingly pay extra baggage fees for, and two filled with gifts from their friends who couldn't yet make the trip—to show their people back home that they were making progress. Until they could return to their motherland with the requisite largesse and grandeur, they went to KAM and spent money and time they didn't have, soothing their souls with Marie-Ange's incredible cooking and Lucien's costly hospitality.

Lucien had been merciful to KAM's male patrons but less so to the women, who lived in profound sadness over having left their children in the care of iffy relatives. He took advantage of those who were willing to give anything for a taste of home. With a few exceptions, he did not allow women at his gambling tables. Only the proven hard-core manly types could sit with the players. He tolerated the ones who drove overnight taxi shifts through crime-ridden Times Square, who owned multiple houses paid for in cash with earnings from transactions with deadly dealers, or who'd amputated all emotion and had not just *left* but had *given away* their children and were therefore thought to be heartless. He would send the softer ones to the kitchen to occupy themselves with gossipy conversations, dish washing, sweeping, and wiping until he was ready for them. In his wife's presence with her back turned, he would cop quick, daring feels while the women stood at the kitchen sink or at the fridge door looking for whatever Marie-Ange sent them to fetch.

He'd had a few trusted ones whom he'd loaned to his wife to clean piles of chicken leg quarters before the scalding water was poured over the poultry. They were never allowed to do anything more with Marie-Ange's chicken, pork, or beef after the hot-water bath. She trusted only Nen-nen, when she visited, and him, who on rare occasions helped rewash and season the meats. Neither he nor she ever wanted the taste of anyone else's hands in her food. He knew that there would have been hell to pay if she ever heard any of these women claim to have cooked anything at KAM. She alone was chef. The only *manman*, although she purposely kept her daughters out of the kitchen and as far away from the late-night action as possible. Friday and Saturday nights belonged to the grown-ups, the strays, and the prey on whom Lucien feasted as he supervised but did not play card games.

Lucien remembered those days conducting the activities at KAM. He'd participated in the weekend fetes only by tasting whatever foods Marie-Ange had thought needed additional seasoning or especially well-prepared dishes that she hadn't wanted him to miss out on before she sold it all. He'd also tasted whatever willing women he could feel up in a dark corner of the front room under the pretext of consoling, lending money, returning pawned jewelry, or triaging legal problems for Marie-Ange to properly diagnose and address during the week. He would sneak them into his garage: the women, feigning farewells, would leave through the front door and walk the dark, narrow driveway to meet him out back for an upright fuck, leisurely fellatio, or heavy petting.

Although the women had thought these encounters were spontaneous, Lucien had planned them by first leering then peering through invisible holes strategically drilled into the

bathroom walls and door. The most convenient place for his lasciviousness would have been the basement, but Marie-Ange had
her temple there. If nothing else, Lucien respected the vigilant
Vierge Marie statues on the multiple altars, at least for a time.
But at the height of KAM's prosperity, he'd kept his crimes
away from the basement.

Flashing back to his past, Lucien told himself that he hadn't
feared the deity at all. He'd valued the vodou practice only as
an additional revenue stream. Whatever Marie-Ange couldn't
fix with her immigrant's knowledge of America's legal ins and
outs, whatever she couldn't deduce or connive to exploit with
her intellect, legwork, or intuition, she diagnosed as spiritual
ailment requiring sacrifices to Ezili. No animals or bloodshed,
just ritual and, of course, money offerings to the goddess. De-
pending on the ailment—difficulty finding a job, a green card
sponsor threatening to back out, a sickness that could not be
cured without long hospital stays requiring health insurance,
cheating/beating husbands, untouchable mistresses or par-
amours, loan sharks or landlords needing to be put in their
places, even policemen abusing their authority like American
Tonton Makout—a patron might spend as much in her basement temple as on his card table. The lovelorn and homesick
patrons sustained KAM as a community center where all their
needs could be met.

Lucien's cab and housemate, Dieuseul, had been introduced
to his wife at KAM. She was one of the few black Americans
who'd gone to Marie-Ange for help with an ex who wouldn't
contribute financially to raising their daughter. The courts
couldn't help because he made all his money off the books.
He used her and her house as a crash pad between affairs with
his flavor-of-the-moment floozies or when hiding from drug-
dealing creditors. Marie-Ange's remedy for her was to move
another man in. She had the perfect candidate: Dieuseul, a hard-

working just-come flush with cash and desperate for papers. Lucien even trusted this man on the day shift with his taxicab.

Dieuseul had been vetted and vouched for, never mind his looks that at least Marie-Ange found attractive. He alternated his shaves between a bald head with a goatee or a low 'fro with a clean-shaven face. He was so dark and fierce-looking that Lucien had nicknamed him Shaka Zulu. His eyes were his lightest feature, but the whites of them had remained yellowish from a childhood vitamin deficiency that had not been cured until he came to America. Marie-Ange had warmed up to him because he resembled her father, who had been tall and dark-skinned, with the same regal warrior carriage and gentlemanly elegance. Truth be told, both men were as sexy, mysterious, poised, and charming as a vampire count. Dieuseul, Boss Dieuseul to most because of the immediate respect his comportment commanded, had large teeth and a mean smile. He was not typically handsome, but his posture and manner of dress made him irresistible to the forlorn single mother. His large hands and atypical size-thirteen shoes told the horny single mom everything else she wanted to know.

Lucien was still wondering where Dieuseul had gone during the fire. He laughed as he remembered the ironic name and the arranged marriage. Dieuseul, "only God," could have saved this woman and protected her daughter from potential predators. Even before Donahue began hosting sex-abuse victims who tearfully recounted their stories before a studio and national audience; before the movie version of *The Color Purple* exposed stepfathers as child molesters; before a fractured Truddi Chase morphed into twelve different personalities over the course of forty minutes with time for commercial breaks during a shocking installment of *The Oprah Winfrey Show;* before Oprah became Oprah, Marie-Ange and women like her had been watching and warning blind, lovestruck mothers of girl-children about men who might be more interested in their daughters than themselves.

Lucien glanced around Leona's room looking for some reminder of Dieuseul's artistic talent, but she'd never hung any of the paintings there. He wanted some reminder of his home, but there was none to be found. He'd respected Dieuseul for being a gifted painter. He'd marveled at the first piece Dieuseul had shown him, a portrait of his six-year-old stepdaughter, Lexus. Dieuseul had loved and protected the adorable untouched girl.

Lucien fondly pondered the unlikely friendship. He'd always known that Dieuseul found light-skinned people distasteful, especially those in authority or in a higher class. Knowing this, Lucien had always respectfully put the "Boss" in front of his name, even though he owned the taxi that Dieuseul rented to make his living. Lucien knew well the reason he respected Dieuseul. He had learned a lot from him—mainly that painting and photography were ideal covers for voyeurism and good excuses to touch and adjust the clothing of subjects. Lucien had never been a painter, but he'd had three cameras in his possession, one his own, the other two pawned objects held for cash-strapped patrons. He'd started taking Polaroid pictures of female visitors to his home, in public and private, so he wouldn't have to have the film developed.

Lucien had also photographed Leona secretly long before she'd ever struck a pose for him in his living room. He had waited for the sound of the toilet flushing to mask the click and wind of his camera as he'd taken her picture from his favorite peephole. He hadn't bothered to puzzle out why such a book-smart woman had settled for being a home-care nurse, why her intellect had not translated into street smarts, common sense, or high self-esteem. He'd just taken advantage of his wife's caregiver who, based on the history she'd divulged within days of working in his house, had indiscriminately tolerated men's misbehavior and lies all her life. She had been and still was desperate to be loved and willing to be his caregiver after his wife died.

He'd been able to tell that Leona had been hurting the first time they'd met from the way she'd held her handbag against her abdomen. She'd held back words as if suppressing vomit. He'd known that she needed someone, a man, despite the love she received from her son and granddaughter, full and half siblings, and church friends. Even the families of former patients who invited her out for meals, who bought her gifts to thank her for giving their dying loved one end-of-life care. When she'd finally spoken, he'd heard more than she'd said. And she'd said a lot! She'd thrown up words as if she hadn't spoken to a prospective lover in decades. He'd known immediately how much she'd wanted someone, wanted the one who was in front of her, wanted him. He'd known that she could have done better for herself. Always the opportunist, he gave her the attention she had been craving and made her see herself through his warped lenses.

Never mind that she was young, younger than Marie-Ange even. She would never know his age. Never mind that her cheeks were as smooth as a sea-worn stone, that her hair caught light and held it on its surface as shine. Never mind the touches, hand holding, and hugs she got from family and friends. Those were not enough. They were not enough. She needed one more to care for. She was a nurse, after all. She needed someone who would reciprocate both her nurturing and her lust that spilled over and into forbidden conversations. She needed a slurred whisper of love breathed on the back of her neck, prolonged and limber lovemaking that made plain sex seem as uneventful and chore-like as mopping up a spill. She needed someone to lick away the loneliness. She wanted something that felt like love, that could keep the lonely from moving around in the crawl spaces where hurt hides, waiting to surprise. She wanted someone to arrest the pain, satisfy the pangs, and just hold her.

Having long ago mastered the inner workings of the female mind, Lucien had known within a week that, when the loquacious Leona fell silent, she was telling herself stories about the future life they would create together. She had been looking forward to the future union that Marie-Ange would generously bless.

Lucien sniffed his armpit as he raised his good hand to slurp his lukewarm coffee. He smelled clean. The VapoRub competed with his creamy, sweet *café con leche*. He waited in bed where he'd been served by Leona. She would join him for a hard-earned amorous breakfast. His narcolepsy and partially lame limbs never interfered with the satisfaction of his and her libidos. In fact, his left hand, partially crippled into a claw, gave more pleasure during foreplay. He'd often wondered how many more women he would have been able to seduce, turn out, and trick at Bar Caimite if he'd had the boon of his post-stroke handicap in his youth.

Lucien counted the minutes until Leona came back upstairs to rejoin him in bed. He needed to make her feel appreciated, so she would acquiesce to his future requests and forgive the new misdeeds he'd already been planning. He filled in the seconds missing on the digital clock on the nightstand nearest him by counting backward in between the clicking minutes. When Leona finally came upstairs, he counted her twitches and groans and the seconds until she fell into a pre-shift catnap. Then he made his way down to her basement.

As he limped imperceptibly around the basement, he carefully assessed every section of that part of the house. Leona lived on a street of identical conjoined row houses. The houses in his neighborhood had more room for modifications than owners had opted for through the years—stilted back porches, expanded living rooms, redacted front parlors. The homes in her neighborhood could not be altered without impacting the ones on either side. Like uniformed Catholic schoolchildren forced to hold hands to keep one another in check on field trips, the row houses had no opportunity for deviation.

Lucien looked around Leona's basement. It was a bright, fully furnished space. Out of its center, a small living room, a kitchen, a bathroom, and two bedrooms sprouted like a horizontal version of da Vinci's Vitruvian Man. Lucien was not focused on the visible rooms, workmanship, or decor. He was studying the layout of the windows to determine how best to get into his own basement and get his girls out. He was also doing something he had never done before in anyone's basement— checking for signs of a hidden safe room. Nothing could be hidden in Leona's too-clean basement. Like her, it was wide open, readable, and innocent of secrets. She kept the doors to the bedrooms locked to keep them especially pristine in case she ever decided to rent the basement, which she never would. Lucien glanced at the doors and thought how a simple butter knife slid strategically between the lock and doorframe would open them. But he had seen those rooms. They didn't even have actual closets, just stand-alone Ikea armoires. No false doors. Just rusted windows painted shut year after year to keep the temperature inside steady. There was a perpetually damp coolness that served to make the air inside feel just warm enough in the winter and cool enough in summer. The windows trapped air in and locked air out.

Feeling his bladder full, Lucien went into the skinny bathroom. Instead of standing up to urinate, he sat down to examine the cracks and corners where the bathroom walls met, in case he'd missed something. He was disappointed that there was no safe room behind any of the walls.

He returned upstairs and sat at Leona's uncluttered kitchen table. With nothing there to count, he found it difficult to plot how to get back into his boarded-up house. He had no idea what he would do, if he were able to get in. Free the girls and lose them and all of his secrets forever? No, he would need a new place to house them.

Lucien stood up and surveyed Leona's kitchen again. He opened her cabinets and found only two or three of everything. Her pantry was not the stockpile that he'd been accustomed to with Marie-Ange. He opened the drawers and found enough utensils to soothe himself. *Zero, one, two, three . . . twenty-one, two, three, four . . . Nothing.* But he soon exhausted the tacky, ornate stainless steel flatware. He needed to get home to his own things, where he could take inventory of the outdated electronics he'd stacked to the basement ceiling. If they'd toppled over during the fire, the tubular path he'd hollowed out would be gone. There would be no way to get from the basement door to the bathroom behind which the safe room was hidden. He thought of how pleasurable it would be to count and restack his fallen property. It would be as if he'd just brought it all in again fresh off the street. *I am nothing. Until I take, until I count, until all of it is mine.*

Unable to mentally sort through the piles of junk or figure out where to relocate his girls to, Lucien looked around Leona's kitchen and found enough bottles to satisfy and inspire him to enumerate what he would need to bring for his Zero, One, Two, Three, and My. Five gallons of water, one for each of them to last one solid week. It would be impossible to carry all of them at once with his good hand and his claw. If he left the Spam and sardines and brought only bread for the confiture, he could force himself to haul the water two gallons at a time. No peanut butter this time. They'd manage. They'd had less in the past when they'd earned punishment for bad behavior. Maybe he could get help. He would have to have some assistance to break into his house. Someone stronger with the use of two good hands and a pair of sturdy legs would have to peel back the wooden boards over the back door.

Lucien picked up Leona's cell phone and dialed Dieuseul on the pretext of collecting the money owed for five full days with the taxicab. Gratefully, Dieuseul brought up the idea of getting into the house to gather a few of his things, his paintings mostly, before Lucien did. The arrangements made, Lucien took the cell phone upstairs to Leona. She was still asleep. He decided not to wake her up for work and turned off her phone.

Lucien couldn't help but shake his head at her peaceful slumber that reconfirmed her obliviousness. But he was homesick for the place where he didn't have to wait for a woman to fall asleep to watch her unabashedly. He had made small strides since harboring Asante in the safe room. Sure, he'd added his three, no, four girls as well, but no one else. And no more spying, stalking, and squirreling away more strays—not since Four.

Lucien climbed back in bed and spooned Leona. He drifted off with Dieuseul on his mind, hoping that his inner alarm clock would suffice to wake him. As he drifted off, he tried to figure out how the fire had started in the first place. He wouldn't have been surprised if Sol had started it. She was the smartest and the toughest. If anyone could have found a way, it would have been her. She would have preferred to kill all of them, had even threatened to do so, just to starve him. Lucien half-regretted taking Sol. He'd chosen her because she reminded him of his first and favorite daughter, Veille. The resemblance turned out to be barely skin-deep. Sol turned out to be as vocal, cunning, and defiant as his second daughter, Clair.

He tossed and turned and finally drifted off thinking of his three daughters. He missed them as much as he missed Marie-Ange, as much as he missed the dewy girls and balmy breezes back home at Bar Caimite. No one could take the place of his daughters, even now. He didn't understand his love for his daughters because he didn't understand love at all. He understood possession but never felt that they were truly his. He'd fallen for them only after he'd figured out how to keep them.

His way of loving them had been to watch them even when they weren't performing. But once Clair had discovered his spying and figured out his mechanisms, she'd turned the tables and enlisted her sisters in games to stalk the stalker. His daughters had become three falcons with a bird's-eye view of a wily squirrel. By the time they'd hit their teens, they had grown weary of stalking their predator to evade his lascivious designs. They'd honored their pact to move out the minute their high school graduation ended. With full scholarships, room and board included, to the best schools they could get into, they'd fled and looked back at only their mother.

In his disturbed slumber, Lucien's mind bumped over memories like wheels over potholes as he recalled the last time he'd seen his girls. Prior to Marie-Ange's funeral, they hadn't spoken to him in years and then only because Clair had served as intermediary to manage Marie-Ange's care in her final days. And, before that, at high school graduation, when they'd kissed their mother good-bye and gotten into their prepacked U-Haul and left South Ozone Park for good.

They had kept their promise to perform at Marie-Ange's funeral in identical outfits that complemented but did not resemble her own. It was Clair who'd insisted that they wear white, as was the custom when someone younger died. The girls had thought it fitting since Marie-Ange had been more the child than the mother. Each played her part and did what she had always done best. Dor sang. Clair spoke. Veille protected, standing soldierlike next to her sisters onstage, staring down at Lucien, daring him to look at them so she could leap on him and rip out his throat.

Lucien could hear his daughters' voices in his dream. Dor had a sweet, clear voice that she sometimes allowed to go breathy or sleepy because she didn't like to talk much. Although she was a born singer, she preferred to shush and soothe. People were always surprised to hear how beautifully and passionately she crooned, given how shy and quiet she was. They were never surprised that she could emote softly like Roberta Flack. But when she belted out ballads like Whitney Houston, people took notice. Clair and Veille had just enough talent to sing backup and harmonize with her.

With her sisters' supportive vocals, Dor had retched up the funeral dirge as if she'd been kicked in the gut by a pimp determined to forcibly abort an unborn. It was not "well with her soul." Her mother had not died peacefully or honorably. Although she'd felt light-headed throughout her performance, the confidence that her sisters would catch her if she fell, pick up the song if she couldn't go on, kept her steady enough to finish. Sensing her weakened state, Clair and Veille powered through the harmony and wailed like reeds that had been ripped from the riverbed where they'd been born. They were mourning their own orphanhood.

Dor's head became heavy and started throbbing the minute she heard the piano's last chord reverberating her last note. She was always like this after performing, as if she had to shed the skin of the entity that had possessed her and produced overwhelmingly powerful sounds that her real self never could have. She all but ran offstage after singing, soaked with sweat as if she had a fever. Relieved to be offstage, she felt no guilt at having left Veille and Clair up there alone.

Clair had fluidly, almost coolly, delivered the eulogy, saying all the right things with the erudition of an overachieving Ivy League graduate, while her anger and grief waited to explode from any unmanned, unplugged orifice. As she climbed off the stage to take her seat in the front pew, a dark spot bloomed on the back of her virgin-white skirt. She bled out her grief. The passion she'd suppressed to keep from crying during her speech gushed out and exposed all she'd tried to hold back.

Still onstage, Veille had stood ready to take up arms to protect her sisters when she saw them in their distraught and vulnerable states. Her pupils assumed the fire red of a car's brake lights on a dark, deserted back road. She knew that if Lucien even looked directly at or dared to approach either of her sisters, her anger would cascade off the stage and flood the church. She would become angry enough to cry, and the flames in her pupils would turn to liquid—first to lava then to blood—in the whites of her eyes and breach her lower lids. She would become a red hellcat and pounce.

To let Veille know that he was not a threat, Lucien had shrunk in his seat and flicked Leona's hand off his shoulder. He knew that he'd turned Veille into a brawler. She'd always been and remained a nice girl, a people pleaser, even when her violent temper materialized. She'd never initiated but always defended her sisters, finishing any fight more viciously than the instigator. Still, most preferred Veille's bite over Clair's bark, including Marie-Ange, whose spirit had intervened during the eulogy to keep Clair's sharp tongue in check. Clair still managed to get in a few barbs at certain oblivious deaf, dumb, or blind attendees, including her father, who'd all but lain down in a fetal position on the pew to play dead in the presence of a grizzly tongue, an armed panther, and a vomiting voice that had brought everybody to tears.

Lucien jolted awake as if he'd felt Veille's threat in his sleep. He gripped the covers with his good hand and covered his head. He had not been surprised that his daughters had been too angry to visit him in the months and years after the funeral. At the repast immediately following the burial, they'd complained about the junk he and Leona had tried to hide at the house. He knew what they thought of him, that he was a stubborn slob who'd insulted their dead mother even further by refusing to hold the second part of her home-going at the catering hall they'd paid for in full. They'd gotten over Leona's behavior. He'd allowed her to act like the woman of the house after her little performance of humility at the church and graveside. She'd looked so dumb as she'd practically curtsied and grinned sadly, offering guests another patty, glass of wine, or bottle of water. They ignored her out of pity because it had been clear that she'd been completely taken with Lucien. They hadn't even cared if he'd been sleeping with her while Marie-Ange was alive, which they'd correctly guessed as true. They'd been grateful that at least the infamous Asante, the basement tenant Marie-Ange had told each of them about during separate too-long phone conversations, had not shown her face. Leona's presence had been tolerable because she'd been useful. They couldn't be angry with her since they had helped choose their father's next wife. They had reserved their disdain for Lucien himself.

Lying on his back, Lucien placed his claw on his chest and felt palpitations. Although he'd always understood why, his daughters' rejections still hurt in the spot where he knew he should have had a heart. To calm the threatening tears thumping rapidly in his throat, he counted the members of his newest family whom he would try to rescue in the morning.

Zero, always start from zero. One, Two, Three, and Four. She's dead. Don't count My. He is not one of them. One, two, three, four, five gallons of water. Twenty-two slices in a loaf of bread plus two end pieces. They have sardines and confiture. In the morning I will count again.

Until then, I cry out of nowhere. I cannot stop or count. There is nothing there.

SOL

———————

Three days after the fire, with the frigid air outside penetrating the insulation, the sweat on the back-room walls had frozen over. The rancid smell of dissipated smoke, molten metal and plastic, burnt wood and fabric, and ruined indiscernible objects turned Sol's stomach. Although these odors were an improvement over the musk, sweat, and excrement fermented in the back room over many years, they were alien and, therefore, nauseating to her distorted nasal palate.

Sol was too cold to sit up. They all were. She let Chiqui, Cocoa, and My huddle together close to but not with her, as if that little distance between them could keep them from catching whatever she had. They were One, Two, Three, and the boy. Sol, Chiqui, Cocoa, and My. They knew better than to invite Asante to snuggle. They let her be. Only Sol thought of and kept an eye on Zero. She understood Asante's preference for solitude. She knew that she'd been in the basement the longest and had spent years with no companions. During the weeks in between visits, Asante had even looked forward to seeing Lucien. Sol also understood Asante's separation from herself, the distance between her self and her mind. How far away from them she had to go so she didn't have to remember where she

was and how she'd gotten there and, god forbid, wonder when
she might get out.

*Zero is not One. He counts from nothing and taught me the
same. Asante is Zero. Zero is not fine. I should not call her that.
Asante is broken. She is of no use, but he uses her still. She is the one
he always comes back to after every One, Two, Three, Four. Even
after My. She has nothing left that he has not taken. She is not me.
She has forgotten the sky. She is not my sister, Two; or Three. She
is alone. And we are not enough. We are three-quarters of a gallon
of water.*

*One-half of one-half of a sardine. The confiture from fallen ap-
ples is too sweet. Apples are easy to count until they meet sugar and
water and fire. They become inseparable pieces of themselves. There
is no bread. Not even little-big-men loaves. Only fish. Can upon can.
There is never rice. Takes too much time to count. Beans are easier.
They grow in the garden only My has seen. We know the season has
changed when he smells like dirt, smells green, smells sweet. Zero
smells like dying. I am already dead. I have died before I die.*

Sol heard Asante start to groan. She didn't force herself to
see from where or from whom the extended growls were coming. She knew Asante's sounds almost as well as she knew her
own voice inside her head. Still, she asked the others to light another candle. She didn't address anyone specifically or directly.
For the past three days, she'd become indifferent to rationing.
It was too cold. Why count? Why save? At least four of them
would make it out before they died of thirst, starved, or were
crushed by the collapsing house. She shivered a little as Chiqui
jumped at the chance to help. Cocoa scurried to plate a sardine
and a generous scoop of marmalade into a saucer to serve her.
Sol nodded, thanking them and asking for water at the same
time.

With her eyes closed, Sol calculated Lucien's next move. He
normally brought rations on Monday, so the water was almost
gone. Asante had been on her umpteenth hunger strike in ump-

teen years, so there was more for the rest. Since the fire, Chiqui and Cocoa had kept their consumption to a minimum to ensure that Sol and little My had enough.

Sol understood their desire to light more candles. Her hallucinations scared them. She fell into the darkness and saw things that were not and had never been there. She would forget what was real and what wasn't. Thinking about her trances plunged her into one again. With eyes closed, she saw the steel wall sweating with an outline of a face traced by an invisible finger. Behind her, another face appeared, crying like a battered woman with hardened lumps and permanent bruises as dark as the mud-stained stone wall. Her mind flipped the reinforced steel wall and laid it flat like an endless kitchen counter. On it, animal carcasses lay skinned and eviscerated, awaiting a butcher's carving. Sol quickly opened her eyes and saw that a second candle had been lit, but it did not light up her mind. She passed her hand just above the steel counter as if soothing the dead animals. She was not remembering these things. They were real to her.

She had never seen a stainless steel kitchen counter. She'd never seen any gutted animals except the odd fowl her mother would buy from the livestock place. She couldn't have been channeling the long-gone ceremonies Marie-Ange had held in the basement because there had never been animal sacrifices to Ezili. There had been one goat slaughtered in the yard during the Louvertures' first summer in SOP. But that had been just for show—to scare the few remaining Italian neighbors and solidify Marie-Ange's reputation among the as yet thin Haitian community as a credible and powerful priestess. But Sol could not have known any of that. Even in her deepest dreams and memories, or with possession, she could not possibly conjure up a sacrifice. Only in her delusions could she see a little light-skinned brown girl gutted, splayed, and waiting for the butcher to arrive and finish her off.

Sol didn't remember much of her early childhood, certainly not before age four. She and her mother, Cara, had started their trek from the Yucatán Peninsula where the corners of Belize, Guatemala, and Mexico fused and confused the nationalities of their inhabitants. She remembered best the time they'd spent walking through the middle of Mexico. Sol had been a misleadingly petite six-year-old when Cara, who was five months pregnant, increased the pace of their journey, hoping to give birth on the Arizona side of the Sonoran Desert. Sol had been more frightened of Cara's wrath after they'd missed their target. Cara had riled for weeks after giving birth in Agua Prieta instead of Douglas. Sol had watched as her mother bled for weeks because of her pulsing rage. Although weakened by the pumping of what was truly life's blood, Cara's adrenaline and drive for survival had pushed her forward with a nursing infant in tow. Since she couldn't have intercourse, she'd perfected sucking, like the baby at her breast, to pay her way across the country to Washington Heights, New York. She'd pretended to have a cousin who would give her a job sorting and selling produce street-side. Sol recalled clearly how her mother had managed to rent a bed in a small room in a tiny apartment in a diminutive squatters' building managed by a Mexican super who was even shorter than she was.

Sol preferred memories to hallucinations. Lying in her own sweat, she drifted in and out of conscious remembering. She could see her eight-year-old self as she'd accompanied Cara on Saturdays and Sundays to sell fruit and flowers on North Conduit Avenue. They'd stood on a strip where the Van Wyck and Belt Parkway kissed and parted at a red light, creating 134th Street and 134th Place. That's where, for years, she used to see Lucien and Marie-Ange driving in a struggling minivan that looked like it might break down at any minute. She'd in fact seen it pushed to the gas station nearby so many times over so many years that the station had borne a different name each time. Sol remembered that Marie-Ange had preferred carnations over roses and always asked for mangos that they never had. She'd rejected the bottled water that Lucien guzzled in one go, preferring to stop at the gas station store for an ice-cold Pepsi. Cara had started stocking a secret stash of soda just for her special customer who spoke Spanglish to her whenever a red light and Lucien's patience had permitted.

Sol raised herself on her elbows and placed her face in her hands to maintain her composure while remembering one of the worst days of her life. She skipped over the weeks Chiqui had spent bawling over Cara's disappearance. She'd tried to console her little sister but could not explain that their mother had vanished into an INS detention center. Sol could see her teenaged self selling flowers on her own. She saw her hand reaching into Lucien's van to hand him change. She saw him mostly alone for months and then later with a new woman, dressed in all black, who sat in the front seat of his van wanting only red carnations. Neither of them had spoken Spanish or cared to explain that the flowers had been for Marie-Ange's grave. Sol had known only that two distant women had disappeared from her life at about the same time, leaving her motherless and more vulnerable than she could have imagined.

Sol turned her head toward the stone wall against which Chiqui was leaning as if listening for exploitable faults in the newly compromised back-room wall. She couldn't believe how grown her sister looked now. But even if Chiqui had been a blossoming woman, Sol never would have taken her baby sister with her to sell on North Conduit. She had been determined to make things different for Chiqui.

Sol had removed Cara's picture from its frame and proclaimed herself the only mother Chiqui needed now that their mother was gone. Sol would wake up at dawn on weekend mornings to hock her wares along North Conduit and try not to lose herself in the sky. She had had to look down more to make the money needed to keep up the appearance of being cared for by an adult. So she'd had to imagine, instead of witness, the miraculous sky. She'd had to believe, instead of reading her story in which she was as much a miracle as the magical intersection of the Yucatán where she'd been born.

Sol sat up again and stared blankly. Her hallucinations slammed the door on memory and took over again. The stone walls were now gushing waterfalls. She was trying to stuff the innards back into the carcass on the bloody kitchen counter. She sewed a seam like a zipper from south to north, from the little girl's pelvis to her breastbone. She ignored Chiqui's and Cocoa's attempts to stop her frantic hands and wipe her forehead. She was sweating more water than she'd consumed all week.

She didn't hear Cocoa singing to bring her out of her trance. Cocoa sang clearer and harder to break the barriers between reality, memory, and hallucination. She was looking for a way not only to pull Sol out of the dream, but to also be heard by those on the outside. The fire had made it possible for sounds from the outside to pour in, but, sucked so far into the surreal, Sol could hear none of it. She was deaf to the hum of idling engines and muffled talk that intoned like a backup choir harmonizing with Cocoa's wails. Together they praised the house, the fire, the remaining candles, Marie-Ange's spirit, and the goddess Ezili for breaking the silence.

In her catatonic state, Sol could not hear Cocoa's escalating exultation. She'd gone deaf to the hallelujahs for the damage to the house's infrastructure that had compromised the soundproofing of the safe room. Sol couldn't break free from her mind's incarceration to feel Cocoa's hands on her chest rubbing her into consciousness. But she wept as if she could see someone kneeling beside her singing an unrecognizable song. Sol gasped suddenly. She took in air like the first breath of a drowning swimmer rescued just in time. She could finally hear everything clearly—Cocoa's singing, the outside noises that came from cracks in the wall instead of Lucien's one-way intercom.

She held Cocoa's hand still on her chest, to stop her singing. They needed to ration their strength because soon a hunger they'd never felt before would suck the sound from their diaphragms. It would knock them into an abyss deeper than the dungeon where they'd been hoarded for too many years.

LA KAY

What had been an ordinary morning of keeping Its eyes and ears peeled for tidbits of news turned into a day of rage and outrage, of tears from men who'd held them back at their mothers' funerals. La Kay leaned in as if to comfortingly embrace KAM patrons who were bawling over the near death of one of their own. Haitian cabdriver Abner Louima had been beaten and sodomized in a Brooklyn police precinct not ten miles from SOP. It had wept over the shoulders of Its occupants and visitors over the bloody beating that had made the front page of New York's major newspapers. Since they hadn't been able to stop talking about what had befallen their fellow countryman, It had learned more than It had wanted about the broom-handle rape and bathroom battery by cops. It had watched closely for Marie-Ange's reaction. She hadn't cried a single tear. She hadn't even choked up at the newsreels of a swollen and disfigured Louima in the hospital. At least not in the presence of anyone at KAM.

La Kay had followed her closely as she'd struggled down the basement stairs into Ezili's new peristyle in the boiler room. She cried then to her goddesses and prayed for justice if outright revenge could not be delivered. Like every good *manbo* and every worthwhile *houngan* in New York at that time, she lit candles and poured *kleren* over the altar and then rubbed the rest on her face to help right the horrible wrong. La Kay had kept quiet while dancing with her during truncated but potent ceremonies in a space barely bigger than a bathroom stall. It had been in lockstep with her every movement, including her final gesture spitting a last swig of *kleren* at the basement door behind which Lucien had been hosting his tenant, Asante.

Less than two years later, It had mourned two deaths with the people at KAM. Marie-Ange had succumbed to cancer one week before Amadou Diallo's murder. It had been surprised that her death hadn't been memorialized by even an obituary in a single newspaper. It figured that she had been less important since she hadn't died at the hands of the NYPD. But, like the people at KAM, It had wept equally over her departure as over those who'd suffered at the hands of evil, empowered authorities.

It had learned that police beatings were nothing new to KAM. Some had fled the same at the hands of Jean-Claude Duvalier's Tonton Makout before immigrating. At least in America there had been a semblance of justice painted in the media. Even if it wasn't real, the gesture had meant a lot to those who could never have hoped for the same in their native country.

Lying prostrate after the crippling fire, La Kay remembered the record Lucien used to play about Makout abuse. He'd blasted it for the entire neighborhood to hear. But no one had been able to play it in Haiti without fear of a sound thrashing while Baby Doc occupied the Palais Nacional.

La Kay had heard no songs for Marie-Ange or Louima. But, later, Diallo would get a well-deserved, but ironic, twenty-one-gun salute in one of Wyclef's songs. When KAM had learned that Diallo had been murdered by police in the vestibule of the Bronx tenement where he'd lived, every taxi driver in SOP had wanted to pack up and move back home. If that had happened, half the houses in the neighborhood would have been left vacant. Under the pretext of preventing a recurrence of the Louima and Diallo incidents, La Kay had pulled together a huddle of Its associates owned by taxi drivers to learn exactly what had happened in the Bronx. However, Its real purpose had been to learn if that might be a way to get rid of Lucien without having to kill Itself in the process.

It had marveled at the randomness of the Louima and Diallo incidents. It had read about and watched national news broadcasts about another cabdriver, Rodney King, who had been beaten on the side of an L.A. road by a bunch of cops. Sixteen-year-old Yusef Hawkins had been shot to death in Bensonhurst. Trinidadian Michael Griffith had been murdered just up the road in Howard Beach. Willie Turks had been stomped to death in Gravesend. It had wearied of going back through the previous decades up to Its birth date. It couldn't have even imagined what had happened in the centuries before then.

La Kay had gathered Its closest associates to find out not only why these murders had been perpetrated, but why those men. It couldn't have known if they'd done anything besides being poor, black, and/or immigrants. It had deduced, based on the newspaper articles and the television news, that these had been good, innocent men. So why them? Why not the hundreds of murderers on Rikers Island? No, not the innocent ones serving sentences for petty offenses or crimes they hadn't committed at all. Not the ones framed by corrupt detectives or a racist district attorney. It had been thinking of the ones who had taken lives, committed rapes (no, not the wrongly accused teenagers who'd been tricked into making false confessions). The real criminals who'd been caught red-handed and about whose guilt there had been no doubt. Those ones. Why not them? Why not a man like Lucien, who'd been preying on women since Bar Caimite? How could It get to him? Set him up to be shot twenty-one times on the side of a road without a day in court. How could It find the right mob or an easily persuaded group of cops who needed no probable cause to go after a black man; to take him out for all of his evil? La Kay wanted to know, to plan, to execute.

It hadn't even learned the worst. It hadn't yet acknowledged the scratching at the steel-reinforced door in Its long-ignored coccyx. It hadn't yet heard the cries or the songs, or felt the movement of four, maybe five women, a child, and god knows who else Lucien had been keeping for an unknown number of years. While lamenting Louima, It had had no idea that Asante had already been locked up in Its back room. KAM had been talking about Asante's shop that had just been raided by the police and sent her running to nobody knew where.

Things had gone quiet in the wake of Marie-Ange's death. After the initial parade of people who'd started their immigrant lives at KAM, only a few diehards and hang-abouts had continued to visit Lucien. For the most part, La Kay had felt the presence of only Dieuseul and Leona. A few patrons would stop by periodically with takeout containers from local eateries. La Kay had joined them, missing the smell and taste of Marie-Ange's cooking. It had gleaned more from their foam food containers than their newspapers. The restaurants in SOP had been enjoying an uptick in business since her death. They'd gone from merely catering to Caribbean tastes with a few items on their menus to being owned by Guyanese purveyors who provided all manner of delicacies from all over the West Indies. Only the Chinese restaurant had held its own over the decades. La Kay and the few KAM stalwarts had gagged on the smell of Leona's cooking and watched as Dieuseul stockpiled appliances in his bedroom to prepare his own meals.

La Kay had perked up every now and then at Lucien's visitors, new immigrants who'd heard about KAM from their people in New York. They'd been disappointed to know that KAM's heartbeat, Marie-Ange, had stopped. But they'd brought news of Haiti's politics and natural disasters, which It had found satisfying enough not to look in Its basement for traces of Asante.

The next catastrophic distraction came on 9/11. It had been easy to slip someone past It then. It had been ducking from low-flying planes into and out of JFK. It could not be faulted for missing a lone girl and a fading woman in Its basement. The entire world had been focused on the four planes flown over and then into U.S. soil, so how could It have known that Lucien had been preparing to take Sol and then Chiqui two years later and then Cocoa after seven dormant years and then Four. While It had been mourning abuse after abuse, death after death, four, maybe five women had been futilely pounding on Its doors. If It had known, It would have found a way to off Lucien long before It had attempted a murder-suicide in the middle of winter. Now that It could feel their presence, It was determined to end their terror. It tried to figure out how to get to him before he came to make them disappear or make them dead, which were one and the same.

Four

LUCIEN

———

With the rescue of his family on his mind, Lucien couldn't fall asleep properly. He tossed and turned in Leona's bed trying not to fall into the crack between the sadomasochistic twins of narcolepsy and insomnia. A former night-shift driver, he'd fought both for decades. They were like single beds brought together to deceptively form a tortuous king. His narcolepsy had been uncontrollable and incurable with over-the-counter solutions. His insomnia had been easily addressed with all manner of accessible tried-and-true herbal and chemical remedies. He'd often preferred the sleeplessness, had even prolonged the mania because the accompanying energy and acuity had helped his overnight hunting. At two in the morning, he didn't so much as wake up as open his eyes to find his way out of bed.

Lucien dressed himself in the dark hallway outside of Leona's bedroom. He climbed down the stairs and sneaked past the second portrait Dieuseul had painted of his daughters. It was different from the first one that both men wanted to rescue from the burned house. The one at Leona's house was wilder, more abstract, like a collaboration between Casimir and Picasso— a Haitian *Les Demoiselle d'Avignon*. The deconstruction and distortion of the girls' bodies was a style Dieuseul had developed as

a reminder of his childhood spent bent before the tourists pur-
chasing his paintings. Before then, the portraits of the neighborhood girls had all been realistic, merciful, and soft, proof
of an art produced out of tenderness and empathy. But Lucien
preferred the later works in which Dieuseul had manipulated
the female form in a way that conveyed a desire to break the
girls whose figures would not bend for him. Lucien had found
the paintings fantastically violent but orderly, bodies crowded
into the canvas, curved into the painter's preferred positions.
He'd always appreciated the way the painter had dismembered
then reassembled his subjects into figures that pleased him.
Maybe, Lucien thought as he traced the forms in the painting in
the dark, Dieuseul would know how to squeeze and contort the
women to get them out of the basement.

Lucien dismissed the thought before getting into his cab
with Dieuseul. He quietly closed the car door so Leona wouldn't
hear. Even if Dieuseul's paintings intimated the empathy of a
kindred spirit, there was no way Lucien would invite him into
such a precious confidence. He had never and would never
share the knowledge of his girls with anyone, let alone allow
someone to see and touch them. Lucien scarcely trusted his
own shrunken conscience with his secret. What he knew of
Dieuseul made him only half trusting.

Lucien didn't need to ask Dieuseul any questions. He knew
that the former soldier could keep a secret because he had done so
under the most severe commander in chief Haiti had ever seen.
The only secret Dieuseul had not kept had been his life story,
which he'd recounted during their long discussions between
shift changes. Lucien had listened closely for elements he could
exploit. He'd confirmed that soldiers at war had to be guardians
of the clandestine and, when required, the keepers of prisoners.
He'd also understood Dieuseul's hunger for superiority. Before
Dieuseul had entered Baby Doc's pitiless army, he had been a
victim of many oppressors: Haiti's light-skinned upper class,

who'd kept an artistic prodigy from the right schools because he couldn't speak proper French; the white tourists in Cap-Haïtien, who'd paid for his portraits with hard-to-get junk food instead of cash, who had praised, pampered, and groomed him until he'd sold them his own body rather than those in his precocious portraits. They'd paid him in greenbacks for his bareback, leaving him HIV positive and with a taste for all things foreign and an entitlement to scarce luxuries. He had been so distracted by the things he'd been able to afford that he'd stopped visiting his family in his hometown of Cité Soleil. He'd sent them American money, food, and clothing instead of giving them the present of his presence. He'd even started to swear that he would never return to the slum where no light penetrated, not even the ubiquitous equatorial sun. Inhabitants had easily forgotten that the sky was always beautiful no matter what lay beneath it. They'd stopped believing that whatever the sun shone upon became light because it seemed to skip over them. Sunrise and sunset were the privileges of other Haitian towns. In Cité Soleil, there was no distinction between day and night. The sun always seemed to sleep late into the evening, forgetting to wake itself up.

Lucien knew Dieuseul's family history well. Despite being a decade older, Lucien had acted the younger brother by pretending to be the deferential boss. Dieuseul had never recovered from his brother's murder in Cité Soleil. The news had forced him to go back. He had reactively developed an odious rage directed at adolescent boys like the ones who'd killed his brother—the ones who had no visibly natural gift, no pedophilic patrons, no means of making money, even bareback, no homes away from home. The ones like he could have been and really had been mere moments before his baby brother got shot for failing to hand over a pair of new Nike sneakers. Dieuseul had sent them to him after being allowed to run through the commissary on the American base where his most committed customer had lived. He'd hated boys more after becoming a stepfather in New York, wishing he could disband the teenagers who'd chased his stepdaughter like wild dogs after strangers' exhaust-smoking cars.

Lucien had held a mild disdain for adolescent boys himself but hadn't been able to hate them outright, because he loved the boy he used to be at Bar Caimite. Still, he empathized with Dieuseul's desire as a former Tonton Makout to take up arms and slaughter any teenaged man-boy, including his former self.

Lucien looked over at Dieuseul as he drove from Leona's to their home. He didn't know what he would find besides the sawdust boards and KEEP OUT signs. These were just barriers to get past quickly, so he could get inside. Inside, Lucien could indulge in his preferred pleasures: penetrating the barriers of women's minds, bombarding the obstacles of their emotions, shattering their exteriors, and wreaking havoc on their defenses. He'd succeeded in doing the same with Dieuseul, who'd willingly picked him up in the middle of the night to assist in his adventurous trespassing.

Lucien never forgot Dieuseul's status. Without having to say the three-letter acronym, he leveraged his knowledge to get Dieuseul to do his bidding. Dieuseul had never been typically symptomatic and had discovered that he had been a carrier only after four years of marriage. By then he'd secured his green card and had gotten his wife pregnant. Lucien remembered her running to KAM, bent on murder and suicide, straight from the ob-gyn. She'd kept herself alive and out of prison only for the sake of her daughter and her unborn son. She'd immediately banished Dieuseul to keep him and herself out of danger.

Lucien chuckled at his talent as a master manipulator. He'd managed to keep Dieuseul's status a secret from everyone except Marie-Ange. He had also convinced her to rent their daughters' vacant bedroom to the heartbroken painter. Lucien had never stopped grooming his wife, preparing her to do whatever he'd decided and keeping her with him despite all manner of evil deeds. He had gotten her used to Dieuseul as his co-driver. She'd thought of their tenant as a harmless forlorn artist reminiscent of her father. Lucien hadn't understood or cared about Marie-Ange's attraction to Dieuseul. If he had, he would have seen the painter's elegance, his relaxed, confident walk, and the easy way he seemed to collapse his six-foot-three-inch frame into a body an entire foot shorter. He would have known that the style of his later paintings had not evidenced a desire to break others but reflected his body's memory. Dieuseul had been bending his long joints into small frames since his days sitting outside of tourist traps in Cap-Haïtien selling paintings and himself. He had folded whatever joint he'd thought might be in someone's way. What Lucien had judged as effeminate— Dieuseul's seated pose, with one leg crossed over at the knees— had been a remnant of a childhood spent bending for buyers. Lucien had never seen the man in private when he painted, imitating the postures in his paintings to ascertain how much he could fit on the canvas.

Even if Dieuseul had not told him, Lucien would have deduced the secrets, including the most shameful. He'd known better than to ever expose the fact that Dieuseul could not speak French. No one at KAM would have guessed that the well-spoken gentleman who'd passed his GED exam the first time around, who'd always carried a book or *The New York Times* under his arm, and who'd kept threatening to take community college classes or lying that he actually had was barely literate in what had remained Haiti's national language. But when he spoke Kreyòl, which was added as a national language out of an act of common sense in the late '90s, he spoke it with an imitation French accent that fooled everyone. Lucien had helped Dieuseul weave the lore that he'd completed all of his classes in Haiti and had been about to graduate from university when he'd gotten a chance to come to the United States to continue his education. This was the story all of KAM's visitors believed and perpetuated until it became truth. Dieuseul maintained the façade required by such a lie. To explain his faltering French, he'd told KAM's patrons that he had decided never to speak the language of the colonizer. Lucien had backed him up, insisting that French was useless in America and the majority of the world.

Lucien didn't mind taking his time getting to the house. He could sense that Dieuseul needed the air and space to let his mind and body roam as much as he did. He looked Dieuseul over as he turned the steering wheel into the many right-hand turns required to get from Ozone Park to SOP. He tried to see what Marie-Ange had seen in the man and concluded that it could only have been the resemblance to her father. He looked at Dieuseul gratefully for the times when he'd dutifully cared for Marie-Ange during the night shift. He wouldn't have cared if the two had had an affair. By that time, Lucien had had little use for her body except when her ailing hands had cooked what he'd liked when he'd liked. He'd accepted and reciprocated hand jobs just to appease her but had been uninterested in her sex. Dieuseul had done him a favor by flirting with and collegially caressing the ailing but still beautiful Marie-Ange. Lucien didn't even care that she'd confided in Dieuseul his affair with Asante. He'd always known that the painter would never breathe a word. He'd eavesdropped to find out how much Marie-Ange had divulged. The furthest she'd gone had been his promise to get rid of his basement bitch and hire a nurse to care for her. He'd done so much worse over the years that his quick fucks and few affairs should have been the least of her worries. Lucien had waited to hear her tell another soul what he'd done and explain why she'd stayed with him after all. After all.

Lucien had both witnessed and been the beneficiary of women's tolerance. Marie-Ange hadn't been the first and wouldn't be the last to stay with an unemployed man. She'd nursed Lucien through his on-the-job injury for more than the workers' comp windfall that had gone straight to repaying their debts. These had been her loans, taken out behind his back with his steady job as collateral. The steaming steel pipe that had fallen on Lucien's leg had completed the khaki tan he'd acquired while working at the factory for nearly a decade. He'd stayed home for three years figuring out if he wanted to return to work at all, anywhere, for anybody. With leftover money from his workers' compensation claim that he'd hidden from Marie-Ange, he'd bought a taxi medallion and a yellow cab to slap it on. He had had no shortage of candidates coming through KAM willing to take any offered shift for six to seven days per week. Dieuseul had won out for the day shift and Lucien had gladly taken the night. While Lucien's injuries had completely healed, Marie-Ange's had just started to form, fester, harden, and corrode her insides with what would be decades of difficult-to-diagnose multiple organ failure.

Sitting next to her first caregiver, Lucien could not recall the feeling of watching his wife deteriorate. Dieuseul would have told him, if he'd asked. But Lucien would never ask. He liked being the all-knowing one with answers to every question. His best conversations had always been with himself. Talking to Marie-Ange during her illness had always ended in arguments. Her illness had come with the erosion of her verbal filters as well. She hadn't been able to censor herself to save anyone's feelings. Years of repressed emotional venom had attacked her body, plunging her in a chemo chair while still in her early thirties.

Lucien started to grow weary of Dieuseul's slow driving through the neighborhood. It wasn't like they needed a tour of SOP. Nothing had changed there, except for his house. He wanted to grab the wheel to make Dieuseul pull over, so he could take the wheel and get to the house faster. He didn't want to think anymore, to remember why he was where he was at this stage in life. He didn't want to drift into memories of his daughters. He'd been dreaming about them less than an hour ago and, as beautiful as they'd been, he did not need to see them now. Thinking of them while fully awake would force him to feel. Not guilt or shame, which would have been appropriate. But something he couldn't name because his insides were both hollow and corroded. *I am nothing.*

His daughters had been different. By the time Marie-Ange had been deep into her first round of sickness, his daughters had started evading and then watching his every move. Marie-Ange had turned a blind eye to her daughters' self-protective maneuvers until knowledge had slapped her in the face. She'd known that Lucien had loved his daughters, especially Veille, more than life itself. She had been their first, the one who'd most resembled him and his kin.

Veille's birth had been unexpected and inconvenient. But she had also been a comfort to them; one more reason to stay together. Lucien had felt prepared to be a father and had fallen in love with his firstborn. A first daughter herself, Marie-Ange had understood that love. She'd also needed additional comfort, someone to love while continuing to mourn her father and Lucien, who'd been set to leave for the United States. But everything changed when she learned that she was pregnant again with a baby still at the breast.

Lucien had always known what Marie-Ange had never been able to admit—that neither of them should have ever been a parent. They hadn't known what true parenting was because their own had loved and abandoned them irresponsibly. But, unlike Marie-Ange, he'd been fine with his view and treatment of his daughters. They'd both seen their children as props, possessions, and extensions of their own egos. Lucien had worshipped Veille and her sisters like the imported figurines in his aunt's glass curio, with which he'd been obsessed as a child. His pursuit of women at KAM and innumerable affairs had been attempts to distract himself from his unnatural attraction to his girls.

Lucien knocked back the thoughts like a child fighting off a forceful and determined bully. Just as they crossed Liberty Avenue, he reclined his seat. He allowed sleep to fight on his behalf and closed his eyes while Dieuseul continued their redundant tour of the neighborhood. Losing his battle against the onslaught of memories, Lucien crawled backward into his dreams like a soldier retreating into a foxhole. Once the shelter collapsed, he had no choice but to dig through the dirt to excavate visions of his exquisite daughters. This time, they were younger, not even in their teens, Marie-Ange's little dolls done up like pedigree show dogs. They were the primped, pretty overachievers; the prizewinners into which their mother had turned them. How could his adoring stares not progress into leering? How could he not touch?

Why was Veille so sad? Why was Marie-Ange so angry? Why was she shaking the girl? Did she need the details? Something to compare with her own father's behaviors? Of course, she would rationalize that her father's affection had been nothing like what he'd done to Veille. Of course, her general had never made her do what he'd made Veille do. Of course, he'd known better.

Wake up! Wake up! Lucien shouted inaudibly to himself while attempting to tunnel himself out of the dirt threatening to bury him alive.

Was that any reason for them to watch me the way they did? Was it enough to make her sick, to make her body begin its shutdown? Was it enough to make her threaten me the way she had? With severing? Abandonment? Did she have to say those words? Had she been choking on them for years? And her questions—how could I possibly respond? How could I tell her while she lay in her sickbed? The way she looked at me, she had clearly been thinking these things before asking, before cutting. I need to wake up! I have to wake up! I don't want to know. I don't want to hear her again! I don't want to go there again! That's where she hurt me with questions I could never answer. Not truthfully to a mother in her sickbed.

Wake up! Wake up!

No sound except for her questions:

Did I make them too pretty for you? I gave birth to them that way. That's how they came out. Me mixed with you, but with more traces of me. That's what made them so pretty. Especially Veille. Did I keep her skin too smooth until she learned how to properly lotion her own body? Did I make the parts in her scalp too straight? Did I comb, brush, and style her tresses too temptingly? Did the hair on her head turn out so thick, so black, that it made you think that she had something more for you? At six years old? Did it remind you of what's between mine? Were the edges of her flannel nightgown too lacy? The cotton too soft? Her panties too roomy?

Did I dress my girls too nicely? Like presents for Papa Noel. Did they look too joyous? Like Christmas? Did I make too many of them? Did you think it was okay to break just one? Did you have plans for all three? To strip them after church? Take off their matching suits? My favorite, fine herringbone fabric trimmed with white? A dress suit with a hem that hit and hid past shin and calve. Covered. Knee socks that vanished under the hemline. Covered. My favorite outfit, high neckline, mock turtleneck with white trim that hit the lower part of the throat. Covered. I found one for each of the three in the right size. Sleeves that fell just below the wrist. Covered. Shoes polished with Griffin black. My special trick, a thin coat of Vaseline. Covered.

Were my girls too shiny for you? Smoothed eyebrows, glossed lips. Covered.

Did I teach them to stand too still? Did they look like mannequins? Flawlessly dressed, prettier than any black dolls Mattel had ever made. Putting white dolls to shame. Perfect. Did I make them too perfect? Manners, mannerisms, poise onstage? Did you think

*they operated on batteries? Did you see them through glass panes?
Covered.*

*Were they too much me and not enough you? Did you forget
that they were yours?! All three? Did you plan to stop at her? Were
the twins next? Take two at once. Did I make too many? Enough
for you to count? Did I make them too fucking lovable?! Pretty, po-
lite, performing at church on those special occasions when you came.
To stare. Glass figurines behind God's curio pane. Covered! Were
you curious? Did you just want to see? What would happen if you
touched? Just one? Did you know that she was real? Did you know
that she would break? Did you know that she could speak?*

Lucien startled himself awake. He did not want Dieuseul
to see him trembling. He would never explain his dreams to
anyone, not because they seemed real, but because they were
the truth. How would he ever explain the tears? His haunting
himself with soft sounds wafting like smoke, *I am nothing*. As
they drove up Rockaway Boulevard, he counted the streets
until they reached his house. He climbed out of the taxi and
into his van as quickly as he could. He signaled for Dieuseul
to follow him. Lucien drove and then parked the van in front
of an abandoned house on the corner of 135th Street, just off
the Conduit. He panted as he struggled to get himself out of
the van and back into the taxi. He gave Dieuseul a look that
said, "Don't ask. Just drive." Lucien closed his eyes and slowed
his breathing. He knew when they reached 126th Street, three
blocks from his house. He opened his eyes to signal for Dieuseul
to slow down and turn right. He placed his hand on the steering
wheel and guided the taxi into a parking space. He didn't have
to explain why they weren't parking closer to the house. They
both already knew that they needed to keep their presence hidden to achieve their separate ends. Lucien sat in the warm car
until Dieuseul finally knocked on the passenger-side window.
He waited for Dieuseul to open the door and help him out. Not

that he needed assistance. He wanted to prepare Dieuseul for the work ahead.

They walked the three blocks to their street as quickly as Lucien's limp allowed.

Dieuseul nervously interrupted the silence to keep his lips from freezing shut. "Did you ever hear from that hairdresser again, the dealer's girlfriend? I can't believe she was Haitian."

"Not a word. That ingrate." Lucien was not interested in saying more. He dropped his chin into his coat, covering his mouth.

"Asante! Ingrate . . ." Dieuseul said, then let silence prevail.

The men turned into the driveway to get to the back of the house. They crept around looking for the easiest way in. Lucien let Dieuseul yank the board off the back door. He didn't need to be there to help or to watch. He needed to get water, five gallons, and bread, gone stale over months, from the freezing garage. When he returned with two gallons of water in his claw, Dieuseul seemed ready to talk again.

"You plan on staying?" Dieuseul nodded toward Lucien's struggling grip.

"For Ezili. Marie-Ange said so." Lucien wouldn't let Dieuseul help with his charge. "My penance. I moved the angel to make room for my things."

Dieuseul understood vodou rituals and accepted Lucien's explanation.

Lucien sunk into his thoughts, plotting his next maneuver. If he could soundproof and insulate his garage to keep the cold out and the heat in. But, mostly, contain Cocoa's singing. Damn, that girl could sing! She had a voice that the world should have heard, but he'd kept it to himself. He could turn the garage into a recording studio. He had all the equipment. No one would question the kooky old man who'd somehow convinced himself that he could make records out of his garage like it was the 1950s. He would have to move them one by one . . . He would leave

Asante, Zero, whom he'd used up. He would take the loudest one first. One, if Sol was well enough. Then Two, Chiqui, to keep Sol in line. Then his favorite, Three, Cocoa with her singing. He'd allow only breathy whispered songs—"This Woman's Work," "Killing Me Softly," "Time After Time"—or use chloroform to keep her quiet for a while. He would allow one more song because he didn't want My to miss "American Boy." The neighbors might recognize her voice since she'd sung at every school, church, picnic, and talent show ever held in SOP; but so many years had passed since then. His mind wouldn't allow him to move them out of order. *Please, remain on the line and move your girls in the order in which they were received.* Zero, One, Two, Three, My. He could keep the boy out, bring him to Leona's. He was his "grandson," after all. She'd have to take him in.

"I forgot." Lucien put down the water and limped back to the garage to where he kept his finer, more salable things. He started to calculate what he would need to make it suitable for his girls. He grabbed two more gallons of water.

They would have to settle for water, leftover sardines, and confiture with bread. At least they'd have water from a spring, not the tap. He thought of how kind he was to his family in the safe room.

LA KAY

La Kay could feel someone walking Its perimeter outside. It was both too late and too early for the demolition crew to be creeping. It was so cold that not even vandals would be outside. Only someone with a hard fixation would brave the single-digit temperatures. It was desperate for a peek. Unable to open Its eyes, It tried to catch the person's smell in the arctic clean air. It inhaled, held Its breath, and deciphered two familiar scents. Its former inhabitants were seeking entry. It tried to play dead. It sucked in air, trying to seal every opening more tightly. It knew that the sawdust boards could be easily removed. It wanted to do something to keep Lucien and Dieuseul out. It knew that the latter could only want his precious paintings and memorabilia from his long-defunct marriage. Lucien, It knew, had to be there for more.

Since It didn't know exactly where the voices had been coming from, It couldn't barricade whatever trapdoor they were crouched behind. It had to let Lucien in, so he could lead It to the right place. But that would be too risky. What if he had come to kill them all? What if he could get to his gun? The one on display in Marie-Ange's china cabinet. What if he'd come with kerosene and matches? It had to find them before he did. It thought of making some loud noise to send the neighbors running out of their homes into the predawn freeze. But It knew that nothing short of another fire would get anyone outside in the cutting cold and disheartening darkness. And certainly not to see what was going on at a place made uglier than it had already been.

La Kay had heard from Its associates how their owners resented the addition of insults to injuries—the turning of a hoarder's house into pure urban blight, boarded up, inviting graffiti. They would never come. Not even a nosy neighbor awakened by a full bladder would bother to press a nose against a frosty windowpane to see what was going on in that place. It didn't have the strength to make noise. It was barely conscious. Its aluminum siding had become a glacier. Its insides were still burning in certain pockets where sparks refused to die. Its only consolation that night was the simultaneously scary and thrilling entertainment of Lucien limping around It in the January cold. It wanted to wake up the houses to see the crazy old man and his cab pal trying to break in. Although It hadn't told them much about Lucien over the years, It had told them just enough to make them look down on him. And he had done just enough to secure their owners' pity and disdain.

LUCIEN HAD also made improvements to his basement before moving Asante into the neat subterranean apartment. He'd sealed off the slim bathroom, the only entrance to the safe room, to house her and his secrets. La Kay had missed that part. It had been too busy minding Marie-Ange, missing the daughters, and hoping for music to focus fully on Lucien's redesign. It had been trying to cheer Itself up to keep from jumping off some invisible cliff. It had forgotten that, given Lucien's cravings, there would always be women needing protection.

La Kay forced one back window open to watch as Dieuseul

pried a board off the back door. Its one eye followed Lucien as he hobbled to the garage and back. It watched as the gallons of water swung from his good hand and his claw. It held Its breath as Dieuseul ran inside first with Lucien hopping in behind him. It felt Its back door close. Two sets of Its stairs creaked and collapsed. It searched and discovered that the agile man going upstairs had succeeded. It trembled nervously, attempting a chuckle that made It choke as Lucien slid down the stairs to the basement and got stuck like a fishbone in Its throat.

SOL

"Turn on another one. Go ahead and light two more. We've been in the dark too long," Sol whispered to Chiqui, who was closest. She squeezed her hand. "It's okay to touch me. I won't be here much longer. We won't."

"No, *we* won't." Chiqui returned the squeeze.

"Let me look at him." Sol raised herself on her elbows and, with Chiqui's support, sat upright. She peered around Chiqui's body to where My had fallen asleep with his hand knotted up in Chiqui's cloth belt.

Sol choked on her tears. "*He* took that away from me. I should have been better, not cried as much. He wouldn't have brought you here too."

"I have always been and will always be your gift. Remember what Cara used to say? 'I gave you a sister. What more do you want?'"

"Everything I'd ever wanted. But not here. Not this. It shouldn't have . . ."

"Sh-sh-sh. Don't. Don't. We're getting out."

"Will he even be able to see by that time? He's never been to school. He can't read."

"He can count." As soon as Chiqui said the words, she swallowed them back and went silent.

"Cara should be here. Not us." Sol always referred to their mother by her first name instead of Mama, and Chiqui had done the same.

"She was in her own hell. Who knows what happened in the detention center?"

"At least she had lights, a bed, regular meals, something normal. Hope."

"We have that now."

"I'll freeze to death first." Sol coughed until she had to lie down again.

"Have some water."

"Save it for him."

"You need it more."

"Not really, love. Not at all. I have no needs. Everything I care about is here dying with me."

"Don't say that. We're going to get out. I'll make sure he wears sunglasses. The ones he bought him the last time."

Sol didn't respond.

"He finally ate the sardines," Chiqui told Sol as reassurance. "Cara is better suited to this sort of thing."

As Sol drifted back into the half consciousness of fever, she saw herself sitting on the bed the three of them had shared. Chiqui had not been able to grasp what their mother's disappearance had meant. No papers. None of them. If Cara had said anything about having children, they would have been scooped up and brought to her in no time.

At fifteen, Sol had known that they'd needed to move. She'd left the super's place in Washington Heights and found them a bed in Jamaica, Queens, an unlikely place for two "Mexican" girls. But at least it had been closer to work. She'd continued her mother's roadside purveyance seven days a week. She'd added mangos, keneps, and hard-to-carry green coconuts on the weekends for her Caribbean patrons. She'd brought flowers only on Sundays and holidays for visitors who didn't want to arrive to family dinners empty-handed, procrastinating suitors trying to impress skeptical brow-cocked parents, and eager-to-please boyfriends of high-maintenance girlfriends who'd demanded hundred-dollars-a-dozen roses on Valentine's Day. Sol had not had the heart to charge those prices on Mother's Day. Not when Cara had vanished. She had not been the best, but she had still been her mother.

Sol thought, *Cara could hold her own.* She tried to piece together the shards of the broken window that had been Cara's life, things shared during drunken outpourings and angry cleaning binges. If Cara had been drinking and in a cleaning mood, she'd become as frantic, determined, and loquacious as a swarm of bees. She would hold back nothing from her young daughters. Sol followed the vision of her mother wherever it would take her. Anywhere was better than the back room.

"*Imaginaté!* I was always this short, but always pretty too. With all of this!" Cara would run her small hands over her breasts, trace her waist and hips, and end at her buttocks.

At four feet eleven inches, Cara's shape had been curvy from the waist up. From pelvis to toe, her boxy shape had given no indication of what bulged above. Her long, wavy jet-black hair hanging to her waist made her flat backside forgivable. Underneath the T-shirts brought to her by repeat tourists, her EEs had sunk and then just sat down at the same time. She would later learn the size bra cups that would accommodate her abundant bosom. Her chubby, round face and wide eyes hid her cunning.

Even remembering her mother's gestures made Sol blush.

"*Gracias a dios!* I've never had to do the things I did to get us here. Never again! But I'm still that girl from Isla Mujeres. In case we ever get sent back, that's where we're from. Like Wonder Woman and the Amazon. *Entiendes?*"

Sol had always wanted to see the place where she'd been born but had settled for hearing about it during Cara's buzzing moments. Now she made do with recalling her mother's story through a haze. She had watched as Cara had cleared the crowded dresser in their tiny tenement room. With the housekeeping bucket close by, Cara would soak tissues with Windex and wipe each cheap glass figurine like a jeweler cleaning precious gems. She'd lay them on the bed carefully, so they wouldn't touch or break. "We come from the beach. Tourist money was never enough. And the things they would throw away." She'd carefully lift the lace doilies to reveal a lacquer dresser with barely enough dust on it to require cleaning. "They always liked me. Tourists, family, my compadres, boys." She'd chuckled. "All of them. I was something."

Sol could see every bit of Cara's story. She welcomed the vision of the beach with its sharp sunlight, creamy sand, and soapy waves chasing the shoreline.

Cara had sold fruit on the beach with her sisters and mother. There had been enough wandering tourists to sustain a healthy trade. But Cara had refused to imagine remaining in a place with no hope of anything better. She had not seen the true wealth of the tourists, so hers hadn't been envy of the material. It had been the idea that these visitors had left their homes, the places where they'd been born, and had come to see somewhere different, somewhere they'd considered better, if just for a moment. Many of them had claimed they wanted to stay there on the beach forever. To Cara, the homes of these tourists had become a distant other place, a paradise that was the opposite of her own, where she wanted to go and stay forever. The idea that she could eventually have enough money to support herself, eat regularly, spend on vacations, had appealed to her. But it had been the freedom, the vision of choices, that had made her salivate.

The Belizean ferryman who brought foreigners to Isla Mujeres from Cancún and Mérida had seen Cara's mouth watering for something better. He promised her passage to other places far away from the Yucatán. She fell in love with that promise and months later gave him a daughter and naming rights as a firm down payment. He tried to provide for his Solange, but Cara wanted to leave the island. She wanted him beheaded when he refused to take a job in California picking whatever crop was in season. Since he wasn't man enough, she decided to leave their infant behind with him. Her large milk-filled breasts would never be enough to feed a family of three, let alone her mother and sisters. She had been responsible for the survival of many, not just her own. She wasn't trying to get to America simply to satisfy her wanderlust.

Cara had brooded over the missed opportunity to leave Isla Mujeres. Even after her milk dried up, her breasts felt heavier than ever. If her ferryman couldn't get her to America, she would bed every tourist until she made one of them fall in love with her. Her cleavage had easily convinced men that she wasn't bright enough to take advantage of them.

Cara had not managed to secure a suitable American suitor because she had been too quick to take what she wanted from them without permission. She didn't have the patience to persuade them that she could fall in love, if they brought her back home with them. It was her stance, shoulder blades pinched behind her to hold up her breasts, feet planted as if she feared toppling forward, that made her posture like that of an alert cobra. She would start out alluring, then still, and after deciding that her target had no intentions of supporting her immigrant ambitions, she would strike with a request, an offer, or an insult that pushed her further away from her goal.

Weary of her indiscreet infidelities—prostitution, really— her ferryman had paid an American woman $1,000 to get them to Mérida and then to Mexico City or as far north as possible. At the last minute the American insisted that she had room for only Cara and the little girl. Once in Mérida, the woman ditched both, leaving Cara to sell herself for cheap to pay for every mile northward. Cara resented her daughter, not so much because she was a slow toddler, but because she was never coquettish or cooperative enough to woo potential suitors with her cuteness. Solange refused to smile or tolerate touches no matter how innocent, friendly, or solicitous her mother's companions.

By the time Cara had sold everything worth anything and arrived in New York with a six-year-old and an infant, she had been too exhausted to be a mother. A provider? A survivor? A hustler? Yes, she had always been expert at these roles. A mother? With two unsellable children in tow, and absent the flexibility to quickly learn enough English to get a housekeeping or nanny job, Cara had spent more time caring for her one room than her children. Sol barely missed her when the greatest fear of every illegal in America came true.

Sol felt something approximating longing for Cara now. Everybody misses her mother when she's in irreversible pain or when she's dying. She missed their bed more, the room too, even Cara's tacky dresser with the cheap little white-glass ballerinas and fragile lambs. She grinned at what had been Cara's orderly process of caring for these things. After wiping the dresser with Pledge, she'd lay the doilies in their places and then rearrange the glass ladies and animals around a small statue of the Virgen de Guadeloupe. Cara had cared as much for the flowers she had sold on North Conduit, even the fruit she washed and cut up every morning in preparation.

Sol had barely missed a day before settling into selling after Cara had been taken into INS custody. She'd stared at the sky above JFK, knowing she was meant to be there, was, in fact, already there but hadn't yet been able to see her spirit self, disembodied and dispersed throughout the universe.

She had not seen Lucien, who she later learned had been watching her for years. He had only once looked up trying to deduce what she had been staring at. She hadn't known that, to him, she had been the treasure, down there, on the ground. She had not surmised his desire to force her to lower her eyes.

Sol got lost in visions of her sky. She knew that that was her true home. Isla Mujeres was merely a small place where her mother's small dreams had been formed. The sky was everywhere. Even when it hid the sun with its clouds, even when it rained.

Sol remembered how the sky had forced her to look down. But it wasn't the downpour that had made her get into Lucien's van. It was her memories of getting in and out of crumbling cars northward from the Yucatán through the whole of Mexico. Her height, intellect, and years of watching Cara take on all manner of men had given her a false sense of invincibility. And she'd known Lucien for years. Had told him that her name was Solange when he'd asked. She'd stuck her hand into his van and practically ridden in it. She'd felt protected on the North Conduit whenever he'd approached, not knowing that he'd spent hours watching her with and without Cara, before creeping up to a red light to make a purchase. He had been the harmless cheapskate who'd counted coins into her outstretched palm and taken back even an extra penny when he'd overpaid. She hadn't needed to see him in his taxicab to know that he could afford to give her a few extra cents. She'd been able to tell by his always-full gas tank that she'd peeped while waiting for his mumbled counting to cease.

SOL STARED into the darkness with the imagined sky in her eyes. "I am not Zero!" she shouted, startling Chiqui, Cocoa, Asante, but mostly My. Thinking of him had always made her nervous, but she'd tried not to show her fear to the others. Instead, she'd crawl inward to remind herself who she was. She needed to after incalculable years in the safe room. Time was hard to determine.

I am One. I am here where the sky is not. I am not hungry. I will not break. Not for food. Not for anything he has to offer. I am rage. Biting, kicking. I am not lying down. I am not quiet. I will kill. Myself after I kill him. I am not darkness. I am inside of it. This is another box with sixteen wheels. I am riding. Far, far with Cara. Chiqui is still inside. We are still inside Mexico. Far from where Cara wants to be. I won't break. I won't be like Zero. I won't bend over or open. Mouth, legs, eyes. I stop seeing everything. Red sky, colored carnations, green keneps, white buckets, metal cart, highway, and planes. I stop hearing too. But I refuse to be Zero. In the box I make myself everything he hates. I shave my head. I refuse to wash. I do not eat. I scream.

And then I stop. No more kicking, biting, screaming. He brings Chiqui as a gift for me. So I stop.

I become everything he wants. I am smiling, sucking, riding. So he won't hurt her. I beg, "Put my gift back where you found her!" Better wherever Cara is than here.

I am knowing that we will go from here. But when we leave, will I disappear into Zero? Will I be One? My self? Or him?

Five

LUCIEN

Lucien leaned against the frame of the back door and watched Dieuseul open the one leading to the main floor. He waited for Dieuseul to disappear into the darkness before he hopped up the one step to get his body into the house. He paused in the dark stairwell to get his bearings before closing the door behind him, shutting out the icy air. The fingers of his good hand fought to hold the gallons of water. His partially numb claw miraculously managed to hold on. Somehow, he stabilized himself to go down the six brittle steps to the basement. He held the tips of two loaves of bread in his teeth. He thought about bringing peanut butter later and possibly sardines. They didn't like them anyway. Weakened, he dropped the heavy load, and everything toppled down the stairs. The gallons of water hit then split against the basement door before him. The water quickly iced over, making that area more slippery.

He could hear the door behind him creaking as it hung partially off its hinges. He turned around and jacked it upward and slammed it as if to spite the recalcitrant house. He ignored the house's laughter at the cold air and predawn light bleeding through its cracks around the door. He looked so pitiful hobbling down the steps. Tears from cold and fatigue streamed down his face, freezing everything from his lashes to his gray mustache. His hands were too frozen to wipe them. He didn't care what his face looked like. It was always too dark in the back room for them to see him. No one wanted to see him. He stopped and searched for the two required keys. He cupped his good hand and blew into it, warming it just enough to grip the key to the first door. He would get the second key, the one that unlocked the safe room, out of his pocket when he got to that door. He started to climb down the steps but lost his balance on the iced-over stairs and slid all the way down to the bottom. Breathlessly, he paused to orient himself. He struggled to stand up and tried by holding on to the stairwell walls that seemed to press inward toward him. In one motion, he stood straight up and pushed against the first door with his shoulder. It wouldn't budge. On his second, more forceful attempt, he slipped again, landing on the steps behind him. Although he was hurt, he didn't scream. He'd always preferred to surprise them. From where he sat, he tried kicking the door with his strongest foot. He knew why it still would not open. His collection had toppled over on the other side.

He knew that his neighbors could not have imagined the incredible mess in the basement or what he'd collected in the back room. If they could have, every ounce of pity they'd held for him would have evaporated. They'd always resented the unkempt houses on the block, the ones with more than one broken-down car in the driveway. Their absolute wrath against him had been quelled only by his tenure in the neighborhood, his past and present kindnesses toward anyone needing help, his grief after his wife's passing, and his having had not one but two strokes. They'd ignored his hoarding as long as he'd kept his mess contained in his house, garage, and van and never left the doors of any of these open, especially in warm weather.

Thinking of the junk that was keeping him from getting to his captives, Lucien considered how and when, but not why, his hoarding had begun. It had started a few years after he'd begun driving the night shift and escalated when his daughters left for college. Having lost the better part of his harem, he'd first started storing his street finds in his garage, then in the girls' closets, under their beds, in the drawers of their girlie dressers and armoires—anywhere Marie-Ange had been too sick to search.

The stuff barring his entry was an endless collection of worthless and redundant electronics. However, he'd found a few valuable items over the years. A collection of eighteenth-century first editions of Shakespeare's complete works that had been discarded by its dead owner's housekeeper who'd been unaware of their value. A pair of genuine ivory statues chiseled before poaching had been illegalized. Two antique Tiffany timepieces, a clock and a platinum pocket watch, presumed fake by their inheritors. His favorite had been one of the first gramophones ever made in America. Most of the original owners of these tragically discarded items had been dejected, unloved wretches. He'd always feared he'd end up the same way, which was why he'd escalated to collecting women who might care for him in his old age the way he'd cared for them in their youth.

Although he hadn't known their exact worth at the time, he'd known enough to have certain items appraised. He'd taken the first offer he'd gotten for the Tiffany clock. He'd held on to the pocket watch that was eventually stolen by one of KAM's patrons to whom he'd bragged about his finds. He'd given his daughters the Shakespeare collection at Marie-Ange's funeral, but they'd purposely left the books behind. Besides these, his only remaining prizes were the ivory statues of a man and woman that he thought of as him and Marie-Ange, and the gramophone. He'd played it once for his girls over the intercom.

Stuck on the basement stairs, there was no way for Lucien to reach Dieuseul, who'd made a beeline for his room the minute he'd gotten past the kitchen. He was jealous of Dieuseul's agility and imagined him easily adjusting his quick and eager gait to navigate the hose-soaked burned mess in the other rooms. He could see him climbing over the debris and the holes in the floor as he made his way up the stairs in the darkness. Through Dieuseul's eyes Lucien surveyed the damage. He could see where the fire might have started. The melted power strips and extension cords, and the many appliances that were still connected, especially the hot plate, could have sparked the blaze. He felt the tremble but knew that Dieuseul would be less cognizant of or interested in the house's reverberating laughter. He knew what Dieuseul was focused on finding—the small portrait of his stepdaughter that he'd painted to memorialize the little girl he remembered.

Lucien had peeped through a hole in the bedroom wall to watch as Dieuseul worked for weeks to capture the innocence of his little girl. He'd been trying to reassemble the likeness of the brown girl whose heart was broken as much as his after the divorce. She hadn't been his child, but he'd always felt protective and possessive of the girl. Without the painter's knowledge, Lucien had fallen in love with this realistic portrait of a ladylike brown girl in Victorian attire, her smile as subtle as one of Vermeer's subjects or those on the faces of the Vierge Marie statues in the boiler room.

He had always deduced what Dieuseul had never been able to explain. He had gotten into the artist's mind to find what he believed to be the reasons for the drastic change in his style of painting. It had only made sense that Dieuseul had lost all his patrons, parents who'd come calling at KAM for gentile reproductions of their children's First Communion photos. The new disfigured, quasi-abstract impressionist interpretations of women and girls had left him with only two Haitian fans, his landlords. Marie-Ange had been schooled in European fine art and developed an appreciation for the undervalued Haitian artists of her father's generation. Lucien had visibly shown his preference for the deconstructionist style that broke women down into more manageable pieces. He had been especially fond of Dieuseul's reimagined renditions of his stepdaughter. Dieuseul had kept on painting for himself, sometimes leaving his bedroom door open and accidentally sharing new pieces with Marie-Ange. He'd given her three of them as payment for the increase in her electricity bill. He'd turned his room into a studio with kitchenette so he could stay inside for days without encountering his landlords except to use the bathroom. Lucien had seen the electricity-siphoning stockpile in Dieuseul's bedroom but had kept quiet because of the silent agreement he'd made with his tenant.

Lucien shifted his weight onto his good side to get out of the freezing puddle beneath him. He tried to strategize how he would get himself back up without falling again. He knew that the longer he sat, the colder he was getting and the harder it would be for him to get up and maneuver in the narrow stairwell. He tried to divine whose revenge his present predicament was. Marie-Ange, whose defunct peristyle stood in the boiler room to his right? Or the women in the back room, whose bad thoughts had somehow landed him on his ass? Or Dieuseul, finally, for those times years ago?

But they'd made peace over his leering at his stepdaughter. Lucien had started before Dieuseul had moved in. He didn't bother trying to figure out why Dieuseul hadn't laid him flat on his back with a backhand or a punch for his obsession with the girl.

Lucien decided to at least try calling out for help. He shouted the name that seemed alien to him because he left off the "Boss" before "Dieuseul." He knew that his friend would ignore him. Maybe Dieuseul had finally decided that Lucien was an undeserving deviant who'd used the guise of art to ogle and touch the women who'd come to KAM. Maybe Dieuseul was getting back at him for disrespecting Marie-Ange with the mistress housed in his basement under her nose. Lucien listened to hear if Dieuseul was coming down to get him, but all he heard was a thud outside. He assumed then that Dieuseul had half climbed, half jumped from the upstairs window rather than make his way back down to rescue him. Surely he'd been saved by the apple tree and backhoe that allowed him to tumble rather than crash into the ice-hardened ground.

Although he knew that he was gone, Lucien panicked and called out to Dieuseul. In between his screams, he heard Cocoa's insistent singing. He thought he was imagining or remembering the sound. His heart raced even faster when he realized that the fire must have compromised the safe room's soundproofing.

If he could hear her, then . . . But he still wanted to hear her sing. He wanted to hear all of them. Not scream. He hated their screaming, especially hers. Not Zero. One. He regretted taking her more than the white girl. If he made it back there, if she was still alive, he would take the opportunity to get rid of her before moving the others. He'd taken her because she'd looked like Veille, his Veille. But she'd turned out to be almost exactly like the vociferous Clair. He wished he'd known better.

Clair had been the outspoken one, irrepressible, defiant. She'd gotten him in trouble. But she'd been the prettiest, the one he'd liked to look at most, the one who'd looked like her mother, with all that hair. She'd gotten rid of it to spite him.

His mind allowed him to travel only so far at one go. He was already broken, stuck on the stairwell steps, unable to get into the basement proper. The thought of Clair and Sol was not helpful. But they'd both been so beautiful with so much hair. They'd become his enemies. He didn't want to think of enemies in his position, but all he could see were his girls. Even if they made him angry. Even if they made him cry. Even if they made him freeze to death in a puddling sheet of ice with the subzero cold coming in. Even if they gave him nothing to hold on to. Even if they didn't let him in. Even if they were his undoing.

Even if they'd stayed alive out of pure spite. Even if they made it out and he didn't. He would always have them in his head even if they finally locked him out of theirs. Like his own daughters. He never got to touch Clair. She had made herself ugly.

She had even shaved her head. Just to spite me. Can you believe it? All that beautiful hair, long like the women on my side of the family, but thick like my angel's. She didn't even go to the barber. And that One, she used a dull edge of a sardine can. No scissors. No scissors. There are plenty of candles. I don't remember how many. Matches too. A lighter even. The fluid is probably too low to strike up a flame. Marie-Ange's lighter from the boiler room. Four, One, apple jam, Spam jelly, sardines, no bread, maybe a gallon and a half of water. The one who shaved her head, she knows how to ration. She knows how to count like me. She hates me. They all do. Why did she have to die? My angel. My girls. Do they have to die? I have to get in. I have to get in. She shaved her head, but she can't cut anything else. No scissors. The top of the Spam can, the spiraled rim peeled back. The rolled-up lid of the open sardine can. She can't cut. Even if she wanted to kill herself, it wouldn't go deep enough for her to bleed much. It's a nice room. A safe room.

Lucien tried to shake off the frostbite creeping over his toes. He twisted his body to see if he could get moving. Each limb felt as heavy as an industrial steel pipe. His fingers didn't move at all anymore. He could feel his insides going cold. Or had they always been that way? He had long stopped feeling his face. He couldn't touch it even if he wanted to. He was too cold to fall asleep, but he knew that his one friend would eventually take him over. It always did. It would shut his eyelids, nod his head, find him something to lean against. It would slide a pillow under his head, turn his breathing into snoring, let him turn to ice, let him die. He fought it off with thoughts of rescuing his girls. If he dared touch One, it would be a death match—Two and Three against him. He wasn't as strong as he'd been when he'd taken her. She'd even ignored his pistol, his gift from a soldier at Bar Caimite. He'd finally subdued her after two loud bleeding years by bringing her a little present, Two. And then his second stroke had happened. Before Four. He'd lowered his sights and standards, except for the race of his next victim.

He'd wanted a white girl when he'd first come to America, but he was too light-skinned for them. They'd all wanted the genuine article, a true Mandingo, Shaft, Huggy Bear, Shaka Zulu type. For the first time in his life, he had been undermined by his complexion. He'd laughed when KAM men whom he'd considered inferior would tell him about their exploits. They'd described it all in great detail while pointing at the life-sized Farrah Fawcett poster on the garage wall just above the card table.

"Not by the color of my skin, but the content of my character!" he exclaimed, overenunciating in a thick accent. The men had assumed that he was referring to their bias toward white women, not his own feelings as a victim of prejudice. "I have a dream!" He laughed so hard tears rolled down his face. "A wet dream!"

"You're going to hell, man!" one of his darker and, therefore, privileged patrons chided.

"We're already there. You're lying to yourselves if you can't see it."

He had never explained what he'd meant, assuming that the men would never truly understand. Was he referring to the karma for their secret misdeeds he'd somehow found out about? Or did he mean that all immigrant life was hell? Was he talking about their subjugation as black men in this country? Or as married men chained prematurely to first loves who'd never lived up to the porn fantasies fashioned by Times Square peep shows and videotapes Lucien provided as background entertainment in his makeshift casino? Had he been scorched at the steel plant in places they could not see? What hell? What could be worse than Haiti?

Lucien hadn't verbalized it, but he'd believed that their hell was of their own making. Every regret, every longing for anything other than what they had, every twinge of covetousness, the greed that had brought them to his card table to gamble away hard-earned paychecks for a chance at a jackpot, their lusting after poster girls and deep-throat flick tricks, their shaking of heads when they entered his house through the front door and walked past Marie-Ange standing in the kitchen, their shaded eyes silently complimenting her fineness, the way they gobbled down her cooking, desperate and hopeful for refills on the house. These were the poured cements, wood frames, and aluminum siding for their personal infernos. Whatever they believed they'd settled for, instead of counting themselves blessed, they had sealed their deals with devils of their own conjuring. Their fantasies of a better heaven—that was hell.

LUCIEN WOKE up only because of the sunlight that started bleeding through the cracks of the back door, illuminating the snow packed in the corners. He knew the demolition team would not come, as Leona had predicted. He didn't need his claw to thaw to grab a plastic-sheaved loaf of bread beside him. He grabbed and tore it open with his teeth, savoring a dry mouthful of bread. He could see a torn gallon that still had a few drops of water, but he couldn't reach it. Still, he thought that captivity couldn't be so terrible with a little bit of warmth and bland food. At least they weren't out in the elements. He'd rescued at least two from bad weather. *Tonère!* He'd saved one from serious jail time and, worse, death to silence a potential DEA informant. *Engras.* What if he'd left them out there in the biting January cold with the piling snow breaching their Payless shoes, summer flip-flops, non-water-resistant high-tops? What if they were out there, straight, gapped, crooked, or decayed teeth chattering, in their tight jeans and T-shirts, flimsy house-dresses, low-rise leggings, cutesy crop tops with their pierced or pristine belly buttons out, or braless with their thongs hiked up their asses like that ingrate.

None of them had been wearing coats when he'd rescued them. None of them had had more than two dollars to their name let alone in their pockets. Who gave a fuck about them but him? The Jean-Baptistes with almost a dozen kids and grandkids cramped in their Section 8 welfare rental? The other neighbors obviously weren't paying attention and didn't give a damn about anything except when they could get rid of his trash house and buy his land? Or the damned public schools that took attendance and just dropped them from their rosters after a week, figuring they'd dropped out? Or the cops? Shit. That was a good one. They'd just been here with the fire marshal to ensure he didn't try to break into his own house. No one had even cared about the white girl. Yeah, he'd had a white girl. Finally. But he had had to get rid of her because she was trouble. Nothing but.

My. Zero. One, she's as good as dead. Two. Three. Four, she's been gone. I cried for her like I still cry over them. They've never seen me cry. Ever. I never made a sound or let the water fall onto their backs. So they never cry with me. They scream and then, after, I hear them cry from somewhere inside that I do not have within me. I am hollow like the things La Belle kept. I am a figure crashing into a wall, revealing nothing because there is nothing. But I cry. I have no feeling except the touch of water falling from my eyes. No feeling inside. I don't remember it ever. If it had been there sometime before, I cannot recall. So I am nothing, not even a memory to myself. I will be their memory. They see the figure that I am. They make me into something—fear, father, harm, care, life, darkness. Still, I am nothing to myself. I am a mirror. I am nothing until someone looks at me.

He thought about Nihla. Four. He didn't have to kill her. He could have just left her there with them. She'd done something awful. He couldn't remember with his mind freezing

over. Had she bitten him, maybe? Tried to run? Maybe he'd
done it by accident. Maybe he hadn't touched her at all. Did
she hit her head? He tried to see what had happened. Did the
piles of junk come down on her? He couldn't find the memory
anywhere. Maybe she'd slit her own throat. She'd been high,
having a drug-induced hallucination. Asante would remember,
even if she wouldn't say anything to anyone about it. Maybe
he hadn't killed the white girl after all. Maybe they'd come for
her, charming princes, men in tights or uniforms brandishing
badges, carrying flashlights and a rough blanket to throw over
her shoulders.

He wanted to be rescued. But he didn't want to be held captive. He knew that whoever came would take him to a hospital
because of his condition. That was prison. He hacked repeatedly, choking on the cold and the thought of being hospitalized.
Better to die here in his house. He didn't care if the girls could
hear him. He wanted to scare them one last time, if just with his
grunting and the rattling of phlegm in his chest. He didn't care
if One was also sick, that she would hear him and be jealous because she could no longer cough. He didn't think of pneumonia,
but he knew that whatever was making him cough and even his
frostbite would force him into a hospital. He wanted them to
know that something was wrong, that something was coming.
He called out just to scare them. No name. He didn't call for
Dieuseul. He just shouted Kreyòl curses to make them wet their
panties as they thought of him one last time. He wanted them to
think that he had made it into the basement. He wanted them
to shake at the thought that he had come to kill them all.

SOL

Sol glared at Cocoa with her eyes closed, knowing that the
singer would understand instinctively, after years together in
the back room, what was being conveyed. No need to say, *Shut
the fuck up!* for Cocoa to understand the silence the situation
demanded. He was here. He was coming. Sol could hear and
sense Lucien's approach better than any of the others. She didn't
know to whom or why he was calling out, but she knew by the
tones of the muffled sounds and the chill that was not a symptom
of her fever that he was here. She nudged Chiqui, who'd fallen
asleep holding her hand. She didn't have to say her name. She'd
given it to her.

There had been no other option but to shorten her sister's
given name to Chiqui. Anglos had barely been able to pro-
nounce Chiqui, which they twisted into *Chicky,* let alone Xo-
chiquetzal, the Aztec goddess of fertility after whom she was
named because she'd been conceived and born under the harshest conditions. Much to Sol's chagrin, Chiqui had always explained that her name meant "small," as in Chiquita bananas.
The sisters had been as different as they'd looked.

Sol didn't know what her sister looked like now. The back
room didn't allow for a clear assessment. The years had aged

them both in ways neither could see. Chiqui's hair had been the lightest of browns with fuzzy blond tips that glowed in the light like a halo. She'd been pale, round, and flat except for her bulbous cheeks and small, curvy fuchsia lips like those painted on baby dolls. Her nose and ears were as small as her mouth. Only her eyes were black and slightly slanted like the eyes of the indigenous people of the Yucatán. Most couldn't tell that her lashes were long because they were the same sunlit blond as the edges of her hair. Unlike Sol, Chiqui had a small gap between her front teeth. She had been poking her tongue through that gap when Lucien scooped her up from the same place he'd taken Sol, the same place Cara had vanished.

 While Sol had been raging in his basement, Lucien had been watching Chiqui with her clippety-clop walk twisting her hips because she had never learned to use her arms to help propel herself forward. With a chunky shape—no waistline or hips— she was not his type. Her figure was neither boyishly childlike nor curvaceously womanly. She still had baby fat for breasts and broad shoulders held up by a wide back. Her flat backside made her look as if her pelvis was pushed perpetually forward. At the moment he'd decided to snatch her, Chiqui had been standing habitually with all her weight on one leg and foot, which emphasized her lack of hips.

She'd sat with perfect posture in the front seat of his van as if trying to get the attention of and recognition from a teacher. With little in the way of street smarts and having only been told that she was being taken to where her big sister was, she'd chatted away about her favorite pastimes: video games, chess (she was captain of the club at school), and all manner of board games. Lucien handed her an old Game Boy preloaded with Tetris, to which she'd instantly become addicted. She rattled on during the drive that he extended to ensure that she was too absorbed in the game to notice where she was being taken. Chiqui loved being a know-it-all, to compete and to win, which later irritated Lucien because she would try to find ways to outsmart him to escape. But lacking his patience, his decades of hard-won savvy, the internal motivation of someone who feared jail time, and genuine psychopathy, she was easily manipulated.

Sol had tried to teach Chiqui how to resist, but she knew that her sister loved food and had been accustomed to being well-fed. Chiqui had not had the benefit of deprivation to prepare her for the back room. She could not fight off hunger, and so she'd fallen victim to the seduction of food that Lucien used to control her. Coupled with her fear of the dark and intolerance of loud noises, he'd easily kept her in check. Sol had just begun teaching her how to cope when Cocoa arrived, triggering all of Chiqui's acute pain points and general dislikes.

Sol had remained calm to keep the youngest two from getting on each other's nerves. Cocoa was very pretty, adept at playing dumb, and deliberately coquettish, which had won her privileges from Lucien. But Sol had seen how the new cellmate had come across to Chiqui like the ditzy girls at school. An incredible singer with range from JHud alto to Beyoncé falsetto, Cocoa exasperated Chiqui's chronic earaches. However, once Cocoa proved her exceptional intelligence and showed Chiqui how to use syrupy sweetness to elicit small favors, she won over her would-be secondary adversary. Together, they'd gotten Lucien to leave the back-room door unlocked some of the time, so they could use the toilet in the adjacent bathroom instead of the encrusted buckets. Chiqui's tiny bladder had been more than grateful, especially when she began to urinate more and more often.

She'd worn diapers around the clock until the age of five and at night until age nine. At twelve, she was still a chronic bedwetter, which became her biggest problem and the greatest annoyance to her fellow captives. Accustomed to bunking three to a bed with Sol and her mother, Chiqui would unknowingly roll closer to Cocoa and Asante in her sleep. The cheap black leggings and oversized T-shirt she'd been wearing when she'd first been abducted by Lucien had to be burned in the shower because they could neither be sanitized nor flushed. Comfortable with the smell of her own perfume and good Haitian home cooking, Cocoa was the first to recommend fire as a remedy for Chiqui's clothes. Asante hadn't been speaking to anyone then. Accustomed to her own womanly odors, she'd been captive in the safe room's stink too long to care. Even Cocoa's singing couldn't coax Asante out of her deepest silences.

Lucien had never planned to take a beloved and well-known girl who lived that close to home. He'd known Cocoa's parents for years. Her older siblings had been his daughters' peers. She came from a decent family with close neighborhood ties, although she did not attend the Catholic school across the street. With seven other children, her parents could barely afford their government-subsidized rent. Cocoa grew up believing the lie that Lucien and Marie-Ange were the greatest parents because their children were proven role models who'd succeeded and been able to get out of SOP. She'd been lured into Lucien's house on the pretext of seeing his children, who'd stopped by for a visit and wanted to hear her sing. That would be her way out of her parents' house and SOP.

Cocoa had gone from a tantrum-throwing shrill toddler to a precocious emotional songstress to get attention as the last in a line of eight. In the family order, her only claim was being the baby, but even that was no novelty to her exhausted parents. They were devout Haitian Christians who did not believe in contraception. In over their heads, they had plunged headlong into the U.S. welfare system and had never gotten out. Only Lucien and Marie-Ange had known, because they'd helped broker the deal for the Jean-Baptistes to rent the home they'd once owned. Cocoa's parents started to show her affection only when they realized that her voice might pull them out of poverty or at least the grave of loan-shark debt. They'd never thought it odd that Lucien was present at every one of their daughter's public school talent shows even though his children were all grown and had attended and graduated from parochial school. He'd also augmented the contributions Cocoa's older siblings provided to subsidize her dance, acting, and voice lessons; performance wardrobe; and hair salon visits.

Trapped in the safe room, Cocoa had ingratiated herself to Lucien, leveraging their cultural and neighborhood connection. Before and after private performances, she would ask him about Haiti, Marie-Ange, his daughters, allowing him to tell her what she knew to be lies about his close family ties. She was a budding actress, after all. When she grew tired of listening to him, she insisted on singing to transmute her pain. Very early on, she made the conscious decision to use her circumstances to inspire her songwriting and infuse her voice quality to produce something so superb it was transcendent. In the small space Lucien allowed her during her time outside of the back room, believing her performances to be for him, Cocoa was the dance and the dancer. She was the melody and the voice, the lyric and the composer. In the back room, she drummed against the damp dirt floor, a sound that no one heard except her, that no one besides her felt except the sensitive Sol. Her humming became meditative chants that lulled even Chiqui's aching eardrums. Cocoa rubbed the hinge between her cellmate's ears and jaw to allow her soothing, hopeful music to take full effect.

Cocoa knew that she would be missed and searched for after her disappearance. If her parents could not afford even borrowed reward money, her siblings and her committed older boyfriend would cobble together an attractive lump sum. Because of her popularity, she was naïvely convinced that the media would pay attention when a cocoa-colored girl went missing. The one who looked like a demure Nicki Minaj or Janet Jackson from her *Good Times* years. The curvy, busty, but innocent-looking, downright adorable fourteen-year-old who never wore makeup but kept her hair and nails "did." The one who smiled with the deepest dimples while singing in the deepest voice or the highest. The one who walked like she was forever being watched on the sidewalk or the stage. The one who posed like a dancer, spoke like a newscaster, and batted her lashes like a Disney Channel ingenue. She got noticed and people would feel her absence. Someone would bring the local news' attention to the fact that the disappearance of black and brown girls like her did not get the same coverage as those of the blond, blue-eyed lost then found Elizabeth Smarts of the world. Someone in the neighborhood, or maybe on the South-side, and desperate for diapers, formula, or just their next fix, would break ranks for the reward money and call in a tip. And they did. But how could anyone know that the highest contributor to the growing reward pot had been her cunning captor.

Sol remembered Lucien bragging about his coup. She wondered what was keeping him from coming through the steel door. If he could put up money to undermine the search for Cocoa, then he could fight his way through the cutting clutter blocking his entry to the back room and slit all of their throats, start a second fire to incinerate their bodies, and, this time, feigning senility, continue crying that children had been trapped and burned up in his basement. He'd done things almost as bad. He had killed one before. With Asante's help, he had murdered Four.

Sol held her breath, but it was shallow, so she quickly exhaled. "Go ahead. Sing if you want to. It might be the last time."

"Stop saying stuff like that!" Cocoa shouted.

"You mean the truth?"

"When did this happen? When did you stop trying?"

"You don't get it. I am already dead."

"I'm not singing at anybody's funeral."

"You think there'll be a funeral? Who's gonna bury me? Next you'll talk about scattering my ashes in the Gulf of Mexico." Sol's utterances left her breathless, so she could not laugh.

Cocoa didn't bother to argue.

Chiqui ignored both of them.

Asante surprised them all with her mad laughter. "This house is coming down. If he makes it in here first, he's going to get rid of all of us. There will be nothing to bury or scatter or sing over, you simpleminded bitches. I know better than all of you what he's capable of. Twenty years. Or has it been more? Who the hell knows?" Asante stopped. She could feel an enormous gas bubble form and rise up from her stomach into her sternum. She wanted to vomit but had nothing inside and she hated to dry heave. She pressed down where her rib cage met and parted like wings, forcing the gas bubble back into her stomach, through her colon, and out of her body.

"Why do all of you insist on saying these things in front of My. He might only be four, but he understands more than you think." Chiqui was angry at everyone, including Sol.

"Just make sure he gets out," Sol responded consolingly.

Sol lay back down and thought about Asante's comment. Twenty years back. She could count forward only from the months after Nihla came, stayed for seven days, and then disappeared for good. Even if she hadn't been able to stand the new girl, Sol had never wanted Nihla dead.

I am not Zero. I am not Four. I am not white, hooked, or coming down, down, down. Four wants powder, needle, and pipe. Four tells time. She say, "Monday." He cannot convince, cannot confuse Four. Not like us. Four comes from New something . . . "Jersey," Zero says. Four say, "New York. Best powder, rock, pipe. Best needle." She take him. Again. Again. Again. She do everything for small bills and purse change. She runs and runs. Into his van. Cold. Rain. Winter. He bring her here because he scared. One of us is pregnant. He is scared to touch Zero, Two, Three, and me. He scared of blood like my bald head, shaved with candle glass of cracked Virgen Maria. Four stay Monday, Tuesday, Wednesday. Four cry, she sweat, kick, bang, all the way to Sunday. She bleed in the room where he take Zero, One, Two, Three, before he carry My inside. Nice room. Bed, rug. Nice food. Music. He bring rock, powder, pipe, needle. He bring death. He so scared, he kill Four.

Asante was the one who knew the most about what had happened to Nihla. Although she'd never spoken to any of the others about that time, and because she never would, they'd all assumed that she had done in Lucien's number Four. But all Asante had done was listen to the slurred speech of a jonesing and delusional addict as Nihla recounted just how she'd ended up in the back room and how she was planning to get out. Asante didn't want to admit, even to herself, that she'd done a bit more than just listen. But as the oldest inhabitant of the safe room, she had a right to keep what she wanted to herself and to keep things from herself to save what was left of her sanity. She didn't like to think about Nihla, not even the nickname she'd given her in anger. The last time she'd uttered "seven-day slut" out loud had been the day after Lucien had followed her instructions on how to get rid of the girl. Asante didn't even allow the name Nihla to flit across her mind. She didn't count to four or five ever. And she'd softened what was left of her memory of the girl and remembered only that she'd been there six, maybe seven days. She'd wiped the word "slut" and all its versions from her mind and mouth ever after in the safe room. She would not let him make her call out or count women, even if it meant that she had to stop speaking altogether. Of all the horrors of the back room, Nihla and My were Asante's biggest regrets. She had covered her ears to shut out the sound of him since his birth. That a child had been born in that place was an unendurable fact she wanted to deny. But My's voice was ever present. His crying. His counting. At least she could mute Nihla's noise when remembering her story.

Monday.

Lucien had not waited long to pounce. Nihla was
still high and drunk from the third Long Island iced
tea to which a john had treated her earlier in the day
when she'd stumbled into the freezing rainstorm.
Lucien had known her from his frequent trips over the
George Washington Bridge for discarded furniture
in Fort Lee. Snowbirds who'd finally had enough of
the Northeast threw away so much well-preserved
furniture that their hired movers were unable to fit
into their loaded trucks. He'd forced his van to make
the trip from Queens to New Jersey in the freezing
rain to keep from missing bulky trash day. Nihla was
a bonus pickup. He didn't like to take her while she
was high. But he'd felt something approximating pity
when he saw her roll out of another customer's clean
used car that night. He usually picked her up on the
Jersey side and drove her to Washington Heights, so
she could score. Since his van was light—most of the
furniture had fallen victim to early spring ice pellets—
he'd diverged from his normal routine. He could tell
that Nihla didn't know what side of the bridge she was
on when she crawled straight into the back of the van
and waited for him to join her. He didn't. He wouldn't
let her do him while she was so high.

Lucien drove over bridges and under overpasses,
along highways and then the narrow two-way streets
to his house. Nihla had no idea. When he unloaded
her into his basement, it may as well have been another
cheap motel or cluttered back seat. It wasn't until she
saw the other women, one of whom she could tell was
pregnant, that she realized that the dungeon she'd
been brought to was anything but safe. The brain fog

from drunkenness had started to wear off by then.
Only a more lucid manic high persevered, making her
crave something to help her maintain that state.

Asante hadn't known what Nihla had been running
from, but she could tell that the girl desperately needed
another hit. She didn't want to be in the mind of
someone that strung out, but neither her experience
nor Lucien had given her a choice. To solve what
had become a crisis for all concerned, including the
pregnant one, she'd had to figure out how to get
Nihla one of three things—another temporary fix, a
murderous overdose, or a way out of the basement.
Without heroin, Nihla had had no choice but to talk
her way through her thoughts. The only one in the
back room she'd been allowed to talk to had been
Asante. Poor old Asante, who'd been in the back
room for over two decades, had had nothing but time
to listen to Nihla as the girl started to unravel into a
bloody pool in the clean room where Lucien had taken
each of them when he'd wanted and how he'd wanted.
Somehow, he'd decided *when*—halfway through
Nihla's tenure—and *how* would be the most fucked-up
thing Asante had ever been forced to do by any man,
including Lucien. And Asante had been forced to
listen to Nihla's words drooled from her sobering,
slobbering mouth.

Nihla had always had another hit before she could
start to remember her parents' house in Maywood,
her mother's hyper-polite Macy's customer-service
voice, her father's serious bookkeeper tone, and the
welts from their corporal strictness. They'd both
worked their way up to managerial status at their
respective jobs after completing community college
night school degrees, affordable on working-class

salaries. Nihla rubbed her thigh for the scars left by
overprotective parents who'd tried to beat every ounce
of superstar aspiration and tween rebelliousness out
of her. Materially, she was spoiled, but her parents
never spared the rod, especially when her preferences
were for Nikes, hip-hop gear, and iPod downloads of
rap music. When she tried to bring home black and
Latino peers, they pulled her out of public school and
practically cuffed her to a desk at Paramus Catholic, a
school they sacrificed to afford.

Asante had wanted to hold Nihla's hands to keep
her from peeling her skin. She couldn't hear the
voices that made the girl slap her itching upper arm.
She didn't know the sounds that were worse than
hallucinations. The sounds of parents who'd told her
that she wasn't pretty, graceful, or talented enough to
be a model, singer, or dancer. She watched as Nihla
scratched at her scabs to rub out the memory of the
first time a white student had offered her H in a corner
of the varsity gym. None of her black or Latino friends
had ever even offered her weed, just musical highs
and the drunkenness of video-chick dancing. PC had
expelled her sophomore year for stealing credit cards
from more affluent students and trading those for weed
that she blatantly smoked on the football field. Zero
tolerance. Her mother had given her a sound thrashing
when they got home, knocking her straight into the
arms of welcoming dealers across the bridge. Her
parents had tracked her down and bounced her from
her grandmother's home to her uncle's, then finally
to her most tolerant aunt's until she was eighteen. She
had never finished high school or bothered to take the
GED exam. She had simply couch-surfed from high to
high.

Through the darkness Asante had seen what the
others couldn't: Nihla's shaky smile, an almost snarky
grin that simultaneously conveyed her persistent
naïveté and inexpressible anxiety. *Zero tolerance, my
ass.* The smell of her unwashed backside permeated the
safe room with an intolerable odor. Cocoa hummed
into prolonged exhales. Nihla looked at Cocoa, the
newest before she'd arrived. How could she sing in
a place like this? Although she could barely see the
other women, she knew that she was the only white
girl there. She could tell that they'd become a little
hopeful, since no one ever stopped looking for a white
girl. She knew better.

Only Asante had known that their new cellmate
had been about to crash from her high. In the half-
light of the votives, she had seen the girl peering at her
through matted strands of hair. She could feel Nihla's
embarrassment as she scanned her from head to toe,
the dirty dreadlocked tresses, the plaid flannel pajama
pants with cuffs so wet they almost dripped, the once-
white mud-encrusted sneakers. She could also see
Nihla's scabs from tearing off skin when drugs were
scarce. Asante had never injected anything herself, but
even coming off the pipe, frequent joints, and whisky
soaks had made her flip out during her first dry days in
the back room. Compared to withdrawal, hunger was
as easy as a child's chuckle.

Asante had only imagined how itchy Lucien had
been while waiting for Nihla to settle down. He had
not touched any of them since the pregnancy. He'd
needed someone he could violate without being
reminded of babies, his daughters, and the family
he'd lost. He'd needed someone whose condition and
very being would not interrupt his pleasure seeking.

He'd wanted no reminder of his past life except for
his Farrah Fawcett fantasies that still flickered against
his closed eyelids when he'd fall asleep penis in hand.
She'd deduced that he had to be as hungry for Nihla as
the girl had been for a hit. Both of them had been on a
hunt for different prey. Both had been starved enough
to kill for their next piece.

Tuesday.

Asante had been able to tell that Nihla still had a
little bit of a buzz when Lucien had come to check the
back room. Asante pleaded with her eyes, begging
him to get rid of the malodorous new prisoner whose
scent rose above that of the slop bucket. She'd known
better than to ask outright. Only Cocoa had been
able do that, batting eyelashes he could barely see
but remembered from the times he'd watched her
on junior high school stages. Asante shrunk back
listening to Nihla beg. He dragged her out to keep
the others from hearing the dirty talk but didn't shut
the door completely. Asante couldn't stand hearing
Nihla plead with him to fuck her any way he wanted in
exchange for a hit, a smoke, a sip, anything to keep her
from sweating, scratching, thinking. Nihla told him
how terrible it was to feel her cellmates judging her
like the brown and black girls had in middle school.

Asante heard the despair in Nihla's voice as the girl
begged him not to take her back to the safe room. She
heard her hope as she explained how willing she was to
go to whatever room he took her to as long as it wasn't
that place. She understood Nihla's optimism that she
would soon be numbed out, if not high. She heard
Lucien quickly throw the girl into the skinny shower,

forcing her down so her bottom could soak while
the water rained down on her. Nihla yelped when he
poured the cold bodywash directly onto her head.
Asante sighed as loudly as Nihla when she heard him
walk out and slam the bathroom door behind him. He
had gone upstairs to host an oblivious Leona. Asante
could hear Nihla fighting the shower's sobering effect,
thrashing about as much as the cramped space would
allow. The others continued to ignore Nihla's antics.

Somehow, Asante had known that she would end
up responsible for whatever happened to Nihla, so
she remained alert, even attentive, to the white girl's
mumblings. She heard Lucien come back to the
bathroom to turn off the water that had run ice cold.
Nihla banged her fists on the walls of the shower
stall as he slapped her with a clean but damp towel.
Asante knew that he had to have been repulsed by the
girl's naked body. She'd seen the beginnings of the
blue bruises, red scratches, and skin that was as gray
as white underwear washed without bleach. Asante
knew him best. He wouldn't want to see the battered
nakedness that would destroy his fantasy of having a
white girl. When he threw Nihla into the back room,
she figured that, despite Nihla's clean state, he still
could not touch her.

Wednesday.

Asante watched as Nihla rose high and came down
low, from mountain peak to base camp, hurting
nobody but herself. Sol pulled Chiqui closer. Cocoa
followed uninvited. Asante stayed in her spot, daring
Nihla to touch her.

"You know, he's really nice." Nihla tried to befriend

the only one who would look at her. "He bought me
all kinds of things. He always fed me. Gave me rides.
He's a good guy."

Asante stared but did not respond.

"I won't tell nobody about this when he lets me go.
Where are we? Any buses run through here?"

Silence.

"Bet y'all just ain't tried to get out. I used to dance.
Bet I could kick down this door." Nihla paused to
scratch. "My boyfriend's black, you know. So I ain't
no racist. Y'all ain't gotta look at me like that. I listen
to hip-hop. I can shake it for a white girl. They called
me 'wigger' at the private school. But them snobs did
more hard drugs . . . I'm gonna get clean after this.
Damn, it smells back here. That bucket. What the
hell? How long y'all be down here?"

Crickets, if any outside sounds could have
penetrated.

"When are you due? I ain't got no kids. My
boyfriend fixed me the last time. Do I look like
somebody's mama? Meth rotted out my teeth. But I'm
only . . . let me see, twenty-one. You know, it's already
Wednesday? He said he'd let me go this weekend.
I'm just gonna do my time. I did six months a while
back for shoplifting a Debbie's crumb cake. Can you
believe it? My lawyer made me take it or I'd go down
for possession too. Now y'all gotta know I'm black.
I'm one of y'all."

As much as she'd wanted to, Asante had held back
from slapping the last bit of lingering high out of
Nihla. She knew that the others were waiting for her
to completely lose it and slam the girl's head against
the stone side of the room. The steel side wouldn't
have drawn blood. Although she doubted Nihla's

fantasy that Lucien was going to let her go, Sunday
couldn't come fast enough.

ASANTE HAD been grateful that no child had been born
while Nihla was there. No innocent deserved to have that as part
of its first encounter with the world. The back room was bad
enough. Knowing the child who'd come to them, she thought
of how My would have offered their desperate visitor a twig or
a rock, something to remind her that there was life outside. My
would have brought in snow. Asante curled up on the floor, not
sure what year it was, if My was alive and Nihla was gone or
if Nihla was there and My was still inside his mother's womb.
Neither was better than the other because both had been devastating for her to witness. She found herself by smelling her way
through. There was the piquant odor of burned things, the cool,
delicious scent of freshly fallen snow. The fragrance of the outside world, no matter how cold it had made the back room, gave
her comfort. Not hope. She didn't dare hope. But she felt like
she could die there without regret because, after all this time, she
could taste the outside on her desperate tongue. She fell asleep
feeling the icy air nibbling the tips of her toes, tinting them a
blue no one could see by candlelight.

LA KAY

La Kay lay flat on Its back. It was conscious, listening to Lucien snoring on Its stairs. At least he'd accepted the fact that no one would rescue him and ceased his histrionics. Up until the fire It hadn't felt any movement in the basement besides his in more than twenty years. But that didn't mean there hadn't been anyone there. It knew well enough that there were secrets folks didn't even tell themselves. Hurtful secrets stashed in the back rooms of minds and hearts, held as closely as an infant marsupial in its mother's pouch. Things folks dared not even acknowledge lest they burst into tears at inopportune moments over evils seen or done. Although It didn't want to know, It decided to search Itself if just to assuage Its guilt. It didn't want to be accountable for having killed innocents scratching at Its sealed doors.

It had ignored the strange sensations coming from the basement for so long, believing that they had been insects or rodents or Lucien. But Its near-death stillness now forced It to feel. It was afraid of the four muffled voices and the occasional whisper of a child. It wanted to believe that the sounds were just auditory hallucinations. But what if they were real? What if they had been real all this time and It hadn't searched out the source? It wanted to turn up the volume, so It could find them now. But It could only lie prostrate with a chest still burning with embers. If It could get up on Its knees, It would pray. Unable to do so, It remained still and played Its favorite game—counting the number of times It heard Its name in a single day.

It could only guess the time because Its eyes had been boarded shut. Now blind, It could hear better. But no sound came, not even a whisper. The only thing left to do was to go back and remember the times It had heard Its name spoken or sung several times a day. Lucien and Marie-Ange had said it most frequently. *"Nou la kay lan"* or *"Nou pap la kay lan."* "We are at the house" or "We won't be home." They'd made no distinction between "house" and "home" because there was none in Kreyòl. It hadn't thought of Itself as a home at all after their daughters moved out. After Marie-Ange died, It hadn't thought of Itself as much of anything at all. It had merely listened to Lucien letting Leona or Dieuseul know when he'd be in or out.

La Kay tried to roll over on Its side but could not move. Its aluminum siding had partially buckled during the fire and was now stiff from the freezing cold. It didn't want to remember the number of times It had heard Lucien coming and going, descending to and climbing up from the basement. It had heard him say *"Men kay lan"* to a newcomer, usually a woman he'd picked up for sex. Sometimes he'd said it in English, "This is the house." La Kay had ignored him because It didn't want to witness his private business with women half his age. It hadn't paid attention to their departures because It had always assumed that they would leave whenever he was finished with them. It now hurt with the realization that some of them had not come willingly and, worse yet, had not left at all. It regretted having been consumed by the distractions of the outside world. It lamented Its deliberate ignorance and wished that one of the unknown ones might say or sing Its name.

It needed to reach far back, to the summers before Lucien had committed his first worst deed, to hear Its name in a song.

It could see two drunken men sitting in Its backyard. Their personal bottles of Barbancourt and their shared six-pack of Miller beer warming by the legs of their chairs in the sun. Each man had caressed his own guitar, serenading their instruments and their homeland at the same time.

M'prale la kay mwen
M'prale la kay mwen
Wou, wou, woy, woy, woy
M'prale la kay mwen.

The House had been convinced that they'd been singing to It. But these forlorn visitors to KAM had wanted to go back home. KAM be damned, they wanted the real thing. The true Ayiti Cherie. The red and blue with no white. No cookie-cutter houses, no basement peristyles, no stove-cooked meals. They wanted wood and charcoal fires burning outdoors, blackening wide pots of cornmeal with red beans and coconut milk. They wanted year-round summers, not seasons. They wanted unscheduled leisure, not hours of factory labor. They wanted to be the majority with no white people turning them into minorities within a minority. They wanted their familiar brand of oppression, an unambiguous dictatorship that made them cower in corners in their often wet pants, sometimes bloody shirts, and always tear-streaked and sweat-stained faces. They wanted an invisible but well-known occupation by foreign soldiers that had made them territorial and nationalistic, while inspiring fantasies of greener grass and money growing on trees. They wanted and sang about going back home, not just home, not just a house they wouldn't own for thirty years, not some solitary apartment that kept them caged.

La Kay had tried to understand the curious nature of these human beings. It had wanted to know who these people were who'd sung to It about It without knowing that It had feelings.

But It had had no way of knowing that It had been the furthest thing from their minds when they'd sung about *la kay*. Its feelings would have been hurt, so It had opted to believe that It had been serenaded. It had swayed and stepped, mimicking the bolero It had seen Lucien dance with any willing partner in public. It had waited for the drunken duo's sad ballad to end, so It could dance to one of Lucien's favorite records that had told It to watch and learn how to properly dance to kompas.

It had marveled that what had started as a sweet afternoon lamentation had broken into a full *bal* by sunset. Lucien had played a full two-hour set of vinyl albums from start to finish. There had been no home-based DJs to slide from one artist to another. So It had simply relaxed and waited to hear Its name in a familiar or favorite song.

La Kay returned to Itself, lying half-dead, eyes boarded up, breath shallow, listening for the sounds of unknown inhabitants. It wanted to hear Its name spoken by one of the muffled voices, whispered by the smallest, sung by the vibrating songstress It now acknowledged had been there all along. It told Itself the things It had long hidden, suppressed things that had forced It to take action and attempt to kill Itself and Lucien. It wanted to know who they were, when they'd been taken, how he'd locked them up. It wanted to match up the times It had turned Its attention to the unnatural outside violence with the horrific moments when girls, now grown women, had been dragged into Its darkest place.

It laughed at Lucien's pitiful cries echoing from the basement stairs. Although It now hoped that the demolition crew would halt its work, It didn't want him to be rescued. It wanted him to shut up so It could finally hear Its name and rescue these as yet unknown women. It needed one of them to call out "La Kay" to resurrect Its rage, kill Lucien, and get them out.

Six

LUCIEN

Although Lucien had been hoping that Leona would come and find him, he didn't want her to contact any of his neighbors, not even the ones who'd called her the morning after the fire. Anyone who came would be looking for an exploitable opportunity. His neighbors passed the house not knowing that he was stuck on the stairs to the basement. He knew that none of them would have cared anyway. They certainly weren't sad that his house was going to be torn down. Some were waiting for him to put it up for sale. He knew what they were thinking. One or two were wishing he would eventually pull them aside to offer them first dibs. The more merciful ones were hoping he'd rebuild and augment rather than diminish their property values. He had enough land with the second lot to build an additional house, if he wanted. Some who'd always been covetous of his insultingly extravagant garden were thinking that the same next to a new house would be a blessing. An in-ground swimming pool would be lovely but out of place in their neighborhood and expensive to put in. The excavation for a pool with what was required to rebuild the house's crumbling foundation would not be covered by the insurance money. He knew that they were talking, could almost hear them from where he sat freezing to death, unable to move anything, including his mind. It drifted between thoughts of Leona coming for him and the vultures with whom he'd shared the neighborhood for decades. They were waiting for him to make a move. They could easily get fifty to a hundred thousand more above asking price for their own homes in the post-recession market. But the digging out required before any construction could start would bankrupt a buyer. He knew that selling was not an option, not to any of them, not to anyone at all. No one but him knew about the safe room. Even that didn't matter since he was never going to get back there. He was going to die on the stairs. The house would be torn down on top of him. He would be crushed and scooped up with the rest of the debris. But the back room would likely remain intact. It would take months to break down the postwar bomb shelter because it could not be blown up.

Lucien had also been hoping that Leona had not gone to the police. But, being as naïve as she was, she had gone in and reported him missing. He could imagine how her request to find him had been received. The officers had probably all but laughed at her even after she'd explained his partial paralysis and possible dementia. No one cared that she didn't want him to die in the eight-degree temperatures made colder by two feet of snow. No, it had not been seventy-two hours since she'd last seen him. Yes, he still drives. Yes, his vehicle was also missing.

He could see her in her too-tight coat with the buttons hanging on for dear life. She was shapely for sure but had gained weight. She walked out of the precinct dejected but not hopeless. She drove around the neighborhood trying to find his van. But it was nowhere to be found. Neither was Dieuseul or the taxi they had driven for the break-in. Leona had already tried to call. Lucien knew that Dieuseul, feeling guilty for having ignored his cries, would not have answered the phone. He tried to warm his claw while praying to who knows what that Leona would find him before his frostbite required hospitalization. He perked up when he heard the soft thud of footsteps in snow, knowing that it could only be her walking down the snow-packed driveway. She made the first footprints leading to the back door. Lucien heard her calling, but the vibration of sound funneled painfully into his frostbitten ears, the canals of which had become miniature bobsledding tunnels.

He could hear her calling to him loudly enough for the latchkey kids of his immediate neighbor to hear and peek outside to once again rejoice in the twenty-six inches that had given them a snow day. Leona spotted the sawdust board hanging by a single screw. The door itself was off its hinges but mostly, miraculously, still in place. She rallied the strength of her youth to pull it toward her, revealing Lucien, half-conscious, slumped down in the crack between the basement door and the slanted steps. He stirred but could not lift his hands to shield his eyes from the brightness of snow reflecting sunlight. Her shadow mercifully blocked it as she struggled down the stairs. She spread her arms like airplane wings and placed her palms on either wall to keep from sliding down. She sat on the step behind him and tried to wrap her arms around him. Failing at that, she dug out her flip phone and called for an ambulance.

He didn't want to think about Leona's assessment of where she'd found him. He hoped she'd assumed that the four and a half gallons of water and the loaves of bread were a function of his hoarding. She understood his condition well, not because she was a hoarder herself or because he'd explained it to her, but because she knew the things immigrants from the poorest countries did out of a perpetual, irrational fear of scarcity. She empathized with this profound sense of lack in the presence of excess, because she'd taken him as a lover while surrounded by a loving and appreciative child and grandchild. She wanted a companion. Loneliness was hell too. To her, it was a hunger of the worst sort.

He felt like a rag doll in the hands of the EMTs as they lifted him up and out into the cold. He couldn't tell the difference between the inside temperature of the stairwell where he'd been and the outside air through which he was being carried.

He felt when he was rolled and then lifted into the waiting ambulance, where they took his pulse and temperature, listened for the breath in his chest, pricked his fingers and toes to see if he would respond. He was conscious only long enough to feel the tires dip into greedy potholes. The ambulance did not think that his status warranted blaring sirens and let its silent lights move them through the traffic along the Van Wyck Expressway to Jamaica Hospital. Minus the disturbance of noisy sirens, Lucien allowed himself to be dragged deeper into the more than two decades he'd spent adjusting things in his dungeon. He kept hearing the *crack, crunch,* and *purr* of his intercom, the only way he'd been able to communicate with his girls without going into the basement. He could think clearly enough to be proud of himself for figuring out how best to keep and enjoy his captives.

Lucien woke up in the hospital shivering in the warmth. He was babbling about his things and his girls. In the years since Marie-Ange's death, since the day he'd last seen his daughters, his hoarding had escalated. The redundant towers of dysfunctional stereo parts in his basement had been one of dozens he'd built throughout the house and in his garage. His desire for collectibles had driven him to grab girls whom he should have known better than to snatch. Nihla had been his first absolute miscalculation since his successful testing with Zero. The white girls he'd previously prospected had resembled the porcelain figurines in his aunt's curio. Cocoa had been a mistake made too close to home that he'd resolved with his donation. The neighborhood search had nearly cost him every penny he'd had in the bank as well as his first three captives. His contribution to the reward pot had been money well spent. She had always been a treasure. She'd reminded him of all three of his daughters—

a multi-event track star, a poised dramatic orator, and a singer a deaf man could feel. She was as pretty as an animator's film-screen invention.

If his daughters had been Disney characters, Veille would have been Nala. Clair—Lady. Dor—Bambi. Veille was the lightest of the three, her complexion the closest to Lucien's. During winter, she would get so light that she looked biracial, shining like the brightest on the scale of sepia photography. She tanned easily in summer, her skin a glowing peach. Her only flaw, if it could have been considered that, from head to toe had been a small black mole in the middle of her forehead that made it appear as if her eyebrows met. She had the long, curly hair of the women in his family but kinkier like Marie-Ange's. He remembered her slender frame with a high behind that had made her look like she had curves even as a little girl. She'd been a late bloomer who didn't acquire the accoutrements of full puberty until age nineteen, when she'd left home for college. Her body had waited for her to be out of her father's house to come into its own. She'd survived the years since the first and last incident, mastering her limber stealth walk that had made her steps inaudible even when she and her sisters had run around playing tag in the house. She had been the feline who could stalk her predator, sense his approach before he even knew where he was going, and alert her sisters to dress faster, pull the belts of their robes tighter, avoid the bathroom, lock the bedroom door, close the closets so he couldn't peep through the holes. She had always stood poised to pounce, her body tilted forward like a sprinter awaiting the sound of a gunshot to take off racing. She had been hypervigilant because she was easily startled, a remnant of being caught unawares that time before. She had always been ready to flee or fight because, during that first episode that was also the last, she had frozen. Never again.

Running track had come easily to Veille in high school, but she could just as well have been a pole-vaulter or a boxer. Her body's energy had been divided evenly between her feet and her fists. However, female boxing had been an oddity before being legitimized by Laila Ali, who brought it into the mainstream. After laying waste to several ignorant and arrogant boys in elementary and middle school, Veille had become afraid of the power in her hands and lunged at the track instead. She had achieved the rare feat of concurrently holding records in long distance and meter dashes in college. She had opted out of the Olympics to remain close to her sisters, with whom she'd shared everything. Even in college, she'd talked to them every day, several times a day, in her soft voice that sounded like hair through a brush.

Hair, brush, and comb. Nala, Lady, and Bambi—Disney's animal princesses. Veille had been more than the hair on her head. She had been the hair itself: untamed, temporarily subdued, quick to rise up and fight off oppressive hot combs, recalcitrant against relaxers, finicky and compliant for the right strokes and pomades. Even Marie-Ange hadn't been able to manage her, especially not after.

Veille had not craved her mother's attention since having been cast aside at eleven months for the twins. She'd clung to Nen-nen and suckled at the childless *lugawou*, who'd figured out how to produce milk from breasts that had never experienced the required biological changes. Veille's precocious walking at six months old had gone unnoticed until it was developmentally appropriate, which is to say when everybody had taken notice of her sisters pulling up on frail furniture in imitation of what they'd seen her doing.

By the time Lucien had returned to Haiti to christen the twins, primarily, and her, incidentally, she'd already been running laps around the perimeter of Nen-nen's hut. She had neither sought nor missed the recognition of the adults around her. But the loneliness of being excluded from the oneness of twin sisterhood had made her settle for any gesture that brought her into the closeness Clair and Dor shared. Veille rejoiced when Marie-Ange bought her a third, slightly larger size of whatever clothes she'd chosen for the twins. She'd showed an unusual gratitude for whatever adult affections approximated love, including Lucien's. By age six, Veille was clearly Lucien's favorite, his firstborn, pleasantly compliant, bright, and needy to the point of desperation. Like any lonely child would, she eventually fell victim to the emotional trap he'd been laying for years. She was already his first and he had been determined to be hers.

Lucien hadn't expected Veille to tell Marie-Ange. He had not expected that single experience, in which there had been no penetration, digital or otherwise, to change her. Afterward, she'd regressed and failed at school. She'd been left back in the third grade, so she and the twins had ended up in the same class. This had made people mistake them for triplets even more often, which Veille loved. She was officially bonded to the pair, which was why she'd told her sisters first what their father had done and finally told Marie-Ange much later.

Clair had been the catalyst and accelerant for the disclosure. As a precocious five-year-old, she couldn't wait to tell. But she'd waited until she could be part of the solution. After overhearing Marie-Ange threaten Lucien, she took it upon herself to confront her father for a crime she could not yet understand. Out of well-deserved disrespect, she started calling him by his first name and convinced Veille and Dor to do the same. This hadn't felt natural to her twin, but it had given Veille the emotional distance she needed by eliminating some of her confusion about the father-daughter connection, at least where titles were concerned. The three would come to understand the degree of Lucien's aberrant behaviors in high school after reading the only black-authored book in the tenth-grade curriculum, Toni Morrison's *The Bluest Eye*. Clair had even alternated between calling her father Lucien and the name Cholly, although he had had no idea that she'd been referring to the unforgivable rapacious father in the novel. She had taunted him with reminders about the goddess in the basement that had precipitated his nightmares. She'd also dreamed about making good on Marie-Ange's threats.

In his half-frozen state, with fear filling his chest like smoke behind a closed door, Lucien was desperate to expel the thoughts of his girls, past and present. He hadn't been able to get to the latter and the former had excommunicated him once again after Marie-Ange's funeral. He'd always known that they must have heard or somehow been told what their mother had said to him, how she'd questioned his manhood and paternity after finding out what he'd done to Veille. Especially that Clair, that saucy, vindictive, beautiful brown girl. She must have been the one who'd heard and then conveyed her mother's venomous lambaste to her sisters verbatim.

Lucien couldn't move his limbs. Even when he coughed, he could not expel whatever had invaded his chest. He could not summon the stamina to silence the memories that moved through his entire body like blood. As he lay on what could have been his deathbed, he heard Marie-Ange's threatening upbraiding through every pore and felt her unanswerable questions pricking every nerve, despite the numbness of frostbite.

Marie-Ange had lowered her voice and come so close that he'd felt her breath and spittle hitting his nose. She'd wanted to snatch his Adam's apple from his throat. She'd spoken to him in a low growl only accessible to fearful, injured, and protective she-cats and -wolves, mother bears, and lionesses.

Didn't you love her enough to hold back? Like my father? He'd held back. He waited outside doors while I changed into the fine things he'd brought back. He insisted on sealed doors for the room he'd built and furnished for me with things paid for in francs. He didn't have to count. There was only one of me. He didn't have to touch finger to finger, skim or steal from the excess in the president's Swiss bank accounts. I know that he'd imagined the flawless French ladies he'd dared not touch. His eyes never touched me. It was enough to hear me breathe as smooth and fluid as French. His one requirement in public: no Kreyòl, except to him in private so he would remember that I was not the saleslady who'd brought him clothes he hadn't been allowed to touch until he'd paid for them. Kreyòl covered up his little lady in impeccably tailored grown-woman gowns. White gloves for First Communion. Lace veil. White shoes. On ordinary days, barely tinted light-colored fabrics that almost looked white. A reminder to hold back, lest he leave an imprint. I was covered.

Mahogany door. Covered. Windowpanes with double wood shutters. No storefront. No curio. Nothing to see! His height, his brown skin, his uniform, especially his beret for generals only, his guns, his heart, his eyes watered over, his lips parted to show teeth. Not a smile. A threat. He would help me alight from the car, walk me to the classroom door, shake every teacher's hand, letting them know who and whose I was, in case they hadn't heard. He'd pat his sidearm as a greeting and trace the strap of his machine gun while telling them my name. His palm on the leather sheath of his machete to make them understand. Duvalier's second-in-command. First to see the president in the morning, the last at night. Same with me. His first and last. And he, mine. His lawful wife, my second-in-command.

Lucien backed into the memory blindly, splitting his head against its wall, letting its grit penetrate into the cut in his scalp. He wanted to think about her, not the things she'd said to him. He didn't want to hear her any more than he wanted to hear himself say, *I am nothing.* Her stories about the man he could never measure up to echoed his own. Her first love. Perfect because he'd been disappeared or made dead. A martyr, although he'd murdered more and deserved worse. He didn't want to see her perfect father. *I am nothing.* He wanted to see her. *I am a mirror, nothing, until she looks into me.* But all she'd done since that morning in Bois Droit was talk about the man whose features he knew by heart. Dark-skinned like cocoa dust. Too dark to have been president in a country that still honored light skin.

Tall, over six feet. Always in uniform or a suit and tie. Perfect posture. Always strapped with several weapons. He'd come from money and added more as the president's most trusted. As smooth and gentle as his fencing sabre. Composed. Restrained. Perfect French. Exceptional Kreyòl. Imposing. Threatening.

He didn't want to hear as Marie-Ange had spoken through clenched teeth with balled fists, standing in his face, poised to pounce.

He never would have allowed me to marry you. Look at what you've turned me into. Look at what you've done. You could never be him. I wish I'd inherited his weapons—his side piece, his machete, his long gun or AK . . . I would not hold back. I wish you and I were in Haiti. I would rip open your throat from ear to ear without reprisal or jail time. I'm holding back. And you will too. Or I will send Ezili's hands down your pants to stroke you to your last coming before she does what should be done. A blood sacrifice to the Vierge Marie.

Thereafter, Lucien would suppress his own questions. Why did she stay? It had been the same question Marie-Ange had asked herself until the day she died. Veille, Clair, and Dor had asked it, even at her funeral. He'd never wanted to know the answer because it had had less to do with him and more to do with the good man, the best man, her first and last love. She needed security. She could not manage on her own with three young daughters in a foreign country she had not yet figured out. She did not have enough money to live and support them on her own. She needed what he had provided since rescuing her from the backlash of the coup in Port au Prince. Although he did not fully understand or feel love, he knew she had never loved him. He had been her indispensable crutch and later he'd become a part of her, a permanent prosthetic that she could not do without.

Lying unable to twist his stiff body on the hospital bed, too cold to count, too numb to feel the warmth of an electric blanket, let alone a sensation as elusive as love, Lucien felt trapped. He knew somewhere inside himself that what Leona had shown him was love, but he could not imitate it well enough to feel it inside him. He wanted to show her that he was grateful. More so, he wanted to show her that he was getting better, so she wouldn't insist on keeping him in the hospital. He did not want to be imprisoned at the mercy of people with absolute control over the flow and consistency of his blood, when and whether he ate or starved, wet or soiled his bed or got up to use the toilet, breathed or suffocated because he could not move a single limb.

Frozen inside and out, the only thing Lucien could move was his mind, and it kept forcing him backward to Marie-Ange's threats. What if she'd done it? Taken the prize between his legs and left him lying in his own blood? What would he have told the people at the hospital? They would have called the police or sent him to some precinct to explain to a uniformed audience. How would he have explained it? Worse yet, they would have asked him why a wife would do such a thing. Infidelity? Or something worse? He would have plausibly copped to cheating. But how he'd lost his prized appendage would have drawn the crowd's curiosity. He would have appeared more senile than he seemed now. Unable to move his lips, Lucien laughed a little inside to imagine his explanation.

"The statues in my wife's vodou temple. Yes, she's a vodou priestess. Yes, the spirits in the statues cut my . . . Yes, the statues came to life. Well, not like that. The spirits inside of them. Yes, inside. No, they're not stuffed into the statues themselves. No, the statues can't walk." Sigh . . . "No, they can't talk either. My wife . . . Yes, the vodou priestess. She sent them to cut . . . Yes, Percocet, Vicodin, and morphine. Yes, they found it. No, she didn't throw it away. Yes, the spirits cut . . . No, I didn't see them. I just woke up and it was hanging. No, I wasn't bleeding. Not when I woke up. No, I couldn't see the stitches. I can't really see down there. My stomach . . .

Yes, my wife, the vodou priestess, was there when I woke up. No, she didn't have a knife. No, I didn't see scissors. Listen, I could barely walk. Yes, I was conscious. She sewed it up. Or they did. Before I woke up." Sigh . . . "The doctors reattached it properly. No, I can't. No, it doesn't. Yes, I'd like to speak to a detective. Yeah . . . I'll wait here. No thanks, I can't sit down."

Zero, one, two, three, four, five . . . eleven, twelve . . . eighteen stitches. They are not real. They are not here. I am not there. I am nowhere. I am nothing.

Lucien's body was completely numb and immobilized. He began to worry that Marie-Ange had posthumously carried out her threat. She could have sent Ezili to do it while he'd lain incapacitated on the basement stairs so close to the boiler room. He dismissed the thought. The only person who would have and could have executed her mother's promise was Clair, and he had not heard from her since her mother died.

He could imagine Clair, especially, laughing at his predicament. She would have been gleeful to know that Marie-Ange had made good on the threats. She would have doubled over at the comical monologue. She would have regretted only not having done the deed herself.

Lucien had correctly judged Clair as the angry but rational one. She'd believed that anger was a wasted emotion only when unaccompanied by sane, strategic action. Well-channeled rage was deadly, even when irrational, which was to say she would have acted on her mother's promise to lop off his most treasured part so that, fearing for his very life, he wouldn't have even dared to go to the police. He had taken his daughter more seriously than his wife for reasons besides her overt challenges. First, she was a twin, an immediate descendant of the violent Marassa *lwa*. He'd grown up knowing their power as vodou's invincible sword-wielding deities. Therefore, Clair had been born with a machete in her hand. When she was a child, he'd had to explain her temperament to the people at KAM who'd forgotten what it meant to be born a twin. He'd always say that she slept with a dagger under her pillow and a cutlass by her bedside. Clair needed no introduction.

She had been their wild child, the boisterous and flamboyant middle one who convincingly and formidably played the role of the eldest. She'd openly challenged him, Marie-Ange, and other adults on behalf of her sisters and herself, whipping out the harshest truth at the most critical moments to halt reprisals. She'd spoken with the sweetest smile, through the whitest teeth, which caught people off guard. It had taken manly schoolboys several hours to realize that she had just stripped them of their skins with a flirtatious voice and a kind visage. Despite her seeming coquettishness, Clair had not been interested in dating or making friends. Her pretty face and niceness had not only made people fall in love with her at first sight; it had made them believe that she was in love with them as well. She'd learned early on to use her attractiveness as a mask to get away with saying and doing the impermissible.

Lucien liked to imagine Clair with her Lady-like dark brown eyes, her pupils taking up most of the space in her irises. Copper flecks made them look like they were lighter in the sunlight. Her sweeping long lashes, Carib-Indian complexion, naturally tinted lips that were the color of her skin with a dab of red clay, and small nose rounded out her cuteness. She'd been gifted with Marie-Ange's hair and a full, womanly height and shape by the age of twelve. She had been the same height as her sisters then, but she'd looked shorter than five foot five because of her curves, compared with their slender builds. She'd been too shapely to be a tomboy, but she'd thrived as a strong swimmer and volleyball player on her high school teams. Fittingly, she'd been drafted into both the drama club because of her poise and looks and the oratory club and debate team because of her polish and articulateness. She'd participated in these activities to dodge Marie-Ange's three-days-a-week church schedule until they'd finally had it out and landed on her attending church only to sing backup for Dor on special occasions.

Her schedule had meant that she was always in a rush and walked like a New Yorker— purposeful, determined, almost running, and always knowing where she was headed. Even her heavy backpack hadn't slowed her down. The textbooks and sports gear had pushed her forward as if she'd been trying to catch a bus to the future. A life outside of KAM and SOP with her sisters in tow had always been one Manhattan sprint away.

Lucien remembered the standoffs Clair would instigate against Marie-Ange. She rarely argued because it was clear who would win. He'd avoided Clair as best as his driving lust had allowed. She'd done everything she could to stand out, so she would always be seen by someone and not become his prey. She'd experimented with girlie punk, Cyndi Lauper and Madonna style, all-black nearly Goth (but more Greenwich Village than Satanic), and imitation Michael Jackson with tight pants, pleather jackets, spiked belts, and silver studs on every possible accessory and article of clothing. She'd finally discovered the one look that repelled him and shut Marie-Ange up for good. Before it had become vogue, Clair had shaved her head.

She'd become known as her school's black Sinéad O'Connor until Roshumba Williams made her mainstream debut with a low 'fro in the *Sports Illustrated* swimsuit edition. When Veille and Dor realized how much their father hated Clair's cut, they'd shaved their relaxed tresses and gone natural as well. He'd loved the wigs that Marie-Ange had made them wear to sing at church. But, true to form, Clair agreed to the teenaged *Dreamgirls* look only if she could wear makeup as well. She hadn't asked for permission or negotiated with her mother. She'd simply put on lipstick and eyeliner, made her sisters' faces up as well, and stepped onto the church stage to bask in Marie-Ange's and the church's disapproval. Drawn by his daughters' adult wigs, Lucien attended church to leer at them while pretending to be the proud father of the talented trio. He'd witnessed how Clair had used her painted face to challenge Marie-Ange. She succeeded at threatening him in the process:

Go ahead. Say something. Climb onstage. Wipe my mouth and I will tell. All of your secrets. What he did. What you know he did. How you know he watches. How he came here just to stare. Unless we show our nappy heads when we get home, we might find him in our closet or behind the shower door. Smear my lipstick. I will unmask you both. Before God. Forget man. I will undress myself. Right here. I will pull down my panties, as our people say, and spout some name-in-vain curses that Ezili would appreciate. I will unveil her and testify about your worship and her true power before your despicable, hypocritical, pathetic congregation.

Lucien had squirmed while looking at Marie-Ange for a cue. She hadn't known what to do—have three nappy-headed girls onstage with fades and 'fros or three secret-hoarding, silky-wigged baby dolls wearing devil-red lipstick in church.

Lucien remembered how, as a baby, Clair had been Marie-Ange's favorite. She'd maintained that status until she'd started speaking in full sentences at eleven months old. As a newborn, she'd cried just as much, which had given the women in Bois Droit a reason to hold the pretty, chubby infant. Her cries and subsequent silence had saved her twin's life.

The midwife hadn't known that Marie-Ange had been carrying twins. In the forty-one weeks of pregnancy there had been no movement or throbbing from the other lump. Dor had been stuck in the womb. When she slipped out still inside the afterbirth sac hours after her twin, Nen-nen and the midwife were gaping-mouth, wide-eyed shocked. The midwife cut the cord, but neither woman said anything to alert Marie-Ange that she'd been carrying twins and that one of them had perished. Outside, the midwife cleaned Dor as if she believed she might survive.

She sucked blood and mucus from her nose, wiped, washed, and wrapped her. She placed her on the stoop next to her tools and the bucket of afterbirth for burial later that night. She attended to Marie-Ange and an inconsolable baby Clair. Despite feeding, rocking, swaddling, shushing, and singing, the newborn firstborn twin cried for hours straight. The women misdiagnosed her as colicky. The baby quieted down only when the faint cries of the other baby outside wafted in through the closed door more like a scent than a sound. Clair wanted everybody to hear her baby sister, the one presumed dead, the one Marie-Ange didn't even know existed. She silenced herself to create space. Out of her quiet, Dor's cries perfumed the room. Without realizing it, the women heard two babies in conversation with each other. Clair's silence spoke to Dor's astonishingly delicate cry. Dor was a miracle, but Clair was the heroine who made space for her sister to be heard, then seen, then held.

Dor had grown up resenting the attention she received as the ugly twin, the darkest of the threesome, and became determined not to be the quietest as well. Her skin was just a few shades lighter than her hair, which was black and tough and tight. She'd begged her mother to press her hair, so she could don the same styles as her sisters. She hadn't needed that to be seen. The whites of her eyes were exceptionally bright, the eyes themselves black with crystalline pupils. She had her mother's full plum-colored lips and a thin, barely visible gap between her front teeth. In high school, everyone said that Dor looked like a supermodel, but no one could figure out who until she was in college and Alek Wek debuted. She was the thinnest, least curvaceous of the sisters. With her athletic build, darker skin, and coarse hair, Lucien was less interested in her than the others initially. He would gawk at her only when there were no other women in the vicinity. She learned to regret not being the runner, the watcher, or the screamer in the family, because the absence of these talents made her the most fearful.

She displayed her vocal talent to ensure that she could be heard in the dark even if she couldn't be seen. Children flocked to her wherever she went. Despite the rigidity that adults observed at first glance, she was always open to a hug from willing little ones, the nicer visitors to KAM, Marie-Ange, and her sisters. She learned never to hug Lucien. She hardly wanted to perform in front of him.

She was born for song with a gift that had chosen her like a barren woman adopts a child. She sometimes allowed her voice to go breathy and sleepy when speaking. But when she belted out ballads, she shut people up better than her twin. Her voice surprised and transfixed people in ways her ordinary presence never could. But she was not a fame seeker because she hated the thought that thousands, if not millions, of men like her father would always watch her in that way.

LUCIEN HAD never told Cocoa that he'd taken her because she was the most akin to his daughters. He'd let her figure that out based on neighborhood lore, old pictures, and his own stories about them. He'd known that, at one time, like most Haitian girls in the neighborhood, she'd aspired to be like Veille, Clair, and Dor. Until now. Until he'd shown her who he really was. He'd watch as terrifying thoughts proliferated like dandelions in an unkempt field. He relished the look on her face as she imagined what he might have done to his own daughters during their first eighteen and nineteen years of life. Having perched himself to peer into her mind, he'd let her torture herself with unspoken questions: *Had he ever gotten any of them pregnant? Had they turned appropriately hateful and vengeful? Had he hated the brown hues of their skin so much that he'd had to take a white girl? Had there been four or five daughters? Had he killed one or two, leaving three? Had there been an incest-conceived grandchild? Had he or they suffocated the evidence to keep it secret? Or had the three simply cut off all ties, leaving him to be and do? Why hadn't they called the police? Had him arrested? Saved others?*

LUCIEN LAUGHED behind frozen lips at the absurdity of being arrested back then. Police involvement was something he feared now but not then. He'd seen the police as as likely to be the culprits as he was. Like many of KAM's patrons, he'd viewed the cops as useless, especially in matters concerning *those people:* immigrant, black, and/or female, just name it. And the neighbors? He wanted to let out a hoot when he thought of them. None of them, including Cocoa herself, would have ever guessed what he had been doing to women in his house long before he'd outright snatched girls off the street. They minded their business because they didn't want anyone meddling in their affairs.

They were Caribbeans, after all. They didn't need anybody knowing and then judging them for leaving their single-digit-aged kids home alone or for spanking them for disobedience. If they slapped their kids and spouses around, they didn't want any intervention. It was impossible to know and not to judge, so it was better not to see, not to criticize, not to feel accountable, not to speak up, not to take action. It was easier, like their new lives in New York, sort of. The semblance of choice and ease allowed them to rationalize why they'd chosen racism in America over hunger in their homelands, why they'd chosen indentured servitude over tourist-trap slave wages. He knew why no one had ever bothered to find out and would never ever know. It was always easier not to. It was always easier to do nothing.

SOL

———————

Hunger is hell. All the women in Lucien's basement had learned that they'd never truly experienced it until being taken. Even Sol had not understood. Although she'd made the trip through the desert, she hadn't really felt hunger until after enjoying America's abundance for half her life only to be deprived. She'd watched Chiqui break down. Cocoa hadn't even been able to sing away that pain. Asante had done 180s and 360s from failed hunger strikes to gorging on a week's rations and anything else Lucien had fed her. Nihla's hunger had been of a different sort, but by her fifth day in the basement, with no chemical sustenance, even she'd become desperate for ice cream of all things. But none of them had ever experienced the hunger of being in the third trimester of pregnancy with no access to timely or decent food, let alone the stuff that would satisfy raging cravings. The murderous symptoms of pregnancy mirrored some of the symptoms of withdrawal. All the women had watched and empathized with the pregnant one most. But they'd all been there in hunger's hell.

In the beginning, hunger had been the most acutely felt sensation, but not the first deprivation to hit. There was the absence of fresh air and its extreme—odors that made them want to vomit. The cold and damp of a cramped cube made of steel, stone, and trampled dirt had made them long for the humble places they'd lived. The cold was incurable even with covers that each had to earn from their captor. They'd slept upright, unable to acculturate themselves to the hardness of the bare floor made of semidried packed mud, decomposed and hardened shit, and the frail bones from carcasses of things they couldn't decipher. The darkness—not merely the absence of outer light but the terror of the unknown—had outstripped the fear of the unseen. The acknowledgment of a total loss of control over their environment and their bodies messed them up worse than their captor's touches.

Sol had not resigned herself to her circumstances until Lucien had taken Chiqui and brought her to hell. She'd finally accepted the absence of light to comfort her sister, who was still afraid of the dark. He had always controlled the darkness. He'd leave with the matches or inexplicably rescind the sundry of sanctified votives. He'd vacillate between luminous generosity and the tightfistedness of a Third World post-storm blackout. Without warning (there was never any warning), he'd plunge them into a darkness so deep it wiped away sound. He might crack the door, so they could see slivers of the bathroom's light that had not only alleviated the darkness temporarily but had given them hope that they might use the toilet or the shower. On a whim, he might let one out into the habitable parts of the basement, the living room cramped with antiquated entertainment options, the rape room graced with an actual bed with blankets, sheets, and pillows; a carpeted floor; mirrors on the ceiling; painted and wood-paneled walls; a breathable scent like a man's tolerable musk after a few days without a shower. The wonder of sound, audible only to those who'd spent months hearing nothing but their own heartbeats and the breathing of Zero, One, Two, Three, or My in utero. He'd downright tease them with vacations upstairs, where windows appeared as if they could be opened or, as a first or last resort, shattered and ecstatically climbed through. They'd dance to see doors, front or back, made of wood that looked hackable, locks that looked pickable, and narrow vitrines that appeared expandable. Sol had tried to escape more than once, only to be thrown back into the back room that he'd try to fortify to prevent that possibility.

Having heard him describe his first test, she'd remained quiet and docile, lest he bring some animal to terrorize them in the back room. Years before renting Asante the basement, he'd performed an elaborate experiment to ensure the safe room's inescapability, to test the efficacy of its soundproofing, and to try out the one-way intercom. A starved German shepherd, a pregnant she-cat, and, later, her litter of six had been his first prisoners. He'd eavesdropped through the intercom and peeked in periodically to check their status and see who was winning. Sitting in the bathroom, he tried to hear the shrieks of the hungry dog as it approached the ex–alley cat. Hearing nothing, and too curious to endure the silence, he'd go to the first intercom outlet installed to listen to their street fights. He shook with glee when the cat went into labor. He waited to hear if the intimidated dog would seize its opportunity to attack. After a month, the cat and her entire litter were all dead. He never found any remnants of the succulent kittens. The only evidence of them was excrement he never bothered to rake up.

He'd then experimented with the dog's starvation over the course of a year. He'd fed it once a week for four months and then gave it nothing but water at the same interval for half the number of months. He would subsequently resume the weekly feeding schedule and then stopped altogether, not even providing water. He listened and peeked daily, shutting the heavy door until the weakened, emaciated dog ceased to approach, saving its strength to mine all edible options, by a starved dog's standards. The longer he waited, the cleaner the once feces-laden floor became. It took an additional three months for the dog to die.

His animal trials completed, Lucien let the remnants of the dog's decomposition and unmined excrement ferment before deeming the environment fit for human testing. He spent one night a week there until he was willing to piss off Marie-Ange by renting the basement to his for-fee, sucky-ducky tenant, Asante.

Sol had tried not to reveal how tortured she'd been by stories he'd recounted to terrorize her into submission. He'd been able to trick Asante into the safe room because of her desperation to be hidden from the DEA and her paranoid, vengeful boyfriend. He'd turned her into Zero and recorded her every move in her new prison. She'd hugged the stone wall nearest the door and balled herself up like a bean. One white eye open in the darkness. The other eye swollen shut. No, he'd never hit her. She'd done it to herself. Throwing a tantrum, knocking over the lone candle, then knocking herself unconscious against the moldy stone in the self-created darkness. One eye open, searching out a crack of light. The other turned inward behind a throbbing wound the shape and color of a ripe plum.

Asante had remembered *Roots,* the nine-hour miniseries that she'd watched on the new color television set in her mother's living room when it was first released. This was what African captives must have experienced after being seized or tricked (the same thing, really) from their villages, thrown into the hold, awaiting the unknown darkness lit up by smells so sharp they made them see. It lit their way to the pit of the waiting ship. The shit was the least of it. The decay of the abducted ones, living and gone, penetrated the TV screen, and she could smell the death rot. There she was, incarcerated in an abyss she used to rent, battered by her own stupidity, ingesting the dampness of the darkest place, smelling herself dying slowly.

Sol had used every ounce of her courage not to break down while listening to Lucien's tales of the cats, the dog, and his first human experiment. She hadn't doubted their veracity because she'd experienced his worst. She'd wanted to weep, hearing how he'd broken Asante, who had been in the "why did I?" stage of her captivity. Refusing to assume the blame-load alone, and with her misjudgments and his voice in her head, she'd started in on her kind: *Women are simple bitches with simple motivations, easily manipulated and deceived. They feed their own fantasies and buy into anything that seems to confirm or fulfill the tiniest piece of their dreams and desires.* There was no reason to believe that she'd had him on lock, that what she'd had with him was ever a relationship, let alone love. She'd loved that he had chosen her, opted to disrespect his wife and make her the woman of the house, in a way. *S-T-U-P-I-D.* He hadn't beaten but he had, well, cheated. Obviously! And protection? So much for that. There she was, the worst of her kind, worse than a simple bitch with a bad attitude—a simple bitch with no options whatsoever. She could only be who, what, and how he wanted her to be. He controlled everything in and around her. But that was the stupid part. She'd allowed it.

After the activity of her mind had given way to emotion, then crept into the realm of bodily sensation, her hunger had ripped her from the inside out like a clawed beast in a bad horror flick slicing its way out of its cocoon. Hunger had been the self-eviscerating quadruped that left her too weakened to even think. But after it had withdrawn its claws and fallen asleep out of pure exhaustion, thought had returned.

Sol had known this all too well, not just from following Asante through Lucien's lens, but from watching each captive soul break against her own mind. Asante and all the women who'd come after had experienced it. If their hunger had been hell, then the process of thinking had been its ninth circle. And the physical sensation had been felt only after the mind cracked the door to allow that feeling to slip by. Upon being tricked, shoved, dragged, or rolled into the back room, each of the five had tortured herself with thinking. The what-ifs, the why-me's, the why-did-I's had scurried around in their minds, reaching the what-the-hells, the how-could-he's, the why-would-anyone's, and then they'd sprinted and hurdled over to the how-the-hells, the what-if-I's, finally landing on the how-do-I's, the what-should-how-can-we's.

Sol remembered how the answers to these had come later. How the fantastic declarations had come later, much later, after the wounds of self-flagellation had been adequately licked, the calm (not peace) of self-convincing cooler heads had finally prevailed, the self-consoling caresses had been accepted. Later, much later. Long after they'd nearly been broken by hunger, assuaged for minutes with nibbles of fingernails, flesh from fingertips, and flagrant cuticles that had grown wildly in the dark. After they'd progressed to the same edible parts of their toes. After pinches of the dirt floor had become palatable. After, long after, they'd finally paused, forcing themselves not to think but to hear and see, they'd realized that there were things far worse than hunger in the back room: silence, darkness, fear, and getting fucked involuntarily in whatever ways he wanted. At some point, each woman had come to the realization that his preferred position was the one he'd forced them into in absentia. He'd contorted their thoughts and turned them into pregnant she-cats strategizing how to scare off a hungry predator ten times their size before entering the vulnerability of giving birth.

Sol had witnessed the complex and innate masochism of the human mind. She'd known how thought could gain control of a being and drag her everywhere until it tired out or completely defeated itself, opting for silent self-protection. The women's minds had tortured them with thinking about everything they'd missed and experiences they never could have imagined. They'd lamented practical goals and fantastic aspirations—educations, careers, affluence, basic female independence. They'd bawled their eyes out over first kisses they'd never have or that hadn't met their expectations. They'd grieved at never having fallen in love or for becoming enthralled and in lust with the wrong men. They'd tried to imagine what they had not experienced, to rekindle what they'd shooed away out of arrogance and ignorance, or taken for granted as if life owed them something it would award later when they were good and ready. They'd listed: traditionally structured families of their own, hot dates with rich men, entire apartments to themselves, home and business proprietorships, multiple paid-for cars, hotel-and-airfare-included vacations to magazine paradises. *Shiiiiiiiit!* They'd listed: learning how to drive. Flying in an airplane. *Man, oh, man! Damn! Choices! Remember* choices*?* Ham or turkey? Takeout or delivery? School or sleep in? Work or hooky? Sing or rap? Answer the call or let it go to voice mail? Lights on or off? Candles, lamps, overhead, or iPhone light? Pig out or diet? Earrings, necklace, both, or neither? Janet Reno, Hillary Clinton, Condoleezza Rice, Hillary Clinton 2.0, Michelle Obama, or Hillary Clinton 3.0? *Or, damn, that next one?! Dammit! I should have voted!* C-H-O-I-C-E*!* Asante had been on the inside before Condi. Sol had been taken just after Senator HRC caused a ruckus in New York. Chiqui had also gotten a glimpse of 2.0. Only Cocoa had been able to revel during the reign of the greatest FLOTUS ever, MLRO. All of them had had to rely on Lucien to share newspaper clippings with pictures, but no dates, and his versions of stories about one or more of these women. He'd even shown them photos of the most recent, unnamed FLOTUS, a rumored captive Zero in her own right.

Sol had watched the others' reactions to Lucien's political commentary after each had returned from a story session with him. She had seen their anger over his opining on inconceivable aggravations they'd wished they could experience again—heat, cold, rain, snow, traffic, the high prices at the supermarket and gas pump, daylight saving time, winter's impact on solar patterns, too-late sunrises and too-early sunsets, the tardiness of people with payments and for appointments. They'd wanted to slap the stubble off his face, if for nothing else than his complaints about things he caused them to experience in the extreme—insomnia, oversleeping, resentment toward inadequate, absent, and missed loved ones. They'd wanted to headbutt him and knock themselves unconscious in the process for the things he'd said, in part or fully intentionally, to push them into tortuous thinking that had driven them mad.

Only Sol had ceased the incessant, uncontrollable thinking. She had mastered thought; she'd overthrown the mind regime, taken her soul out of the trunk and put it in the driver's seat where it belonged. She'd relegated thinking to merely mechanical and functional—a cup holder, windshield wipers, a hubcap—made important and useful only when the driver chose to drive the car and employ it because it made things a little more comfortable or safer. She'd made it optional like heated leather seats, five-way headrests, powered seat positioning. She'd used it as a rearview mirror when her past would be useful and help her to avoid some perilous situation or individual who might sneak up on her. She'd used it as a paper map she could fold away when she wanted. Her mind was not her. The thinking it did, the thoughts it reproduced (it could only recycle information, not create it), the stories it told and retold and then told again in different ways to call attention to itself, did not define her. She was so much more. That should have been a no-brainer for any simpleton. Soul, which is to say true Self, sublimated space and time. Being didn't just think or believe; it *knew* that transcendence is not the leaving of one's body and mind. It was not a disembodied pair of hands folded in prayer. It was the full integration and harmonization of all parts *within* the purview of the endless, timeless Soul.

Sol had known, knows, and is knowing the five *F*s. That fear generates four, not three, responses: fight, flight, freeze, and freedom. Transcendence. Even before her abduction, before her migration from south to north, she'd *known*. She'd controlled her faculties the way she'd played with light switches to entertain baby Chiqui in their single room. Later, she'd tried to explain to her sister this control over and integration of mind and body to experience life, whatever the outcome. Chiqui had misinterpreted much of the lesson. Sol had been disappointed to watch her sister conduct her physical and mental faculties like instruments, forcing them into perfection, competition with others, and overachievement. Chiqui finally came to understand her cellmates and sympathize with the pregnant one.

During their many post-rape story sessions, Sol had come to the realization that she and Lucien had had to have certain experiences in common, that his evil could not have come out of nowhere. There had to have been something they'd both seen, felt, and known, but her knowing had come differently. They'd both experienced fear, but not only did they opt for different *F*s at different speeds; they'd chosen their *F*s based on a different knowing. Maybe it was because she'd been younger and less hardened or less privileged and more open. Pliant, liquid, and light, she'd gone through, not over, the wall and emerged as pure spirit. At three years old she'd become as knowing as the universe itself. She'd maintained it because of the absence of formal education until the age of seven. By the time she'd started her passage through the back room she could have escaped any circumstances she chose. Mere months into her captivity, she'd even progressed toward the realization that she could get herself out of the back room anytime she wanted.

Sol chose not to reveal herself to Lucien—not yet. She chose to let him believe that she was merely rebellious and cunning, and certainly no match for him. In reality, she was freedom. She just couldn't let him know. Not yet.

SOL DID not say a word when Lucien's rescuers came, hollered, lifted him out, and left. She watched Cocoa break down again and wished she could console her. Cocoa couldn't take it anymore. She could taste the snow outside, she was so ready to be free. She had been counting the days since Nihla's death and My's birth. After the fire, she'd dropped all pretenses. No more coquettishness or pretentious optimism. She was ready to get out. She showed an aggression that, if not managed, would result in a brawl with Asante. She would slap the pessimism and the taste out of the older woman's mouth. Sol reached for Cocoa's hand and held it. That would have to do for now. Now was just a blip to Sol, but it felt like the one-third of a lifetime that it was for Cocoa.

Sol had always known that the restraints that held back the anger of those with Cocoa's sweetsy, cutesy demeanor were tenuous. They were stretched to their limits as they tried to maintain their balance and optimism under the worst assaults. They had to eventually snap. They were never permanent. Sol understood well, and she knew that Asante did too. A belt can hold for only so long. Holding in shit while being force-fed distends the belly. It all must come out of one or both ends unless these are concurrently sealed. Then the person has no choice but to blow herself to bits from the inside out and die. Sol had always known what Cocoa could not see, that Asante's aggression had always been survival. And that Cocoa's purposeful restraint would eventually kill her if she didn't unbuckle the belt. Like all of them, Cocoa was being stuffed with every minute in the back room, her lips sewn shut. The frequency of her bowel movements had always been controlled by him. More than that, he'd plugged her anus just for kicks. "Let it out every chance you get," Sol had heard Asante say even through her angry silences.

Sol knew that Cocoa would crumble or blow, just like Asante had. They'd each had a breakdown. Cocoa had tried to sing hers away. She'd pushed it down into her diaphragm and released it in measured notes. But that was not enough for the kind of hurt Lucien had inflicted. His had never been microaggressions, slights pardonable by devout Christians, women, and minorities everywhere or high-road victims.

It was living four hundred years or more, awoken from death during the transatlantic crossing to find oneself enslaved in the Americas, then killed by whipping or ripping, being drawn and quartered or overworked, then being raised from the dead and transported to the North-South border only to be killed in a Civil War battle, resuscitated again to live through lynching, assassination at the Audubon, raised from the dead again and assassinated again on a hotel balcony, backhanded into a roadside police beating, pistol-whipped and injected with liquid crack, hanged in a jail cell while doing time for possession only to be awoken by a broomstick or plunger up the ass, surviving that then being gunned down for wearing a hoodie a few steps from your own doorstep, waking up to find yourself dead in another cell after a routine traffic stop, shaken up and then choked out in front of a bodega, revived and shot for being unarmed again and again and again across ten states, knocked awake sideways all the way to Kabul, Mosul, or Baghdad only to be stoned, set on fire, decapitated for trying to go to school or rejecting a rapacious husband at twelve, with your head sewn back on you wake up in a secure confessional to be raped, silenced, raped again, and murdered in the name of . . . rising from the dead after three days' rest to find yourself brown or black or female or immigrant or poor or young in a school or a boardroom brothel, sodomized in another safe room while awaiting deportation. The real *real*.

Sol could see what Cocoa could not: that the brown girl had swallowed four hundred years, swallowed harder, sucked in her gut, and emitted silent gas. Sol had never said this but had seen Cocoa's belief. She'd convinced herself that it would all pass, which confirmed the correctness of her conditioned response to adversity. Cocoa had always wanted to be right about herself. She never wanted anyone undoing more than what Lucien had already undone. She'd swallowed until her throat became sore, until she couldn't even sing, until she became constipated, unable to pass anything from any orifice. Her rage would not just pass. Not this kind. Not during or after him. She'd thought that she was saving it all up to appropriately channel it into something beautiful when she got out. She wouldn't succumb to the knowledge that she was a rag doll he could unsew at any seam or rip open at any unintended spot. He could stuff her full of whatever he wanted, including a baby, and sew her back up, leaving no openings for her to relieve herself, not even narrow windpipes or parted lips out of which to sing the way he loved. He understood the need for an outlet for rage. They were all there because of it.

"I'm going to fuck that niggah up when we get out of here!" No one had ever heard Cocoa swear before, but Sol had seen it coming. They'd all seen and heard what they'd believed was the worst in one another. But each time any of them did something to surprise the others, it was like a new cellmate had been brought in.

"Uh-oh. Goody-goody 'bout to lose it now." Asante shrank back a little as she made the comment.

Sol held Cocoa's hand tighter. Chiqui placed a hand on Cocoa's shoulder. My huddled closer.

"If you even . . ." Cocoa started crying before she could finish the sentence. She always cried when she was angry—even with Lucien, who'd interpreted her tears as weakness and submission. Each time, he'd believed that he'd broken her just a little bit more. "That niggah ain't here, but you his bitch. I ain't nevah been on his leash. I've held my own since I've been in here. But if you even . . . I will whip you with his leash instead of fucking him up like I want to. You do not want to get on my Southside."

"I ain't even . . ." Asante didn't get to say *studyin' you!*

Cocoa broke free from what was supposed to be the soothing restraint of her three beloveds. She grabbed an unlit votive and leaped on top of Asante. "You ain't gonna kill me like you killed Nihla."

Chiqui held My as tight as a secret. She sealed her hands over his ears protectively.

"I'mma kill you first. I ain't no Little Orphan Annie, but you can bet your bottom dollar on that." She huffed as she hit Asante with everything except the glass she was saving for the death blow. "I ain't white. I never been high unless you count falsetto or losing it to the music. I've never hoed. I still ain't never sucked a dick. Bam. Not even his. Bam." Cocoa stood up because her words had become harder hitting now. "Bam. Cuz if I deep throat a muthafucka, I can't sing right. Bam. And that muh'fucka believed it."

As much as Asante wanted to scream, *That's not how you get pregnant!* she held back to prevent further blows.

"Bam. Now you know. Now you know, bitch. Ain't nobody gonna kill Cocoa."

Sol understood that referring to oneself in the third person was always an escalation.

"Not him, and Cocoa sure as shit ain't gettin' killed by his little bitch." Cocoa dropped down and got in Asante's face. "You've seen Cocoa, but guess what? You ain't nevah seen Colette Jean-Baptiste. Now that you done made me tell you my government, you 'bout to see both Cocoa and Colette!"

Sol saw Cocoa's hand in the air, pulled back into a fist. She shrunk back and held Chiqui and My, so they wouldn't see what was coming.

Cocoa landed the first ferocious blow into Asante's up-turned eyes.

Blauw! She didn't give her a chance to recoil or recover. She pulled her arm back and launched her fist like an arrow from a bow. One at a time, she spat out her words like bitter olive pits.

"I!" *Blauw!* She synchronized the punch with the word.

"Ain't!" *Blauw!* She raised her fist and dropped it on top of Asante's head.

"Dyin'!" *Blauw!* Asante defensively covered her head with her arms.

"Down!" *Blauw!*

"Here!" *Blauw!*

"Bitch!" *Blauw!* To give her knuckles a rest, Cocoa opened her hand and slapped Asante across the face, knocking her into the stone wall.

"And in case you illiterate, skanky, hateful piece of shit wasn't countin', that was six!"

Blauw!

"Now seven! One for every year I been down here. I should give you one more for good luck. Cuz only luck and my mama coming through that door could save your ho ass right now."

Sol saw Cocoa raise the hand with the glass in it.

"Don't!" Chiqui screamed. "If you're gonna do that, blow out the other ones. Don't let him see it." She had already started smothering My between her breasts.

Sol understood Cocoa's rage. She was releasing everything she'd held back all those years. She had been suppressing her fear of and anger at Asante since Nihla disappeared. Sol was not surprised that Asante had not fought back. She'd felt Asante's crippling guilt since Nihla's disappearance. Sol lay down to rest. She was exhausted from the fight she'd just witnessed. She heard Asante crying over Cocoa's panting. She could feel Asante sinking. Cocoa had knocked her into the full awareness of what she'd done to Nihla.

Thursday.

Like the others, Asante had been afraid that, if Lucien broke his pregnancy-induced sex fast, he would come after them with a vengeance after a long

reprieve. He would rip the pregnant one apart. Asante
figured that he still had not touched Nihla except
to move her from the safe room to the bedroom.
He hadn't fed Nihla, who'd just started to feel and
express hunger for food. But that could have been part
of her involuntary detox delusion. She marveled at
her tattoo of three side-by-side hot-air balloons that
she scratched at continually because she felt the tiny
orange lines of the flames burning. She hadn't been
able to explain to Asante when or why she'd gotten
it and had no idea who belonged to the monogramed
initials in each. At least she was clean, sort of. At least
she'd stopped talking, finally. At least she'd saved her
worst for the privacy of the bedroom, where the others
could not witness her cutting.

   Asante had known why Lucien had left the back-
room door open. He'd wanted them to hear the
sounds gushing out of Nihla. He was daring them to
try to escape. He wanted to test their submission and
their will to live. Asante had listened closely as
if waiting for his instructions. She heard Nihla ask
him for ice cream. She had not had it in years, she
claimed, and volunteered to make him feel good in
exchange. It was either that or a hit of whatever he
was willing to give. She was even willing to settle for
a joint. Asante could hear Nihla jumping on the bed
and talking in a singsongy voice. She heard her hit
her head against the mirrors on the low ceiling and
waited to hear the scream that never came, even when
one broke and fell. Nihla plopped down hard and
excitedly examined a small shard of broken glass. This
was the tool she needed to make her sundae. Asante
heard Lucien let out a long groan and knew there was
trouble.

He ran to the back room and grabbed Asante by the arm. The women knew that something had gone awry with Nihla because Lucien never took them out two at a time. The pregnant one hoped that he was setting a new precedent and that she would not have to give birth in the back room and at least one of her cellmates would accompany her. Asante did not want to be involved in whatever plan he'd devised to subdue or get rid of Nihla. However, she welcomed the chance to get out for a moment. She did not expect to see blood.

She didn't give away her repulsion when he asked her for help without saying a word. Neither of them had ever seen anything like it. Asante looked at Nihla from the corners of her eyes and gagged when she saw the girl cutting herself. Using her tattoo as the stencil, Nihla was tracing the three scoops on her arm. She did not look at them once while slicing off flesh. She laid the sections on the largest piece of the mirror. The girl squealed, and Asante thought that Nihla had finally felt the pain from the cutting, but she had done so not out of pain, but because the blood resembled:

"Strawberry topping! This is just a strawberry sundae. No banana, dude!" She looked up at Lucien for the first time. "Strawberry ice cream too. No vanilla." She smiled at him. "No dulce de leche, no chocolate, or whatever you are."

Asante sat back to watch, waiting for Lucien's invitation to help. She could see that he had stopped counting the cuts. He hated blood. He finally grabbed Nihla's wrist to stop her. To stop the bleeding, he snatched the bedsheet from under her. He decided then and there that he would get whatever drug she needed to get her to stop the cutting.

Friday.

Lucien brought enough ice cream and cocaine
for both women, but Asante never got a taste of the
latter. Nihla was ravenous and, worse yet, willing to
do anything and hurt anyone to get her fix. Asante let
her have whatever she needed, as long as she stopped
trying to get at the mirrors on the ceiling to complete
her strawberry sundae. Asante wanted to save some
ice cream for the pregnant one. She took advantage of
Lucien's predicament and, on the pretext of going to
the back room to get her favorite brush, brought three
of the four pints of Häagen-Dazs to the others. She
returned to the bedroom to Lucien's pleading eyes.
She responded to his request by dictating how they
would handle the situation.

"More coke. See if you can get your hands on some
needles and some H. It has to look like a real overdose.
I'll get her ready. Bring me my makeup bag. I know
you still have it." Under her breath she whispered,
"You probably been trying to dress up in some of my
clothes."

Lucien came back with the bag too quickly, as if he
had not hidden it even after all those years.

"You got my clothes too?" She did not need to tell
him to bring something tight fitting and provocative
because that was all she used to wear. "I need a blow-
dryer and my curling iron, if she's gonna look right."

Lucien came back with everything, the hair
supplies, heroin, plus his souvenir handgun.

"I forgot to ask you for my jewelry."

Feeling her first high in more than five days, Nihla
started to perk up. "I've got my own jewelry. Where is
it, Lulu?"

Asante was surprised to hear his nickname pronounced like a little girl's name. No wonder Nihla trusted him so much.

The rings, necklaces, and especially the earrings looked familiar to her. They should have, since most of it had been hers. The rings Chiqui had counted as her inheritance and Cocoa's hollow door-knocker earrings with her name across the middle rounded out the collection.

"She's ready."

Bandaged, dressed, and made up, Nihla looked like someone Lucien might have considered taking. But she still looked like a streetwalker rather than a homegrown brothel prostitute.

"Do what I told you. They'll think she overdosed."

Asante was not about to let him shoot the girl in the basement. That would be the point from which none of them could return. If he got a taste for blood that he himself had drawn, enjoyed the snuffing out, the silencing, the doll-like stillness of a dead dressed-up girl, then this new fetish might take over. She might be next to take a bullet to the head and fall face-first onto the bedroom carpet. He could kill them all at any time. But, thus far, he'd never used force, just coercion, blackmail, the imminent threat that he would hurt the others if one of them failed to cooperate. If he started outright killing, she would be responsible for two lives taken at once when he turned on the pregnant one. He would save her, his first, for last, and he would take his time. He might not even use the gun again. He would devise some new mechanism or replicate Nihla's slicing so he could see blood that he was no longer afraid of. He'd memorized their cycles, counted the days for each, and avoided menses like a cat dodging a hungry dog. But he acclimated to new situations quickly. Blood no longer scared him. Killing still seemed to. She needed to keep it that way. She would not do his dirty work. She could show him how. She was hoping that Nihla was as hard-core a user as she'd seemed, so she could bounce back from a dose that would have been lethal to a lightweight.

Saturday.

Asante had watched Lucien inject Nihla himself. He half carried, half dragged the girl out of the basement. What he'd done after that, Asante could only guess. She'd given him the instructions. All he needed to do was follow them. He had to give Nihla the final dose at 9:00 p.m. as he stopped pretending to look for parking on Haven Avenue in Washington Heights. Unable to find a spot, he'd pull up slowly to the emergency room doors. He didn't need his .22. The hood of his coat and his scarf wrapped around his face up to his eyes were enough of a disguise. He'd have popped off his license plates. He'd stop and roll her out of the van without coming to a complete stop. He'd be grateful that at least the passenger-side rear automatic door still worked so he didn't have to get out to open and close it.

One day early! Lucien had set Nihla free one day early, which was why Sol and the others continued to believe that their former cellmate was dead and that Asante had helped kill her. Neither Asante nor Lucien knew if Nihla was still alive. Lucien had not bothered to try to find out. Asante had always hoped that Nihla had survived. Lucien had hoped she hadn't. Neither had ever mentioned the white girl again.

Whenever one of the others would ask about Nihla, Asante would quickly correct her: "You mean the seven-day slut, or should I say six? He let her go early."

Sol had asked only once. Like the others, she did not believe that the issuance of such a dehumanizing title could come from a merciful mouth. Asante was a murderer as far as Sol was concerned. She hoped that none of them ever got sick or became delusional enough to warrant extrication from the back room. They'd come to fear a transfer to the bedroom even more than before. Although they'd each wished that Lucien would kill them while raping them, they didn't want to die in whatever mysterious way he'd killed Nihla. The rape room had become the kill room. What a place to give birth.

I am not Zero. I am One. I am knowing voices. I cannot hear. I am not broken. Like this room. Burning. Like this house. I am smelling fire and smoke, snow and cold. I am not begging. I hear him scream, "Help, help, help!" They come for him. Footsteps go. Voices go. Zero, Two, Three, and My are sad. Three is noise. She is cry. She is scream, "Here! Here! Here!" It is not our time. I am knowing. But I feel for Two, Three, Four (she dead), My, and even Zero. Three say to My, "Come here, baby." I am hearing them cry.

LA KAY

The House felt the sound when Its top bedroom floor collapsed. The boom startled It and Its newly discovered inhabitants in the back room. It felt their stomachs drop and knew that they were thinking the same thing It was—that Its insides were about to come down on them. It was trying to puzzle out how to keep that from happening. It wanted to keep them safe until It could let somebody know that they were there.

It was feeling guilty about having missed their presence. For how long? If It retraced Lucien's steps over the years, It could deduce when he'd likely taken each of them. In honesty, It needed only to consider the distractions that would have kept Its attentions away from the back room.

Louima, Diallo, 9/11, the August blackout. No one could have seen anything, let alone those struck blind during a hot summer. The recession a few years later. Then everybody's attention had been focused on the election of the first black president. La Kay gave Itself a pass for missing anything during that period. It had been celebrating with the rest of KAM, especially the ones who had finally become U.S. citizens in the years prior and had voted in that historic election.

And then It had felt the tumult of KAM patrons old and new who'd needed a place to gather and mourn an unlikely earthquake in Haiti. They'd scarcely completed their acknowledgment of their nation's independence when, on January 12, a fault had split open their worlds. Feeling their pain, La Kay had joined in their mourning while watching news footage of the disaster that had knocked an already kneeling country flat on its face. It cried at the sight of the cracked statue of Nèg Mawon, a memorialization of a centuries-old maroon rebel from the hills. Behind its fallen body, the Palais Nacional had split down its middle like America's White House in a Hollywood Armageddon film. It hadn't known what to do, how to help, as Lucien's comrades had sat waiting for phone calls with news of loved ones who may have perished or been displaced by the worst natural disaster to hit their country in over a century. There had been no name for this monster that had risen from the earth's center to devour their capital city and its surrounding provinces. La Kay had listened for a year, hearing about an anniversary that had overshadowed Haiti's independence. It had seen a resurgence of visits and purchases by newcomers and old patrons desirous of inventory from Lucien's stockpiles that they would send to refurbish their shattered land. It had no idea that he'd found new prey to manipulate and victimize worse than what he'd done previously.

La Kay groaned and put away the memories. It tried to figure out the happenings that had usurped Its attention in the years after that. The president had been trying to restore the economy, health care . . . None of that would have been gripping enough to distract It from Lucien's activities. It vaguely remembered him bringing home somebody who wasn't Leona. It should have known about the white girl. It still didn't know who she'd been, how long she'd stayed, if she was still there with the others in Its safe room. But It felt in the pit of Its stomach the boom of guilt that It hadn't been paying enough attention to the women being misled, drugged, or dragged into Its basement.

Now It wanted to stay alive for two reasons, to get the girls out and to ask Lucien why he'd made It complicit in his evil. It hadn't understood what he'd done to Veille or any number of women at KAM. It had thought that Asante had been a passing but important mistress who'd voluntarily entered Its basement. It hadn't known enough about the white girl to pass judgment. It started to resign Itself to the fact that It might never get at the why. It might hear something about the how, if It managed to get the women out. But, like honest help for Haiti, the why would never come.

Knowing Lucien as It did, It knew that there would be no answers. It had learned long ago that Lucien tried not to ask himself questions. And It was right. Lucien would never explain why he'd taken Nihla because he hadn't known himself. La Kay had peeped the posters in the garage, had seen the way Lucien had looked at the white women on the arms of KAM's gamblers in their heyday. But It hadn't gone far enough into Lucien's memories, into his psyche, to know that the white girl must have reminded him of the glass dolls in his aunt's curio. It would have wept to know that the white girl had not survived seven days in Its basement.

It tried to remember her, but so many years had passed. It had seen her only once or twice. It had heard only a minor dustup in Its basement bedroom. It had long ignored that part of Itself, ever since Asante. Nothing but Lucien's endless garbage-quality television sets and stereos were down there. And whatever he'd done with that stuff, La Kay hadn't cared enough to search. Now It had to search Itself for missed clues, for strangers dragged between Its legs into a hellhole. It found only one aberration in a consistently aberrant existence with Lucien— a baby boy who'd grown into a toddler and then a small boy.

La Kay had been trying to figure out to whom the boy really belonged. Veille, Clair, and Dor would have never allowed Lucien access to their children. Now, reeling under the assumption that Lucien had somehow stolen or borrowed the child from one of his strays, La Kay had another reason to do away with Itself and Its owner to keep safe the newest child in Its midst.

Seven

LUCIEN

_____

Lucien knew that he needed a doctor's care to pull apart his fingers and toes, to warm his limbs back to life, to yank the cough out of his chest. He didn't feel like he was dying. He was inappropriately hopeful for a man his age. But he'd survived two strokes, had maneuvered with his dragging leg and permanent claw, and had someone to lean on. He would stay in the hospital for a few days to make Leona happy, to keep her with him, and to get better so he could go back to his house and fix things.

LUCIEN HAD never been an engineer, but he had been a scientist in his own right. He had not built the safe room, but he'd thoroughly checked its soundness. He was unable to explain how the soundproofing worked, but he'd made sure it did before responsibly testing its efficacy on human subjects. He'd known that it sealed light and sound in and out. After two strokes, he'd learned that the room was not as accessible as he'd once thought. But it had always been good enough for his girls. It had functioned the way he'd needed it to. More important, it had made its involuntary long-term residents behave. The intercom had been a different matter. It had been a post-construction fabrication, the lone weak spot in an otherwise fortified penitentiary.

He'd liked to play with it, to hear the yelps of the German shepherd, the screeching of the she-cat, the silence when it had been empty. He'd tested it for himself, making sure the buttons did not work from the inside. Unable to test it from both sides concurrently, he hadn't known about its *crack, crunch, purr,* until My. Then he'd taken pleasure in knowing that he could twist the women's bellies into knots at the press of a button without saying a word or playing a song. He'd crackled the box to life as the signal for Cocoa to sing to him when he could no longer manage the stairs or navigate the junky alleyway more than once a week. He had played music, mostly for her, but even before, so his captives could enjoy the tunes he loved.

He was still proud of his gentleness because he'd never overtly or violently attacked them. He'd never even hit them. He'd pulled their hair or their ears, especially during. The worst he'd done without knowing it was assaulting them with his scent even after he'd showered, when he'd put on deodorant and cologne, powdered his pubis. His smell scared them as much as the sound of him thudding down the stairs, grunting with exhaustion after a few pumps. The weight of him could be ignored. He liked it when they closed their eyes and went with them on the fantasies they created to escape. He even let them plug their ears with their fingers, so they wouldn't hear his low, closed-mouth snarl. But the smell of his body was the worst of him, the part of him they could not flee from. They had to breathe. He tested them. He opened his mouth over their faces. His retch-worthy breath stood erect over the scent of his body. It rose above the smell of the slop bucket in the back room. It was so harsh that it became sound and solid at the same time. It was tangible and terrifying even to Asante, who'd once enjoyed the wake-up breath of her lover's morning tongue. It woke them, made them sit up straight, made them try to run. It was an arresting odor that bound all of their five senses, seizing them where they stood. Even through the steel soundproof door, they could hear it. It announced his presence as soon as he ducked into the room. Even in the dark, without the light from a single candle, they could see its arrival.

It was worse than his touch. Although he'd never beaten them. A bite, yes. A pinch, yes. Dragging from the darkness by their hair or ears? Yes, yes, and yes. But it wasn't like . . . It could have been much worse, he thought.

It's not like I fucked them. At least, not often. I like their mouths. They prefer mine. And my fingers. Rough from cold nights collecting. Zero . . . two, four, six, eight, ten . . . twenty. Pumps. They count with me. One, two, three, sometimes four digits. Sometimes a fist. Every so often I have to give them more. I hear them count strokes like blows, but I never hit them. I don't want them to stop. When they say the numbers, I feel like more than nothing.

He'd pinched them and left bruises, but just so he could count the marks while giving them their weekly shower. He'd bitten them accidentally on purpose once or twice, but that had only been his excitement gone awry. But he'd never ever back-handed, punched, or kicked even one of them. He had never handcuffed or tied them down. The worst he'd done had been to tease their imaginations with suggestions of things he might do *if*. Things he'd shown them in scary movies, and then allowed their imaginations to keep them in check. He'd poked around their minds like a finger in a wound, searching for the sorest spot. He preferred to think that he'd cajoled more than he'd commanded, waited more than he'd coaxed, watched more than he'd touched. When one of them had gotten pregnant, he'd waited nearly a year before touching any of them. And, after that, he'd waited patiently for the lullabies that would come after the *crack, crunch, purr* of his sweet box.

He needed the singing to deafen him to the words he'd been hearing since the period of time that he could not remember.

I am nothing. Between life with La Belle and his first time seeing his disembodied and empty hands and then seeing those
same hands holding a gun. Since then, he'd been quick to cry
behind the backs of women. He'd used his peepholes to hide his
tears from his subjects. He'd closed his mouth so they wouldn't
hear the crying that came from nowhere and the accompanying
haunting syllables, *I am nothing.*

He'd cried when Sol was giving birth. The delivery hadn't
been like his first experiment. He'd even risked the tears and
words flooding then breaching the spot in his throat. He'd been
unable to stomach the thought of so much coming out of a
door that would never heal itself shut the same way again. He
hadn't wanted to witness and rejoice. He'd wanted to stalk,
plot, lay his trap, walk into her mind, and wreck shop. He had
not desired another child. He'd wanted a baby something, a
little thing he could rear or rid himself of at will. But when My
arrived, he'd wanted to give his son himself the way he saw
himself. He'd wanted to draw his version of himself live for My
and thereby give him what he believed was everything.

He'd admitted to himself that his first breakdown had not
started with a stroke, neither the first nor the second. It had
started with My. It had been the inability to control all life under
his purview, to control the first scratch at the thing beneath his
upper rib cage. He had never called it a heart, just the *feeling.*
He still hated it. Except for having to go to the hospital, part
of him was grateful to be numb all over. Feeling had been his
least favorite part of invading the insides of the women's minds
even if he could only imitate genuine emotions and reflect them
back like a fun-house mirror. He'd hated to experience their
thoughts comingled with a sensation that eluded him like an
ice cube through warm fingers. Anytime he'd heard them start
to cry, he would take his finger off the incoming button on the
box. He'd enjoyed only when their minds writhed, when they
screamed the most creative curses they could produce, their

tongues twisting off and spitting words into the air that he controlled. He'd relished his time inside them. Their minds were his domain. Their bodies, his garden maze. But their feelings were the dungeon where they tried to trap him. In the end, it was My who'd dragged him into the prison he could not break out of. He was forced to hear and to cry.

My crying comes from nowhere. I am nothing inside. No hurt. But I cry before and after. And for him, even during. They don't know. They don't see. I am nothing to see. I am only their reflections and now I am his. He makes me. Cry. I want to hold him, but I can't let go. The gun is in my hand. It reminds me that I have a hand, an arm, a shoulder, a body. I hold on to anything to make me more than the nothing that I am. But now my My threatens to make me something. I'd rather cry from nowhere because somewhere inside me is a prison.

LUCIEN WOKE up hours after his arrival at the hospital, shivering wildly. He couldn't feel the warmth of the room that mirrored the rise in the temperature outside. He turned his head to look at the rooftops, where rain was melting the snow. A feeling approximating heartbreak came over him as he thought of the demolition crew members donning slickers the same color as their hard hats to start leveling his house. He lay hoping that they'd wait for him to get out of the hospital and say a final farewell on his front steps. Maybe they'd be delayed, waiting for days for an all clear to start lopping off the aboveground levels of the house. He wondered how far they'd gotten. Had more of the upstairs floors collapsed? Had the weakened and overburdened main floor buckled? Was he worrying for nothing? Although he kept replaying the men grumbling about not letting anyone die in the hazardous house while he tried to retrieve his belongings, he chose to hope that he'd get there in time to halt the damage for a few hours.

He knew that they could never understand his hoarding. They would see it as more reason to tear his house apart. He told himself that even if the house was collapsing downward onto itself, it was also being pushed upward by the compressed mostly metal junk in the basement. Unless they dismantled the house chunk by chunk, they might never get their machinery into the ground to excavate or exhume. He laughed himself into a coughing fit thinking of his secret. Not the women, but the bomb shelter that neither his neighbors nor the demolition team knew existed. Whatever plans the fire marshal may have gotten from the records bureau were not the originals. The plans for the house that they would have in hand were doctored reproductions that had been made by civil servants on the take who'd erased the Mob safe rooms from the blueprints. Lucien satisfied himself that he would have time to at least save My and maybe one or two of the others in the safe room. Although the plan he had made in the days prior had collapsed, he chose to believe that he still had a chance.

He couldn't believe how things had fallen apart, how he had not followed his original plan after the second stroke. He had tried to coach himself to stay healthy enough for My, for his girls. He never again wanted to be reliant on Leona's mercy. After his second stroke, he had sworn not to become her prisoner for a third time.

Do not get sick again, not around her. Do not allow her to become your jailer. Do not give her cause to take you to the hospital. She is one of them. Flex-shift healers of the worst kind, always watching, listening, sniffing. Anticipating every twinge, cough, and ache. Waiting for a reason to poke, fondle, confine. Don't breathe. Stop every sneeze before it happens. Do not take in their salt water or their purified air. Hide your arms. Do not let them stick you. Do not let them take your blood, search your mucus, take pictures of your bones, look inside your chest. Do not let them name your sickness. Get out before they make you worse. Do not fall asleep. Do not let her tiptoe

fault, besides the cutting threat, had been her illness that had forced him to watch her confined under the control of other men who'd called her ailment by name.

"Cancer." The faceless doctor with a foreign accent had refused to sugarcoat. "Surgery is the best option. We think it has spread."

Lucien had looked for the others in the group of "we."

"We can do it on an emergency basis. It's spreading as we speak. We can discuss the options afterward. Chemo, yes. Radiation, absolutely. Both mandatory. Yes, figure out the options later, then determine where and from whom you will receive your care after the hospital. Yes, a long stay. It has, well, spread." He produced an anatomical blueprint of her insides.

Lucien had hung his head and walked out before the finger tracing and detailed explanations had begun. He'd felt more comfortable watching and eavesdropping through cracks, slits in curtains, from hallways and stairwells. He'd peeked and listened.

"Here is where we found the biggest mass, which has these tubes, fallopian, connected. The ovaries. Your small intestine likely. No, not your vagina per se. Really, upward." The doctor looked up from the paper and searched for Lucien. "Can you get your husband back in here? We need to discuss the length of your stay and postoperative care."

Lucien had quickly returned to the room before the doctor could finish his last sentence. He followed the doctor's explanation as if being led on a leash.

The length of the stay turned out to be six weeks. Wife batterers, child abusers, kiddie-porn collectors, even downright molesters who'd pled *no lo contestere* had been given less time. Lucien had had to be on lockdown with her for years of near-death scares until she'd finally died. Worse than jail, although he was still more afraid of that than the hospital.

Lucien looked up at the ceiling, not knowing if he was

through your mind. Keep your head clear of clutter. Remember where
they hid your clothes. Recall the turns out of rooms and hallways.
Count the stairs. Count the floors to the ground. Count the blocks to
the dollar van, the streets to your street, the cars on the next. Get into
your van. Rest. Rest. Drive by to make sure. Stop when you see your
house. Go inside. Get My.

Lucien regained full consciousness in the middle of the afternoon, screaming inaudibly in a hoarse voice for Marie-Ange
and his girls. He shook his head vigorously, like a Saint Bernard
shaking off fleas. He wanted Leona to get the hell out of his ear
canal, to get her to stop trying to crawl into places she desperately wanted to see. *Do not let her in!* He knew that she would
try to stop him.

Go inside and let them out. Get them out. One by one. But not
One first. Zero should go first. Then One. I should kill her, skip her,
same thing. Then Two and Three. Then My. My first. No, he needs
care. Count backward. Always make My last. Three then Two. Leave
One behind. Kill her. Leave Zero. Kill her too. Then My will remain
with two mothers like me.

He didn't know that he was coming undone. He couldn't
see his madness from the outside and so he thought that he was
as he'd always been. He took his hallucination for lucidity, mix-
ing past and present, feeling what he didn't know to be longing
and missing loved ones. He'd understood emptiness more than
hurt and had experienced a bit of sadness when Marie-Ange
passed. Anxiety was new to him. It had come about only after
the fire and hadn't left him since, even when he was daydream-
ing, unconscious, or asleep. His eyes were open, he thought.
But he could hear himself calling for Marie-Ange as if she might
respond.

Marie-Ange had been the best but not his first mother. He
had never considered his birth mother in that category at all.
His aunt La Belle had always held that place as his first and only
mother until his wife. He'd told himself that Marie-Ange's only

awake or asleep. He was high on oxygen. He didn't budge because the small pinprick of the IV hurt too much to snatch out
himself. He also had yet to figure out how to execute his plan.
He had to ready the garage before the demolition was complete
and then transfer the women, at least two of them, and My. He
knew that Leona was just taking a break from his bedside. He
needed to send her away, to make sure she would be gone for
several hours before he acted. He would send her to the court to
halt the tearing down of his house. She would do it. He believed
that she loved him more now that he was trapped in the hospital, now that his girls—all of them, including his delusions of
Marie-Ange—were gone. She might just pretend to try to save
his house but let it get torn down so he'd be left with nothing
except her. He understood well the desire to hold a cherished
one for safekeeping. But Lucien did not, could not, believe that
Leona had loved him, because he didn't know what love was.

With three thin blankets yanked up to his chin, he felt hateful. He hated Leona for believing that her love was true. He
felt as much disdain for her as he did for the inadequate blankets that were given to him in the hospital and those who had
given him the covers, knowing that one paper-thin layer could
not warm a grown frostbitten man. He hated the doctors for
keeping him jailed because of a little cough called by a strange
name, "pneumonia," in an attempt to scare him. He hated the
first nurse who'd missed a vein and had to prick him twice to
get the IV in. He'd wanted to throw her across the room like the
tray of lukewarm, unsalted, misnamed gray-brown heap they
called food, even steak (of the Salisbury variety), with gravy
that was gelatinous and powdery at the same time, mashed pota-
toes (he still had teeth), and Jell-O (what the fuck was Jell-O?).
He hated the circumstances that had brought him to the hospital
as much as the person who'd loved him enough to bring him
there, sit with him, wipe his feverish forehead. The same person who had wiped his ass after his second stroke and who still

gave him sponge baths. He hated sponge baths. They reminded him of his childhood in Haiti when La Belle would try to conserve water that was still being hauled in steel drums for the use of affluent families. At least La Belle could see through him. He hated that Leona believed every lie he'd ever told her. He hated her for her forgiveness because there were times that she seemed to know that he was being deceptive. Rather than confront him, she'd let him have his lie like a pauper with counterfeit money. He hated her for not being Marie-Ange. He hated Marie-Ange too, for more than just dying on him or threatening his treasure. He'd hated being controlled by the responsibilities he had created and assumed.

He couldn't even think about his daughters. He couldn't begin to admit to himself how much he'd wanted to annihilate them from the time they were born. They'd been unruly children, precocious up to the day they'd told on him. Brilliant mimics for mastering how to stalk him. He despised them for having talents that he did not, talents they'd wasted because he never derived financial or sexual benefits from them, except that one time. They'd never sung for him in private, only at church, where he hadn't been able to publicly reveal his hedonism, close his eyes around the luxurious sounds, lick his lips to indulgently savor a cappella riffs, recline into the notes and bask in the private concert, slip his hand downward decadently to satisfy himself. They hadn't even given him that. He hated Marie-Ange for not sharing. They belonged to him as much as her. If she could dress them up and parade them around, then he could have them or, if necessary, buy them, which he'd already done by paying the mortgage, their tuition, and for whatever lessons to refine their talents. He was decent for suppressing his hatred and being a tolerant husband, a mostly restrained father, a generous family and community caregiver.

He'd hated the women at KAM. He'd given the men a pass because they'd all been suffering like he had. But the women who'd passed through on their way to the promised better life, they'd owed him much more for his services. He hadn't been greedy. He hadn't even asked for money most of the time. He had had a pay-it-forward attitude, a "good will come to me" mindset. He'd given and given an ear. He'd loaned them tongues when they couldn't speak the white man's language. He'd advised, wiped tears, translated, found jobs, loaned money, helped feed, arranged marriages—all without requiring a big cash fee. How much would they have had to pay for their papers? Tens of thousands had been asked for the life-altering documents that would have allowed them to earn a better living and to go home to see and, most often, bury loved ones, with the legal right and full ability to return home. Which one was home? Haiti? America? PAP or SOP? KAM? Or the hovels into which they'd ducked while inappropriately dressed in two-piece church suits with high collars, itchy pantyhose, and frilly hats in ninety-degree weather? Home? They'd always come back to KAM. He had been so overly kind that they'd owed him exceptional payment for the things he'd done for them. The documents he'd filled out to get their kids to America. How much would a mother give for her kids? He'd never asked for much money and sometimes none at all.

He hated them for pretending not to know his fee. They'd known how to repay him. They'd glossed over his crass jokes about body parts that he could have only seen by peeking. He'd known the cuteness of facial features by heart after months or years of close observation. He'd always indicated his desire *pou yon ti bagay*, "for a little something," a little touching with lowered lids, a stroke of lips on lips, just hand holding downward indecently, just a *piece* of ass, not the whole thing. They would still be whole after giving it up. There would be enough left over for hungry husbands. They didn't even have to lie down. Slide the panties to the side and give him a slice standing up. Forget the panties altogether. He'd settle for a taste however they wanted to give it to him or take it—on their knees at the side of the house, in the garden, or in the rear of the garage when it was warm. In the boiler room, the shadowy corner of the foyer, the coat closet where he kept the small collection of things he was planning to send to Haiti. He could help them fill a barrel or a shipping container for the hungry ones back home. He could help with his hands on their hips or a palm guiding their stroke. Baby wipes and paper towels handy for the cleanup.

He'd hated the secrecy of it all when everyone knew the need and the deed. In Haiti he'd run a brothel out in the open, where everyone knew that the bar was just a front, a prop, and a necessity to keep the girls loose, willing, forgiving, and grateful for the handful of cash. Everyone who passed, and certainly those who came in, knew. There had been no dungeon at Bar Caimite. He'd spoken to the women face-to-face at will. There had been no intercom. If he'd wanted one of them to sing, she'd done it right in front of him. If he'd wanted more, she'd start before he'd even asked. He'd never had to ask at his old place. Why did he have to do so at KAM? At home? In the safe room? It was safe for him. He had always hated the women who'd made him feel like he had to ask, who'd waited for his request when they'd known full well what he wanted, what they owed him. He had not been a formal creditor. They'd damn well known that. He wasn't going to send a letter in the mail half reminding, half begging for payment. They'd known that they'd owed him, what he'd done for them when and what it should cost.

If I saved your life from the Tonton Makout who disappeared your father, of course you owed me enough sex to make three babies and then some more till death do us part. If I got you to America, got you a job, scalded myself in a steel mill, bought you a house, showed you who to go to for extra money when my paycheck wasn't enough, of course you owed me a blind eye while others paid their debts on all fours, two knees, a slit backside, an open hole. Why did I have to sneak and then ask for what was mine, what I was owed?

The whole concept of permission had always infuriated him, made him want to throw and break things. He never did. He was a docile, civilized, and kind man. Only children asked for permission to touch glass curio cases, fragile figurines, lace doilies. But why ask when the answer was always no followed by a short, superfluous explanation of how these things might break. That was the whole point! To shatter the breakable. An earthquake does not ask for permission to wreak havoc. It simply does what's in its nature. This was in his. He was being himself. Why hide? Why pretend? When everyone knew, saw; when some whispered about it, confronted him in crooked ways?

Lucien railed in his mind, all the while surveying the hospital room for an exit. He was angry enough to hurl himself out the window, onto the landing, into the melting snow down below. He was angry enough to spit. He hated every person he had ever encountered. He knew that they had known. Everybody who'd come to KAM and even before he'd bought the house, they'd all known who he was, what he was. He had visited their small apartments where it had been impossible to walk and stalk. So he'd just gawked. Everyone had had a cousin, a sister, even a mother who'd been cornered in a cramped kitchen, backed into a closet so narrow and shallow it was merely an indentation in the wall with a sheet for a curtain. In SOP, even the neighbors who were not Haitian had known how he rolled, especially if they'd ever known someone to whom he'd rendered a favor. And everybody had seen him watching. They hadn't known about the holes in his walls, but they had seen the slickness with which he'd managed to always be alone with some new prey. They'd been afraid to say it, afraid to name it. It was none of their business. *Even his wife knows, so who are we to say? It was just a little touch, a little piece. He's harmless, friendly, welcoming, helpful, kind. Let his little quirks slide.* He hadn't hurt anybody, had he? All men cheat and at least he wasn't doing it all in her face, taking mistresses out and buying them things or keeping them in the house. Until Asante. He'd given them so much to talk about.

Why is he always in the salon? He'd better be careful 'cause the cops are watching that place. Since when does she do house calls? Even if Marie-Ange is sick and bald, she still needs to get her nails done. But she's real mad now. He done moved the hairdresser into the basement. What about the ceremonies? In the boiler room. When you're desperate you go to the storefront church instead of Saint Patrick's Cathedral. Why's he always in the basement? Where did she disappear to? DEA got her or she's dead. Her baby daddy did not play. What about the salon? She left it all behind, probably all of her things in the basement too. Her daughter? Gone. Grandbaby? Gone too. Woman of the house, my ass. He's all up under his wife now. He got somebody taking care of her properly. She still asks for homegirl, the hairdresser. She's still suspicious. The only one left for him to fuck is the nurse. She's all right. She'll be good enough once his wife dies. She isn't going to die anytime soon. He did the right thing, getting rid of the hairdresser.

He's been in the hospital. Second stroke. My, my! What goes around . . . We don't see him much anymore. Where has he been? He stays in the house mostly, and then, somehow, he comes back with so much junk. As long as he keeps it inside his house. He must be lonely. Wife, kids, gone. No grandkids visiting. Except that little boy. He has his girlfriend, the nurse. Wonder how long that had been going on. Shut up. Don't make me laugh. He's not a bad guy. Life just didn't turn out the way he wanted it. Sometimes you love a woman or a man so much you get a little messed up over them. Before you know it . . . Bad choices. He's quiet and lonely. Does his own grocery shopping. You ever see the hairdresser again? Never.

They've already started tearing down the house. So much junk. It's going to take a long, long time to get that work done. No, they're doing it fast. It's a hazard. It could fall over onto either side. I never liked those people to the left. He's in the hospital again for the third time. Not sure he's gonna make it. He'll end up in there for a fourth when he sees his house. Gone.

Lucien's hatred kept him awake, so he could continue planning his escape. He gave up on saving his girls. He would take only My. He would fight the others and draw blood if he had to. He would find his gun. He would execute them all and take the boy, drive south to somewhere warm like he and Marie-Ange and then he and Leona had planned. The boy was all he wanted. They could start over somewhere new. My was still at the age where he would forget the back room and his mother entirely. He was well trained and didn't speak at all. He already knew how to watch, stalk, hunt. He was adorable and would be excellent bait. He was a collector too—twigs, stones, and leaves were only the beginning. He even knew how to retain enough ice cream on his sticky little hands to feed the others. He already had women eating out of his hands. My was the son he had always wanted. And Lucien wanted to be his father as much as he'd wanted a father of his own.

Lucien's anger flung him upward in his hospital bed. He willed his heavy limbs into motion. He had to get moving. My was his. He reasoned that the little boy was the only captive worth keeping. He hoped that he hadn't gotten sick from being closeted with Sol. Even if My was ill, Lucien was prepared to risk one more emergency room visit where the boy might be posed questions about his home life by a concerned nurse or a trained social worker. He would chance being exposed to have his son all to himself, to make a man out of him. A man in his own image. *I am nothing.*

Having settled on how he would eliminate them, Lucien pushed the other four captives out of his mind altogether. He didn't care if they'd survived several days without food and water, as long as they'd fed My, which he knew they would. Surely they'd had reserves. He couldn't help counting again and mumbled the inventory of rations. He knew that Sol would have planned for a crisis. She'd been sick, so if any of them would be dead by the time he arrived to rescue My, she would be. Maybe Asante too, because she was weak, having been down there the longest. Chiqui and Cocoa were younger, so they were more likely to be alive and combative. But if My was dead from being in the sickroom for so long, he would not know what to do or how to be. For now, he chose to believe that he could get My out and leave behind the women's remains to be buried in his trash, scooped up and dumped with the remnants of all he'd collected—the furniture, TVs, and stereos—and the new debris—the collapsed steel walls, the crumbled cinder blocks, and the floorboards. If he could have My, it would be enough. Just enough feeling to make him into something. He could stop counting. He could stop taking.

Tears fell into his mouth as he whispered to himself.

My fingers are one, two, three, and more than I am. There are too many, too many pieces to count. Too many things in the way to get to My. There is enough food. How many? How many jars, gallons, loaves? There are four of them who would slit my throat with the edge of a sardine can. This always scared me. I liked the taste of my own fear as much as theirs. I dared them, once, twice, three, and four times. But they held back in case they failed. In case I lived through the bleeding. Then I would have to do the things I had never done. Never counted the pounding of a hand, my hand, the cracking of my fingers, one, two, three, and five and then ten against unbruised bodies. I would have to count the hits of my fists and hear the numbers repeated in My's whispered echo. He is one, two, three, four, five years mine. He is the only one who hurts me when I am gone from home. He builds me up, counting the pieces of me into existence. Without him I am nothing except these tears falling into my mouth. I have no eyes for them to fall from. They flow so there are no single drops to count. I let them fall into my hands, between my one, two, three, and five fingers. Between the ten that I can see through, but they are nothing as I am nothing. I swallow and know that I could and must stand on legs that do not exist. Two of them with ten toes like my hands and fingers with nothing in or between them. I have to use them to wipe my face. I have to take the nothing with me. With My I could be more.

I could stop crying. I could be more than hollow. Something more than my weapon. I don't remember where it came from. But My is mine in my memory until I can get him out. He will be enough. I will cry for them because they are mine like my house. They are nearly gone. And so, for now, I am nothing. Until I hold my My.

SOL

I am not Four. Four dead. I am here. Still. But I am dying. I am knowing. No more smoke. No fire. I am seeing rain. Gray day. I am hearing. Driving back, forth. Walking back, forth. I am hearing "stop," "stay." I am knowing. I do not see him. He is gone. He is dead. I hope. When I hear rain and then back, forth, "stop," "stay," I am knowing time. I count since Four gone. Ninety-eight days. Then My come. Two and Three make My.

Three say, "If it's a boy, I will name him Marley." Two say, "If it's a boy, I will name him Prince." Three say, "If it's a girl, I will name her Zoe." Two say, "If it's a girl, I will name her Marisol."

I am hearing Zero. Cry. Retch. I am hearing Three. Cry. Retch. I am hearing Two, my gift.

"Push! Stand up! Stand up!"

We push, stand. Push, crawl. Rest. Breathe.

"My is ours," Two say. She give me My.

And now My. One cry. I hear. Two squeeze. Suck, cut. My is our all. We cry. We all wet with water, blood. My come early. Not chance, destiny. My born easy. Not chance. My not big. My li'l, li'l. Cut, suck, kiss, sing. My born facing west. I scared. I want east. But, at least, My born summer. I am knowing. My is a boy. My American boy. I ask why My born. My sick. My need doctor. My born brown. My sick twenty-one days. I am counting.

I remember Cara. We are walking. Cara big with Two. Three thousand miles. We walk. No ocean. Two born three thousand miles from where we start. I am counting steps. Cara not knowing. I am counting. Every step. No ocean. Big hill. I get high. Cara, "Push. Stand up! Crawl. Cry, Cara, breathe." Cara stop. She walk three thousand fifty miles in place. Back, forth, stop, stay. Give me Two. Two born weekend. Two born fifty miles from where Cara want. Three thousand fifty we walk to get there. Cara sad. Two born early. Not when Cara want. Two born quiet. Summer, like My, later. Two born li'l like My.

My sick. My need a doctor. Two tell him three times. Three scream, "My need a doctor, doctor, doctor." My hot like me. My need ice. Not cream like what Zero bring us before. My need cold. I am knowing. He take My. Three scream. Zero beg, beg, beg. "Don't take My!" Zero scared. Zero say, "Massa, Massa. Take me." Zero pray. Leave My. He say, "Easy. Take it eeee-ʑʑʑ-eeee." I am knowing. My come back. Again, My sick. Three times he take My and always east. I am knowing. My future. Three thousand miles. Plus fifty. I count. He take My again.

After My, he hungry. He take Zero. He take Two. He take Three. He take One. He take and take and take. We scream when he take My. Too many times. My is not dead. My is not Four. My is Five.

Sol shivered from the cold coming in full force into the back room. Despite the freezing temperature, the smell of the outside air consoled her. They would all be frostbitten even if they were found in time. She might not make it. But that was okay, she thought. As long as they got themselves out. She pulled the damp covers closer. Her fever had gotten worse and she still could not cough. She could barely think, but that too was all right. They'd find a way without her. She wasn't sure if she was hallucinating or remembering, but she felt like she knew everything that had happened to them before and since they'd been taken, stolen, borrowed, bowed, and broken by Lucien. She wanted to help them get out. She thought that her death would motivate them to summon their collective strength. She didn't mind. She didn't want to be taken out, burned, or buried, or even healed. She didn't want a life on this earth after all of this. She didn't even exist in America. There were no traces of her anywhere. No documentation to prove that she'd ever been born or existed before and certainly not after this, now. The same with My, except whatever identity Lucien had created for him.

Sol remembered the three times Lucien had taken My to the hospital. Lucien had clearly gotten a high from his trips with the ailing infant. Sol imagined the story he must have told at the hospital to explain how he'd brought in a newborn with no documentation. He must have enjoyed the attention he'd received at the hospital as the doting grandpa who'd brought his ailing grandson to the hospital instead of his crack-head daughter who'd dumped the baby on him. Sol had observed his fiending to make the second and third trips.

Against Cocoa's, Chiqui's, and Asante's tearful protests, he'd continued to steal My out of the back room regularly. Sol had not wasted her breath pleading. She would not give Lucien the pleasure of hearing her beg. Not even for My. He wouldn't have listened anyway.

Sol could tell that something was different every time Lucien brought My back. He had taken My outside a total of fourteen times in four years. Six times in the first year alone until he'd realized his own imprudence. Then four times in the second year. He hadn't been able to help himself in the third and fourth years when he'd taken My out twice each year, despite the boy's ability to speak.

My would bring back scratched toys from Lucien's garbage graveyard. Having been permitted a whiff of outside air, a crawl on raw ground and rough grass, My would bring back souvenirs every time. Sol had counted the mementos from each outing, separating them from the junk from the trips upstairs.

MY BRING things from outside. He take him to the park. I am knowing. He take him to swings, dirt, flowers. Outside summer. My birthday. My bring park inside. My bring leaf, earth, and rock. My bring ice cream on his fingers. One, Two, Three lick. We miss outside. Each time Zero, Two, and Three beg, "Take me!" They want outside more than My. He want My to be like him. He want My take. Count. Take. Count. My hold leaf in two not one hand. Gentle. Leaf break. Rock fall. Stick crack. He break My. My come back. My shake. My cry. My whisper, "No go! No go!" He take My again. Crunch, crack, purr. Cocoa stand by sweet box. My hear Cocoa sing "You'll be my American boy . . ." My stop cry. He make My spy. He whisper, "Count one to one hundred." He want My learn. Sing, read, write. Stalk, count, hunt, take.

She'd taken her turn caring for My, sharing the burden with Cocoa and Chiqui. She'd already known that, although Asante was the only one with any experience taking care of an infant, there was no use asking her. Sol had taken care of Chiqui when she was a baby. But she'd been uncomfortable with infants. Her sweet spots had been Chiqui's toddler and early-childhood years, when Cara had relinquished mothering entirely.

Sol hadn't tried to force Asante back into motherhood but allowed her to join in when My's hair grew long and thick, so untamed that she and the others had not known what to do with it. Sol had held him in her lap while Asante combed his hair. My had also sat in Cocoa's and Chiqui's laps. Concerned about the filth in the back room, they'd held him all the time. They had not carried him because there was nowhere to carry him to. None of them had wanted any part of him to touch the nasty ground. They'd finally put him down when he started kicking to use his legs.

Four years later, dying in the cold of the safe room in the middle of January, Sol was still trying to reconcile My's birth and life in a hell he had not asked for. She thought now, like she had then, that children are not meant to be born in the dark, never to see natural light for more than minutes at a time, never to know who is who except by their scent until they are passed into the arms of the one they recognize by touch and sound as mother. Babies are not meant to be carried until age three, never touching ground, then walking off-kilter, falling down more than moving. Babies are not meant to walk in single square rooms, never to run until they have all of their teeth, are speaking in full sentences, and know whom to call mother. Babies are not meant to be born in back rooms or basements, jail cells, the pits of ships. Maybe some babies are not meant to be born at all.

She had often watched My and questioned whether life was worth living regardless of the circumstances. Weren't there conditions under which it was okay not to allow a life? Weren't there some lives that needed snuffing out, out of mercy or punishment? What kinds of killings were permissible? At what stage in the developmental sequence or the cycle of evil was it okay to end it all, stop it from growing, from hurting? At what point could a person decide and not wait for some higher power to execute its divine plan? When and why? What were the conditions, possibilities, and permutations? Was it too much to ask for a fixed number of choices defined on the preset wedges of a spinning wheel?

Sol had often had to pull herself out of these dangerous thoughts. She'd heard Chiqui and Cocoa discussing the same in their own ways before and after My's birth. But she quickly shut them up because she didn't want the thoughts to start up again. The tragedy of being born in the back room had been obvious. Walking had been as hard for him as seeing, but a four-year-old who still wobbled when he walked had been more obviously challenged. My had never run in the backyard or hopped like a joey on a playground. His deficits had been glaring even to Lucien, who'd also carried the boy during their outings, fearing the concern that he would have drawn from strangers. Sol had known that My would call attention with his exaggerated knock-kneed stance, his slow, wobbly gait that was developmentally inappropriate for a three-, four-, or five-year-old, the frequent falling, his inability to run. She had hoped that some kind stranger would intervene and have the boy taken away from his odd grandfather.

My's trouble with walking had been evident. The progressing blindness, like his mother's and the other cellmates', had not been. His eyesight had been failing long before he could shout-whisper-gasp "No go! No go!" when being taken out of the back room. He'd been going blind even before he started returning to the prison with sunglasses purchased by "Grandpa." Sol had finally acknowledged My's near blindness while watching Chiqui attempt to teach him to read. She had assumed that his struggles had more to do with his age and learning by candlelight. She'd dismissed it, preferring to focus on his strengths as a source of hope in the darkness. She'd been able to tell that My's hearing was impeccable by his response to her humming, Cocoa's singing, and the music Lucien would pipe through the intercom's *crack, crunch,* stuttering static. She'd even seen My count time with the beats.

Even now, as she pulled her legs farther into her curled-up body, Sol could hear My tapping his feet. Cocoa was singing her apology to Asante for the earlier thrashing.

Sol perked up. Chiqui braced herself for Asante's retaliation for the beating Cocoa had dispensed. Asante hummed off-key while standing up to accept the sorry and join forces.

"We gonna get the hell up out of here!" Asante's fury was back.

Cocoa stood up to help. "We are not going to die in here. Not even *you*." She threw her voice over her shoulder to Sol. She had returned to her own normal.

"This fire must have done some damage to this hellhole. It has gotten too cold in here. There's no more food. Not even them muthafuckin' sardines. The damned water is gone! Only a few candles left. I don't even know if this goddamned lighter is going to flick on again."

"I'm going to sing." Cocoa turned to Asante. "You listen for where I fade out. That's where the cracks are."

Asante walked along the walls with her ears primed for sound.

"Hand me a candle, please," Cocoa said with her usual politeness.

"You don't need light to hear," Asante said with residual antagonism and mistrust in her voice.

"Just give me a dag-gone candle!" Cocoa struck back.

Chiqui plopped My on the ground and stood up. "Here. Here!"

"Thank! You!" Cocoa shouted at Asante to make her point, but nodded politely at Chiqui.

"You're going to try to burn the place down again?" Asante squinted.

"Just shut up and sing!" Chiqui's irritability pierced her diplomacy.

"Any special requests?" Cocoa rolled her eyes in the dark.

"Can you rap?" Asante quipped.

Cocoa sighed. "Old school or new school?"

"What you think?"

"Okay then. Tupac."

"Who the fuck is that?"

"Tupac Shakur!"

"I only know one Shakur and she's in Cuba as far as I remember."

"Come on. You haven't been in here that long."

"How the hell are you going to tell me how long I've been in here?! And I wasn't listening to that new-school shit back then. Even if I was, I wouldn't remember."

Cocoa rattled off the artists she used to listen to. "You don't know Nas, OutKast. You definitely don't know Wyclef. Even if you had been out by then, you don't speak any Creole."

"You mean *Kre-yôl*," Asante enunciated with the proper accent.

"Fine! What do you want to hear, then?"

"Eric B. and Rakim?"

"It's just Rakim now."

"Now? Do you even know what year it is? Do any of us? Now? This little girl said 'now'!" Asante doubled over as if she were laughing. She was not. She kept Cocoa talking so she could find the cracks in the walls. She listened more closely when she got to the corners.

"Uh. Uh. Uh." Cocoa gave herself a head start and warmed up her rapping voice. "Check it. Check it. *It's been a long time. I shouldna left you* . . ." Cocoa rapped the lyrics she could remember and mumbled the words she didn't know, then skipped to the end of the song.

Asante filled in the rest and together they finished the song: *"Soul, soul. You got it."*

"Give me another one!" Asante was hyped.

Cocoa leaned into the next lyrics, maintaining a hypnotic rhythm that transported her the way only music could.

Asante was so excited she didn't let Cocoa finish. "I did not know you could do that."

"I can do a li'l sumpin'-sumpin'. Almost anything with my voice."

"Lemme find out you can beatbox."

"I could learn. I can't believe you've never heard Foxy Brown, Nicki Minaj, Lauryn Hill!"

"Lauryn who?"

"From the Fugees! Shit. You've been here that long! Miss Hill!"

"Nope. Just Miss Jackson."

"If you're nasty!" they said in unison.

Sol felt My tremble forcefully. It reminded her of the way he had been after every outing with Lucien. She did not have the strength to ask Cocoa and Asante to keep it down. She just started shivering, her teeth chattering with empathy for the boy. This got Chiqui's attention.

"Chill," Chiqui admonished. "We need to get these two warmed up."

"We can't build a bonfire!" Asante said, reminding them that choking was a horrible way to die.

"Then they're not going to make it." Chiqui shrugged.

"We're all going to make it!" Cocoa threw her body into the declaration. She started singing. *"When I was seventeen, I did what people told me."* She dropped the tune and transitioned to My's comfort song: *"You'll be my . . ."*

Cocoa lifted My up and crooned into his ears. "I'mma warm you up, baby." She cried the next song into the top of My's head: *"Forever mine, ever mine, ever . . ."* She could feel tears obstructing the song's flow in her throat. "That's the last song I heard before that joker made me come in here."

"I got it!" Chiqui crouched closer to hear better.

"Show me what you got, then!" Asante sang.

"No, I found the spot! Right here." Chiqui stood up and pointed to the crack. "I've been paying attention while you two were doing your MTV thing."

"Light it up right here." Asante gestured.

"We got any of those sticks left?" Cocoa reminded Chiqui of My's souvenirs from the outside.

"And rocks."

Sol did not rejoice over the cracks in the walls the way the others did. She wasn't afraid to hope. She just knew that there was much more to be done to get out. They needed more than singing to make themselves heard. They had no sledgehammers or drills to penetrate the stone and steel. Any fire they might build would kill them all before the smoke could be seen by anyone outside. She thought that their best chance would be to ambush Lucien when he came to release or slaughter them. Although she would be too weak to join in the fight, Chiqui, Cocoa, and Asante were hopeful, excited, and fearless enough to take him down. The idea that this might be their last chance had pushed their rage to the surface and it was as strong as it had been when each of them had first been taken. Sol could not feel anger, not while dying. She'd decided on empathy for Lucien to explain his evil to herself in the hopes of getting into his mind to overthrow him.

Sol had come to a certain understanding that she and Lucien were more alike than anyone would ever believe. Although she'd never learned anything about his life before his immigration to America, she believed that he'd gone through something that had turned him.

She knew little of her own origins. She couldn't even name the place she'd come from. She knew that it was somewhere on the Yucatán Peninsula—Mexico? Belize? Guatemala? Some mystical place where the boundaries of three countries came together then fanned out like sunrays. She did not need to understand her beginnings to understand herself. She was timeless. The body she'd been in since birth was just a vessel. That people thought that all she was was only her body, including and especially Lucien, was the joke she did not laugh at. It had offered her no protection, not even from the elements. It did not shield her from inside hurt. It had no special abilities. She could see the shell in the dark. She'd examined it many times while Lucien had showered and touched her. It was the color of roasted cashews. It had a round face, large almond eyes, a broad nose, and thick sucking lips. It was uncharacteristically African given the place where it had been created. She had never met her father, so the question of paternity had floated in and out but left no evidence of its importance. Cara and this man had given her the name Solange, which also did not fit the place where the vessel was formed. Besides the giver of her name, Cara had told her to watch.

"What I do with a man you will have to do too so we can make it. Never mind where. Here and how are what matter. Whatever he wants, you give."

"I want the little one too," a man said, climbing off of Cara.

Sol felt her mother snatch her up so abruptly that it felt like flying. She winced when Cara pinned her wrists down as if nailing her to a cross as a sacrifice to the man. Sol wriggled out of Cara's hold and discovered that she could save herself. She told the body to fight. She instructed it to wiggle and kick. She made it scream. She told it to take bloody bites out of the stubbled cheek. She told her legs to run. She told them to run faster. She whispered in its ears and entered its head. Her body absorbed the voice, swallowed the guiding force, and went where she needed to go.

She found a hiding place in a riverbed that had just enough water to keep her body out of sight. Her body and mind were scared, not ready to lie down again or ever. They heeded her instructions. She told her body to lie still. She told her head to stay underwater. Her mind did not question the water or her body's place in it. She felt the river take her in. She let go and took pleasure in how it closed over her, how its ripples stilled themselves, allowing its surface to turn to glass. She told her lungs when to breathe and not to. At no point did she flee into her imagination. She questioned nothing, not the stillness of her body, not the peace of a painless drowning. Water did not question its wetness.

When Cara had finally found her, Sol had accepted the belt strap on her wet skin. She listened to her mother's wails about the missed ride with the first in what would be a line of *coyotajes*. Sol told her tear ducts not to produce salt water. She told her pulse not to beat fast. She told her heart not to hate or love her mother. After the whipping, she commanded her body to heal and told her hurt feelings to do the same. The whipping primed her body for the journey. But her acceptance prepared her to take her mother's place.

On the last leg of their trek from the intersection of three countries to the jagged border between two, Sol had felt sorry for Cara's resentful body that was still healing from the birth. It had been premature, not because the baby had come before forty weeks, but because she'd been born on the wrong side of the damned desert. Finally, to get them to the other side, Sol gave her six-year-old body to the last *coyotaje* fifty miles from the Arizona border. She did not wonder what else the beating and the rape of her body were preparing her for. She took both in like water.

SOL FELT the room grow colder. She felt the temperature drop even more when she thought about Cara and the things she'd made her do as means of survival before and after arriving in America. But Sol needed to understand how she'd come to be in this place, dying on the filthy dirt floor in the back room of a basement. She lanced her memory as if breaking the skin of a putrid wound and watched it ooze incessantly, unstoppable until it carried her to the safe room.

It had all started on the off-ramp of a highway where planes flew low enough to make the sky seem touchable. Sol had known that it had been wrong of Cara to drag a sleeping baby to sell fruit and flowers under the overpass of North Conduit. But there had been no other choice on the weekends. She and Cara had been the only ones who'd even known that there'd been a baby asleep in the padded crate that lay inside of the stolen supermarket shopping cart. Sol's presence boosted sales until she grew nearly as tall as her mother. She no longer had the stature of a child, and none of their customers, except Lucien, appreciated the tallish little girl for being just that. A year later, she was both old and big enough to stay at home alone with the toddler. She was an ideal caregiver, too calm and levelheaded to ever scream or lose her temper with her little sister. Not yet an adolescent, Sol was becoming a better mother than her own. She even chose the babysitter on the busy days when Cara needed her on the roadside. She went out to sell with her mother only on holidays, which meant that she was always with Cara on Mother's Day.

That is where Sol had first encountered Lucien. She didn't know then that, every time he'd stopped to buy fruit, flowers, and water he didn't need, he'd offered her candy to test her mother's vigilance and also to learn what would best serve as a lure. Sol had obliged him by reaching into his van with hands too small for her body to give him his change every time. She was too young to know that he was testing her, trying to see if she would hold the money tightly, hand it over reluctantly, or look at him with pleading eyes. Had she known, she would have thrown the coins in his face to take out one or both of his eyes. But she was ten, eleven, twelve, then fifteen, and despite her time in the desert, she had not learned distrust.

Sol had never been kissed and was still a virgin when Lucien had lured her into his van. She had grown six inches in two years and developed a false sense of invincibility because of her height. It had gotten her closer to the sky. But her breasts and her constant checking to make sure her unwanted gift had not spontaneously arrived forced her to look down more than up. It was this distraction that sealed her decision to get into Lucien's van. Soaking wet from her sky's downpour, fearing that a pink puddle might form around her white sneakers, she climbed in and disappeared. Had she not taken such pride in and derived such power from her height, had she not been forced into an adolescent identification with her hips, breasts, backside, and a fear of her flow, she would have never fallen prey to an offer of a ride. She had never taken one before. She'd ducked her head to keep from hitting the vanity mirror. She'd swallowed to suppress the sickness in the pit of her stomach and allowed her overconfidence to rise. She'd told herself that whatever the danger, she would be able to overcome it.

She'd held to this even in the back room. Even when Lucien tried to tempt her tears by withholding sugar. Even when he flooded the basement with music trying to figure out the genre that moved her. She loved all the sounds that he piped through the intercom. She held her breath to keep from humming to the a cappella vocals of the folk songs that reminded her of how her fellow migrants had sung to her during her south-to-north trek. She almost broke down with the flute and guitar of norteño subway artists. A crack approximating a smile ran across her face when he'd brought Cocoa to the back room with her tortuously gorgeous voice. But no music could silence her guilt for being the reason he'd taken Chiqui. She wouldn't let him see her agony as he recounted the things he had done and would do to her sister. As much as she wanted to rip his head off with her bitten-down fingers, she bit her bottom lip and drew a thin red line of spit. She knew that, although he could watch all manner of sadistic porn, he could not stand the sight of blood.

SOL SAT up on the layers of damp and dirty sheets. She looked at Chiqui huddled with Cocoa and Asante, scratching at the dirt and stone. They were beyond the point of waiting to be rescued. They figured that Lucien would kill them all before setting them free. After so many years, after feeling the seeping wind and the smell of snow that signaled their last hope, they preferred a death from trying to passivity. The fire they were building would be either a saving grace or a funeral pyre. Either was better than doing nothing.

LA KAY

La Kay curled Itself up like a fetus. It could feel Its roof being
torn off. It wanted to scream, but It knew that the worst was yet
to come. It was now unsure of Its desire to die. It braced Itself
as the crew tore into Its top floor. It curled into Itself tighter—
Its head burrowed into Its chest to hide the tears on Its face, Its
knees drawn into Its abdomen. The unbearable pain made It
weep quietly but convulsively, Its shoulders reverberating the
violent ache in Its chest. It definitively decided that It no longer
wanted to die. It just wanted the pain to stop. It felt the peeling
of Its skin as Its aluminum siding and the foam and fiber insulation were being ripped off.

It felt a little bit of relief when the backhoe scooped out decades of Lucien's junk. It could feel the excavation of souvenirs
from Lucien's twilight pickups from the street-side trash from
well-to-do New Jersey neighborhoods. On the exposed main
floor, It felt the weight of Marie-Ange's stove, which stood staring defiantly at the workmen, reminding them to shut off the
gas from its source before digging down into the boiler room.
It could have blown Itself and them into pieces as delicate as
snowflakes, but It had a final mission to complete. It hugged
Itself to keep Its invaluable bowels from being gutted. It knew

that It would have to surrender Its shell to save Its core and the survivors in Its back room. It let go of Its pain-ridden exterior and held on to the parts of Itself that It started to realize were true and timeless—Its spirit, Its heart, and Its mind—that It would have to employ to outmaneuver the demolition team. It knew that It could not remain intact and also release the prisoners Lucien had locked up in Its back room for decades. It resigned Itself to Its own death to save lives.

It was old, older than Lucien. They'd been born the same month and the same day years apart. It had wanted them to die together too. It had to keep him away from his son to keep him from harming the boy. A tower of TVs had already fallen on top of the child, leaving him bruised but with no broken limbs. Worse yet, Lucien had been trying to turn the boy into his replica. He had already reopened his peepholes that La Kay had sealed up and made defunct years before. He had shown the boy how to spy with stealth, how to count the fingers, toes, limbs, eyes, and breasts of future victims. He had introduced the child to the sweet box from which a beautiful voice had emerged. La Kay now realized that that voice had been coming from the back room, not some miraculously repaired stereo from Lucien's junk pile. It had missed so many clues about the women imprisoned in the bomb shelter that It had scarcely known existed.

La Kay tried to peek into the safe room, but It could not open the door. It tried to break one of the walls with a heavy kick, but it would not give. It decided to shake Its body in the hope of dislodging part of Its foundation. It felt a fault open, and then the seam that joined two walls cracked enough for a cold breeze to pass through. It wanted to vomit from the smell seeping out of the place. It still could not see who or how many were inside. It was hopeful that with a few strong quivers It might split the walls open. But It had to be cautious not to bring down the second floor on top of them. It remained still for a while to feel any movement that It could. It breathed deeply and felt Its chest loosen with the knowledge that It would not die in vain.

It listened closely, but It did not count the number of voices, the hands and feet touching the dirt floor. It did not want to be like him. It would not eavesdrop. It had already let them know that It was alive and willing to help. It had created an aperture for them to work through to save themselves. It remained still so It could feel their activity to determine how else It could help. They were quiet except for the little boy, who torturously counted to one hundred in whispered tones. La Kay became frightened because he reminded It of Lucien. It shook a little to get the child to stop. No one could bear the counting.

A whisper colder than the outside air ran through It and It knew the women heard and felt it too. As cold as the ice crystals dripping from the tips of tree branches, as thin as cotton stretched between delicate fingers, the breath spoke: *I am nothing.*

eight

help remembering La Belle as his first love, if he had ever felt love.

Desperate for maternal affection, he'd followed her commands and stood guard at her door as she'd entertained the husbands of neighborhood wives. He'd waited as she'd bedded a few male in-laws. When he'd get tired of looking out for angry wives who never showed up, he'd peek to see the goings-on in the room. He'd told himself that he was just examining the figurines in the curio that had been directly in his line of sight. In fact, he'd been watching the awkward movements of middle-aged lovers twisting themselves into failed acrobatics.

He'd always felt as if she'd known that he'd been watching. He'd interpreted her reprimands for stroking her porcelain Lladrós as admonishment for his voyeurism. But he'd also felt that she'd excused his inevitable leering because she had placed him in a position of keeping watch. He had been trained.

As he'd entered double-digit ages, La Belle had started closing her doors completely to show him that she no longer required his services. He hadn't known where to go after that. He'd been curious about the small watering hole in town that he'd passed after school. He'd seen genuinely beautiful women of every age calling forth suitors. He'd endeared himself to a few of them and ran errands when they were indisposed. In exchange, they'd allowed him to watch them undress themselves and their suitors, about whom they would make jokes later. He'd found his place at Bar Caimite.

Absent the early intimacy with La Belle, he'd sought out women who might coddle, even stroke him with quasi-maternal adoration. He'd been the perfect specimen, a true *pouchon* with his mulatto looks and new gait that was evolving from childlike to manly with every minute he spent at Caimite. There he'd learned that watching was more gratifying than performing and that directing the movements of women aroused him more than sex itself. Soon his favorite worker, a woman who'd fre-

LUCIEN

―――――――――

Lucien's legs took their time thawing out as if his very blood had congealed inside. He was accustomed to paralysis, but not of this sort. He didn't want to look at his feet. He just wanted them to move on his command. He looked around the room and saw that the bed across from his was now occupied. He knew that he had to keep from waking the man or alerting the slow but watchful and willing nurses. He was grateful that his claw was still functional. It always did its job. He used it to poke the buttons on the remote to turn on the television. The volume was already turned down close to mute. Static flickered on the old set as he changed the channels to see just how deeply his neighbor was sleeping. His neighbor did not stir. He tried to divine how old the man was. He was in his sixties himself, but still agile even with partially functional limbs.

He had been frozen before, long before the strokes, long before coming to America. He'd believed that he'd recovered from his first paralysis as a youngster. He hadn't even had his aunt La Belle to rub his legs back to life, to scream him out of a reverie, to direct his steps. He had managed all on his own with no guidance from caring adults. Despite that, he still couldn't

quently allowed him to watch, asked if he wanted to join her for a bath. He'd willingly accepted the offer and filled the tub. He'd climbed in with her, trying to avoid her toes that searched him out under the water. He rose from the water, turning away from her stare. Naked and nervous, he waited for her to finish. As he dried himself, he caught a glimpse of someone watching him through a crack in the door.

Lucien lowered his eyes as a shirtless figure crept into the room. He fixed his eyes on the man's crisply pressed khaki pants, the ones he'd seen on the soldiers who frequented the bar. A similar gun was holstered in the man's belt loop. He did not want to look above the waist at the man's bare chest, let alone meet his eyes. His heartbeat threatened to break through his rib cage. To calm himself he counted the toes on the soldier's bare feet. He counted the fingers on each hand that hung below the man's pant pockets. When he felt the oiled fingers of his hostess on his shoulders, he counted those too. But limbs and digits were finite, so he counted every beat of his heart. He didn't stop counting even when he felt himself being pushed toward the soldier. He told himself not to look up at the man, to focus on his gun, to watch where his hands went.

Although time had frozen as stiff as his immovable legs, his heartbeat had not. He had reached the limits of his fear. There was no fight, no flight. He closed his eyes and saw a glass wall. He saw two possibilities: madness or death. He would not allow himself to be pushed to either irreversible option. He pressed his nose against the transparent wall and saw his own image staring back at him. He stood toe-to-toe with his reflection. He saw himself mad. He saw himself dead. Tears ran down his face and then abruptly retreated into his closed eyes. He opened them and made the choice to become what he feared.

Lucien lunged for the soldier's gun and managed to wrestle it out of its holster. He heard the soldier laugh. But he wasn't deterred. Without a word, Lucien pointed the gun at the man, gesturing for him to move to the bed. The slippery woman followed without being told.

He'd turned the table on the couple and forced them to stare at their own reflections, their own madness, their own deaths. He did not know how or when he'd learned to handle a gun, but his grasp convinced him that he could pull the trigger and shoot them with ease. Aroused by their fear, he stood stiff as they collapsed onto the sheets. He felt himself become the monster they had made.

Lucien's fear had calcified into an incomprehensible evil. He tried to keep his newly made victims from reading his remaining discomfort with his new self. Like a small child, he closed his eyes to make himself invisible, as if he could turn into a spirit before them. He searched inside himself and did not recognize any of the thoughts or feelings there. He could not reach his true self, an entity he had never really known, awaiting its death. He became nothing. Just a body subject to occupation by whatever survivalist spirit wanted to take over the pretty boy standing in a room that reeked of sex and terror. When he'd finally spoken, his voice had transformed from the shakiness of a boy into that of a hoarse man. He was possessed.

LUCIEN WOULD have never found the words to explain how his fear had crystalized into wickedness. He had never acquired the language to explain that his fear had reached the interior limit before madness, before death. He could not unveil the sculpture carved by hands so full of terror they no longer knew how to hold or hug or hope. He'd become a statue come alive with the ghost of an inexplicable malevolence. Fear had killed the hopeful soul of the child he had been. It was that child's stolen breath that snuck out as a poison mist to lay waste to the souls of future victims. How could he explain what he'd never acknowledged? How could he examine what he'd never allowed himself to know? How could he tell anyone when, where, why, or how he'd learned to watch, stalk, hunt, and seize? How he managed to mirror the pain of others to lull them into the belief that he was an empathic being? Who could he have told? Certainly not Marie-Ange. Leona? Never. Dieuseul? He'd been too far gone by then to have a true friend.

Lucien swallowed secrets like saliva. He was still crying as he tried to lift limbs that would not listen to his commands.

I don't know why or what I remember from back then in Caimite. The tears stop when I think of my place. And then my house. I am like fire; I am nothing until I am. Difé. *And I am crying again.*

Lucien wiped his face and shrugged off the memories to focus on his impossible plan. He struggled to untie the hospital gown with his functional claw. He nearly fell trying to reach the drawer where his clothes were stored. He dressed himself the only way he could, slowly, painfully, laboriously. He kept the pliant but functional hospital slippers on his feet. He pulled himself up on the three-footed cane at his bedside. Most of his journey would be indoors. He would need to wait outside only long enough to get a taxi. He was too numb to feel the cold.

He was grateful that the halls were empty. He counted every belabored step to the elevator and then each footfall to the sliding glass doors. He counted every second until a taxi came. He counted the coins in his pocket. He counted the eight single dollar bills that he paid the driver. He counted his keys to find the right one to open his van. He counted the stuttering of the failing engine. He counted the number of times he pressed on the gas pedal to egg it on. He turned the heat on as high as it would go. He switched on the radio and was comforted by the sound of static. He tuned it to the only station he ever listened to since age fifty, 1010 WINS. Then he slumped down to rest. It was only minutes before he bolted straight up in his seat.

Lucien heard his name mispronounced by the newscaster. He decided that he wanted to go home. Not the house where he'd lived with Marie-Ange and reared his daughters. Not the home where he'd imprisoned four, sometimes five women and his own son across two decades. Not there. He wanted to go to his real home. *Home* home. Back home. The place he had not been since 1975, when he'd reveled at the sight of his set of four girls for the first time—Marie-Ange, his first and favorite, Veille, and his newborn matching pair, Clair and Dor.

He formed his delusional plan. He would go to the airport. Never mind that he had no plane ticket. He would drive up and down the ramps. He knew just where, having driven his cab through the airport for decades. Never mind a passport. He would crash through the fence. Never mind that this was sixteen years after 9/11. He would make it. Van versus chain-link fence. Van wins. He would drive right onto the tarmac. He would get on a plane. Never mind which. He would go to Port au Prince. He would walk to Bar Caimite. Never mind that it had been closed since 1980. He would make his journey. Never mind that it was impossible. Never mind that he'd get shot before he made it onto the tarmac at JFK. Never mind that he would be crushed to death under the wheels of a landing plane, if by some miracle he made it past the counterterrorism firing squad. He would make it home. Somehow.

SOL

Sol listened as the others crawled around searching for anything dry enough to start and sustain a fire. The outside air seeped in, dampening every scrap of filthy bedding. Even the gifts of twigs My had brought back from his outings with Lucien strained to snap. She could hear sticks cracking and splintering between frostbitten fingers. She dug her own into the dirt beneath her and pushed her body into the farthest corner to make room for the work. She heard a few empty votives fall over and, soon after, felt them touch a part of her back that the torn sheets could never cover. Although she knew the answer, she still wondered why she had not made better use of the weapons in the room to wound or cripple Lucien.

She had scalded him with hot candle wax on more than one occasion before he'd brought Chiqui to keep her in check. She'd cracked the faces of many of the Virgin Marys and stabbed him with shards. But her injurious deeds and words had cost her and the others. They'd all paid with bruises from deep pinches that he'd later counted. She'd paid with hair grabs, twisted wrists, and extended trips to the rape room. He'd stopped only when he had been sure that she'd learned the lessons he'd tried to drill into her mind. After his stroke, he'd armed himself with a fire poker and his loaded pistol. Even when he'd only been able to stroke the goose bumps on her bare arm, to pull his claw through her hair, to lick his good fingers and run them across her bruised, trembling lips, the threat of worse had throbbed. She'd squeezed shut her eyes that no longer cried. She'd tamed her aggression and crept around the rim of his temper like a spoon scooping the edges of hot porridge.

She thought that, if he came now, she would find the strength to scuttle to the door, attack his Achilles tendons with a single slice and bring him to his knees. Except for the crawling, it would not be hard to bring him down. The others could manage. Fueled by years of rage, she would take the chance. Especially now. Even she was rediscovering her will to live inside of her weakened body. She was reimagining ways to overcome him and more so to do what he had done to her.

She saw the pile of rags in the corner. The others had finished building their pyre and had been striking matches that would not ignite. She heard the clicking of defunct lighters that had run dry of fuel. She heard their voices but didn't assign them to anyone in particular.

"Put a stick in the candle."

"What if it goes out? We won't be able to see."

"What if it doesn't?"

"Just go do it."

"Be careful!"

"Just put the fucking stick in the goddamned flame already!"

She heard their collective sigh and saw the room light up a little brighter.

"These rags had better catch."

"Cocoa already told us that she ain't dying in here."

"Damn right!"

She heard their coughing before the smoke reached her.

"Make sure you cover up his mouth and his nose!"

"Bring him to me," Sol found the strength to whisper. "Bring him here."

"Look who's alive."

"Never die."

Sol could remember saying those words only one other time in her life. It was after she'd given birth to My.

I am not dead. I am not dying. I am One. Inside I hear two beats. They both mine. Heart in heart. I feel pain. I cry. I retch. I don't want to. I can't. Push! Stand! I crawl. I am the crying. I am the retching, groaning, growling. I roar. Rest. Breathe. Breathe! Make him breathe, Zero. Cut, suck. Water. Blood. I am wet. Suck. "Again! Please, make him breathe!" I beg. Never die. I beg and beg God. Make him breathe for me. He is crying. He is clean in my arms. I am wet. I am bleeding. I say to me, "Never die." I am not One. Now I am two.

LA KAY

La Kay panted then gasped. On Its tongue, the very air tasted like salt, like love, like light, like blood. It took a deep breath and sat up and out of Its own dream only to realize that they had truly left. At once happy and lonely, It lay longing, silence sliding down Its molten walls. Only Its front steps remained erect. A row of brick teeth with slivers of cement in the gaps. A shit-stained smile of dirty dentures to be spat out by a final cough.

La Kay separated Itself from the body in which It had been housed for more than seventy years. It circled overhead observing closely, as police, firefighters, and construction workers held back news crews that had gathered to report an unfolding drama. It had neither wanted nor expected Its demise to be broadcast across the city and then on national and global television and radio stations. But there It was, a hacked-apart mess in the foreground of video and still camera shots. It could only take comfort that It was not and had never been the corporeal collection of walls, rooms, and hallways that everyone believed It to be. It was so much more—a spirit with the largesse to help Its involuntary inhabitants save themselves. It had also surrendered any remnants of fear to liberate Its own soul. It had earned

Its place in the open air, above the clamor of stories breaking over unbreakable spirits.

Before rising into the clouds, It looked down proudly. It had done Its job, finally. It had murdered the place where Its owner's evil had thrived for decades. Now Its exterior was about to become infamous for keeping his secrets for so long. Its spirit hovered over the colony of news crews gathered to report the tragedy that was also Its triumph.

> "Breaking news this morning, ladies and gentlemen. We're live in South Ozone Park, Queens, on 123rd Street just off of Rockaway Boulevard, where fire department and construction crews are working to get to an unknown number of people who are trapped in the basement of the house behind me. As you can see, the house was in the process of being torn down. On Sunday, this house was nearly gutted by a three-alarm blaze. The recent snowstorm halted the demolition work that resumed just yesterday. Today, just before dawn, an attentive member of the demolition crew saw smoke coming from a large drainage pipe in the basement. When he came closer, he heard screams for help. We don't know how many people are in there, who they are, how they survived, or if there are any casualties. What we do know is that they've been trapped in this basement for days. There is no news on the whereabouts of the owner of the house."

Lanfè!

> "First responders are working cautiously but quickly to pull the house apart without disturbing the foun-

dation. The house is at serious risk of collapse because of the work that had already started after the
fire that ripped through here last Sunday. Fortunately, the weather is warmer than the single-digit
temperatures we had two days ago. It is forty-one
degrees now, which is making this very delicate op-
eration much more bearable for the crew working
to free the people in the basement.

"We'll continue to bring you the latest on this
developing story."

Lanfè!

"Breaking news . . . ABC was the first on the scene
this morning, watching what has turned out to
be just a shocking story. Just a few moments ago,
four women and a young boy were pulled from the
basement of this house."

*One, two, three, four, five stretchers. Sheets and blankets cover
heads. Four waiting ambulances so Sol could ride with My.*

"Their conditions are unknown, but we've been told
that they looked emaciated and sooty, as would be
expected after several days in the basement of this
house that nearly burned to the ground. A demolition crew had been working to tear down the house
earlier this morning when they heard sounds coming from a pipe . . . I don't know if you can see the
corner of the house behind me where the pipe was
removed. They pulled five people out of the basement, including, I was just told, a little boy who
looks to be about three or four years old. Again,

four women and a young boy have just been rescued from a house in South Ozone Park, Queens.
They are alive. They are safe. We still don't know
who they are or how they survived.

"We've been told that the owner of the house
is at Jamaica Hospital, just a few miles from here.
He's recovering from an unknown illness. Authorities have not been able to speak to him about the
developments at his house.

"We'll continue to bring you more information as
we receive it."

LA KAY was proud that It had finally done something good.
It had managed to save a few of the generations of lives that had
been entombed in terror, terrible self-blame, unearned shame,
and, most of all, violence so extreme it had eaten them from the
outside in and back again. It finally loved Itself and indulged in
remembrances of laughter and the smell of savory cooked food,
the heat of forgivable loving arguments, the callouses scrubbed
smooth on the bottoms of hardworking feet that had borne the
weight of factory laborers, housekeepers, nannies, and other
stand-up immigrants. It now loved the other houses too, watching them mourn and envy Its end. Hoping to someday expose
their truths and save even one life struggling to breathe.

La Kay's shell lay gutted and splintered like a child's Pop-
sicle stick structure that had been stepped on by raging giants.
As It looked down, It wondered if anyone would mourn It or
find a reason to keep the memory of La Kay alive.

*One room. One, two, three, four hospital beds so Sol can lie
next to My.*

"This story keeps getting more and more shocking, bizarre, and tragic. We just learned that the four women and the little boy who were rescued earlier this afternoon had been held captive in the back room of this basement for as long as twenty years. They allege that the owner of the house behind me had kidnapped and held them against their will. Neighbors are shocked that the man some of them have known for nearly forty years could have committed such a horrible crime. The whereabouts of Lucien Louverture this evening are unknown."

"This is CNN. Another in a long line of tragic stories of abduction and decades of captivity in a house in one of New York's largest boroughs. We're here at a house in South Ozone Park, Queens, where four women and a little boy were rescued earlier this morning from the basement of a house that was about to be demolished. How many more times does this have to happen in this country and around the world? How do we make sense of the evil?

"The owner of this house had held one of the women for over twenty years. She and the others, including a four-year-old boy, are recovering at various hospitals throughout the city. Obviously, their long road to recovery will include both physical and psychological care. Some of their families have been notified. No news yet if the boy was born in the basement or abducted more recently, but investigators are trying to learn as much as they can from these very fragile victims . . ."

Lanfè!

"The owner of the house left Jamaica Hospital in the early hours of the morning as this story was unfolding. His whereabouts are unknown. Police have undertaken a massive search. Neighbors say that he could not have gotten far since he has difficulty walking after a stroke that left him partially debilitated."

Lanfè!

"Police are said to be questioning the homeowner's girlfriend, Leona LaMerci, to ascertain his whereabouts. She was found at her home with a former tenant of the house of horrors, Dieuseul François. The tenant is said to have been in possession of the taxicab belonging to the alleged culprit in these crimes. Both the girlfriend and the tenant are in police custody. Although there is no evidence that they had any involvement in the crimes, they are being held for questioning to determine their knowledge of or what part they may have played in the abduction and imprisonment of the victims."

One, two, three, four leave the hospital. Zero is dead.

"This just in. We've learned that one of the women, Asante, whose last name we have yet to learn, has died in the hospital. We do not know the cause of death. Such a tragedy."

"As the days go by, we're learning more and more about this tragedy in Queens, New York, where four women and a little boy were held captive for as long as twenty years. Like many parts of the city, the neighborhood is a predominantly immigrant enclave of working- and professional-class homeowners who came here to make a better life for themselves and their children. Those who've lived on this street for many years are shocked to learn that one of their own could have been masking such evil and insanity. The man appears to have been bold enough to abduct a young girl on his own block. One of the women lived just seven houses down from where she was kept. A very focused search was undertaken in 2010 to find Colette 'Cocoa' Jean-Baptiste. We're told that her abductor had even joined the search and put up some of the reward money. Her family will make a statement in the next few hours."

One, Two, and My. Only Three is happy. Family hugs, tears, more embraces, whispered "I loved you's," "I've missed you's," "I thought we'd lost you's." Only Three can sing joy.

"A bright spot in this story about the house of horrors. Colette 'Cocoa' Jean-Baptiste is home with her family. They will soon be moving to Los Angeles, California, where Cocoa will launch her singing career. She has been signed by an as yet undisclosed music mogul and performer. We can only speculate who this might be. Such wonderful news coming after a week of learning about the unimaginably shocking and terrifying ordeal."

"We're standing by to hear from the attorney representing the three daughters of Lucien Louver-

separated from their families. As the fate of a little boy and his family hangs in the balance, supporters from the nation's premier advocacy groups have already announced that they will lobby for asylum on behalf of the two women."

And then only three. One, Two, and My to count.

Lanfè!

ture. They are said to be living outside of the New York metro area—three successful career women with families of their own. Let's listen."

"On behalf of the three women who refuse to refer to themselves as the 'daughters' of Lucien Louverture, I am asking the media to respect their privacy. They are as shocked and devastated by what they've recently learned about the abductions and horrors in what was once their childhood home. They have been estranged from the alleged culprit for decades and have no idea of his whereabouts. They are cooperating with law enforcement officials in their search for the man. Like everyone, they want justice for the victims. Thank you."

"Authorities are having difficulty locating the family of two of the women who were rescued a week ago after being held captive for over a decade in a house in South Ozone Park, Queens. We are told that they may have come here from Mexico illegally.

"They'd been abducted as teenagers. We've learned that their mother had languished in a U.S. detention center for years and had been deported over a decade ago. While such actions are not new, deportations have increased at a feverish pace under our nation's new administration. To date over 460 parents, mostly from California, have been deported without their children by ICE officials. That figure does not include the scores of undocumented parents throughout the rest of the United States who have been detained by ICE,

SOL

———————

Sol sat alone on a steel bench in the detention center that had been carved out of a women's federal correctional facility. She did not know exactly where she was except that she was no longer *there*. This place was not far off from where she'd been kept for what she now knew had been sixteen years. She wasn't happy. Relieved, yes. She felt the healing on its way like a far-off mare slowly trotting toward her. She was still imprisoned, just behind cleaner walls, under brighter lights, with less unkind jailers holding her hostage. She bit down on her lip waiting for them to bring My to her. As much as she wanted to be with him, she didn't want him to live in this place either. He had earned his right to live free on the outside that was also on the inside of America. He had been born in the country's dirt, not merely on its soil. Even if they sent her back to a distant and frightening unknown, he, at least, deserved freedom outside these walls. She heard her name being called and stood up quickly, hoping that she would see him finally.

I am not One. I am not Zero, Two, Three, or Four. I am Sol.

Solange is what Cara called me. No last name. I do not remember, or I do not know my father or his name.

"Solange! Solange!" I hear the agent yell as if I am not sitting there close by, alone. "Come with me."

I follow. I don't dare ask a question. I stand at a counter, my face staring at the face of another agent.

"Name?"

"Mine or his?"

"His." She doesn't look down when she types.

"My." I cannot see the screen.

"What kind of name is that?"

I shrug.

"Is it M-y?"

I don't answer. He is My. Because of Two and Three. I mean, Chiqui and Cocoa. They thought he would be a girl. They agreed on Marisol. For a boy they agreed on Mar-y-Sol. I only asked why there, why then.

"Miss? Miss? Is it M-y?" *Under her breath I hear her say,* "Only white people give their kids names like that."

I say, "No matter."

"Last name?"

"I don't know."

"There has to be a last name."

I say, "You like 'Smith'? You want 'Smith'?"

She writes. Again, she barely whispers and shrugs her shoulders.

I hear her eyes say, You barely look twenty. *Her mouth says,* "Is this your real age? Thirty-one?"

I say again, "I don't know."

Her eyes say, "You had him when you were sixteen." She counts wrong.

I say, "Thirty, more or less, not twenty."

I hear her eyes roll. I see her say something I can't hear.

She has no idea. I do not tell her where I have been. She wants to know only where I came from, so they can send me back.

"Are you sure he was born here?"

"Yes."

"But they didn't give you a birth certificate in the hospital."

"No. Not in the hospital." I do not explain. She is locked up like me because she has not heard. The others in here have. They know my story from television. I learn the same way. I know who Cocoa is now. She has family. Not like mine. Not like Chiqui and My. We are in here now and in there again.

"Father's name?"

I don't answer.

Again, her eyes say everything. Her body says a new thing. "Is my shift over?"

I stare. I almost cry.

"You have a last name for him?"

"Doctor's name who saved My is 'Lamar,' " I say.

"First name My. Last name L-a-m-a-r. Middle name?"

I sigh. "No."

"Date of birth?"

I count backward to when I believe Four died. I mean Nihla. I add three months.

"May 21, 2012."

"You seem pretty sure about a child with no birth certificate."

I feel tears in my eyes.

"5-21-12," she says slowly. "I'm gonna play those numbers."

I feel tears on my face.

"That's eighteen dollars and fifty cents. We'll take it out of your commissary. People have been sending you money. You know, a lot of big-shot lawyers are trying to get you out of here, allow you to stay."

My mouth makes a sound like it's about to scream.

"The document will be ready in a few days. Your advocate will pick it up."

I hear myself say, "What about My?"

"Your son? He's waiting for you."

"What about my sister?"

"You have a sister in here? Let me check." She looks down at her screen. "She's somewhere in this place. I guess you'll all be going together."

I do not ask where.

ACKNOWLEDGMENTS

Love is me thanking all of you for loving me:

Ife and Essen, for the honor of being your mother. You have made me grateful for the challenges of single motherhood because I have you all to myself.

Marjorie Momplaisir, my first love and soul mate, who was the first to inspire and encourage me to live and write.

My mother and grandmother, who consistently send me their love and messages from the spirit world.

Matante Tida, for your support and generosity without which the publication of this book would not have been possible.

My special readers who never got tired of rereading my work anytime you were asked.

Mononc Jojo, for being my multilingual dictionary, correcting my Kreyòl, and whispering the secret that I am indeed your "fave."

My soul sisters who listened, prayed, and comforted me as I cried, reassuring me that my time would come: Paula Baia, Angela Mayfield, Kathy McLean, Laverne Marable.

Anuraag Maini, a friend whom I didn't expect to become a friend, who shares his compassionate spirit in a soul-poor place.

Acknowledgments

My life teachers and adoptive parents, Ngũgĩ wa Thiong'o and Pamela Newkirk.

My supporters at Victoria Sanders & Associates for taking a leap of faith and introducing me to . . .

Benee Knauer, who taught me how to build a book and advocated for me when I didn't have the words.

Carole Baron, for trusting me with your friendship and reputation.

Charitybuzz, for giving me an entrée into the book-publishing ecosystem by connecting me with the gracious Jean Feiwel and Monique Patterson.

The Universe that has conspired to bring forth its message through me.

The Omega who is love itself.

A Note About the Author

Francesca Momplaisir is a Haitian-born multilingual literature scholar and writer of fiction and poetry in both English and her native Haitian Kreyòl. She holds undergraduate and graduate degrees in English and comparative literature from Columbia University, the University of Oxford, and New York University. She earned a doctorate in African and African diaspora literature as an NYU MacCracken fellow. She is a recipient of a Fulbright fellowship to travel to Ghana to research the cultural retention and memory of the transatlantic slave trade. Francesca is the proud single mother of two sons and resides in the New York City metro area.

A Note on the Type

Pierre Simon Fournier *le jeune* (1712–1768), who designed the type used in this book, was both an originator and a collector of types. His services to the art of printing were his design of letters, his creation of ornaments and initials, and his standardization of type sizes. His types are old style in character and sharply cut. In 1764 and 1766 he published his *Manuel typographique*, a treatise on the history of French types and printing, on typefounding in all its details, and on what many consider his most important contribution to typography—the measurement of type by the point system.

Typeset by Scribe, Inc., Philadelphia, Pennsylvania
Printed and bound by Berryville Graphics, Berryville, Virginia
Designed by Maria Carella